COTTON
SMITH

THE THIRTEENTH
BULLET

BOOK ONE IN THE TEXAS RANGER SERIES

POCKET STAR BOOKS

New York   London   Toronto   Sydney

This book is a work of fiction. Names, characters, places and incidents are products of the author's imagination or are used fictitiously. Any resemblance to actual events or locales or persons, living or dead, is entirely coincidental.

An *Original* Publication of POCKET BOOKS

A Pocket Star Book published by
POCKET BOOKS, a division of Simon & Schuster, Inc.
1230 Avenue of the Americas, New York, NY 10020

Copyright © 2004 by Cotton Smith

ISBN: 0-7434-7568-2

First Pocket Books printing February 2004

10 9 8 7 6 5 4 3 2 1

POCKET STAR BOOKS and colophon are registered trademarks of Simon & Schuster, Inc.

Printed in the U.S.A.

For information regarding special discounts for bulk purchases, please contact Simon & Schuster Special Sales at 1-800-456-6798 or business@simonandschuster.com

For Sonya, my North Star

"Two shadows be movin' on the roof. Across the street. The fine store that be Doc Williams's." Texas Ranger "Old Thunder" Kileen growled the alert without looking away from the shuttered window in the small Bennett jail. "Unless it be the wee people comin' to call, I'd say we got us some Silver Mallow boys."

The huge lawman could only see through a narrow crack, but it was enough. His nephew, Texas Ranger Time Carlow, looked up from the desk where he was shoving new cartridges into the sawed-off Winchester carbine he carried like a handgun.

"You stay here, Thunder, and cover me. I'll go get them." Carlow stood and spun the lever into readiness. Long black hair paraded across his shoulders. A tailored mustache and brooding eyebrows reinforced his combative appearance.

"No, let me be pickin' the devils off right from

here, me son," Kileen said, tapping the shutters three times for luck. The window closure offered a small gun slot for that purpose. The superstitious Ranger usually told anyone who would listen that such knocking got the attention of spirits living in the wood, so they could honor his wishes. He didn't give the reasoning now; Carlow would've been annoyed, having heard it often.

"They'll stay down after the first shot, Thunder. Shannon and Noah will be comin' back from patrol soon. They'd be sitting ducks." Carlow moved to the jail door and opened it slightly. "If we can capture them, we might learn something, too."

Outside, a bleak November sky was unable to stop the relentless cold shadows that were seizing the winter-nipped prairie or keep the tense border town from hiding within them. A ribbon of dust shot through the opening and spun erratically across the planked floor, pushed there by a dying red sun. Time Carlow pointed his weapon at the tiny dust whirl. "If you're from Silver Mallow's gang, you're in trouble. Bang."

His chuckle was met by a grunt from Kileen. " 'Tis a warnin', it is, from the wee people for ye to stay put," the big Irishman said, without turning away from the shuttered window.

"Which side are the 'wee people' on, Thunder?"

Carlow's confident manner belied what they

2

faced. If the notorious Silver Mallow and his band of outlaws attacked the town of Bennett, it would be tonight. If they came, it would be nearly thirty heavily armed bandits against four Rangers. Bennett's sheriff and his deputies left soon after the Rangers brought in the eight Mallow gang prisoners. The sheriff cited pressing family concerns a day's ride away. His two part-time deputies refused to stay in the jail with the Rangers and were last seen drinking, playing cards, and enjoying the lilac-sweetened girls in the rooms at the Corao.

It didn't matter. Kileen and Carlow had prepared themselves for the challenge from their position in the city sheriff's adobe-and-timbered office and jail, while the other two Rangers patrolled the town. Once a hardware store, the stand-alone building sat more or less in the center of the primary retail street, augmented by a heavy door and shuttered windows. As dusk seeped into the room, a weary candle was the only thing they could find to enhance the solitary oil lamp. The candle's uneven flame was an indication of its short life.

For the first time, Carlow was glad the jail was gray; the outlaws on the roof wouldn't be able to detect the door opening so he could study the store and what he had to do. He could see them now, too. Or at least two shapes trying to stay low and out of sight but not quite accomplishing the feat. Unasked questions rushed into Carlow's mind as he gauged the distance between the doors of the jail and the Williams Drugstore: Were the two alone? Or just two of an entire gang coming? Could he make it without them seeing him? Or shooting him?

Yesterday's arrest was a first. No one had been able to catch any of the Mallow gang doing anything before; no county or city peace officer wanted to try. Acting on a tip, the four Rangers had captured a few Mallow gang members pushing a stolen herd of three hundred cattle toward the border yesterday. To the dismay of town leaders, they brought the rustlers into the Bennett jail with the intention of hanging them publicly as a warning to other outlaws. The recovered cattle were grazing on a hillside outside of town until their rightful owner could come. A messenger had been sent with the good news to rancher M. J. Cahal, a day's ride to the west.

Throughout the day, stories of the gang's threats to break their friends out of jail floated through the trembling town. The bustling settlement of Bennett itself sat proudly along the edge of the Texas border, part of a turbulent region where ranches were attacked and burned, entire herds of cattle stolen and run into Mexico—and honest citizens murdered or driven away. Cattle rustlers, bank robbers, gunmen, and thieves—from both sides of the border—were threatening the region's stability.

"No thirteenth bullet be loadin' in that fine gun, did ye?" Kileen asked, rolling away from the window and resting his back against the wall. A hard frown followed. "Thirteenth bullets not be shootin' true. Ye know that."

Carlow raised the hand-carbine like a Comanche warrior signaling an attack. "No thirteenth bullet, Thunder."

Of course, both knew he hadn't counted the cartridges to avoid the thirteenth as he loaded. And never did. Superstitions were his uncle's domain—and his best friend, Ranger Shannon Dornan. Lowering the gun, his eyes caressed the stock with its strange Celtic carving. The same marking was on Kileen's and Dornan's rifles. Kileen said it was an ancient war symbol for victory, and neither younger man challenged his interpretation. Besides, it was an interesting design most thought was Comanche or Kiowa. Carlow liked what this gun gave him: the stopping power and accuracy of a rifle combined with the quickness of a pistol.

Carlow's uncle, a former bare-knuckle prizefighter and now just "Old Thunder" to his Ranger friends, stood like a hulking bear, watching his confident nephew. The huge brawler's concern for the striking young man he loved like a son was all over his hard, ruddy face. In the musky oil-lamp light of the jail, the ex-prizefighter looked older than his forty-two years and larger than his six-foot-two, 220-pound frame. A thick mustache sported flags of gray. His nose had been broken at least twice; his cauliflower ears definitely displayed the effects of fist combat.

He knew there was no use arguing with his nephew. He recognized Carlow could fight better than any man he'd ever known. He also knew Carlow's idea to attack was right. That's why he insisted on the four Rangers taking turns patrolling the town. If they stayed in the jail, they would be surrounded by morning. But it angered him that at least two outlaws had already slipped into Bennett unnoticed. "How ye be figgerin' on doin' this—without gettin' your fine head blown to kingdom come?"

"Watch me. They won't expect this." Carlow grinned mischievously, the grin that signaled everything was fine and he was in control, even when neither was so. "When I start running, spray the roof with bullets. That'll keep them from seeing me."

Men were often intimidated by Carlow's easy confidence, but not "Old Thunder" Kileen. Of course, Time Carlow wasn't bothered by the huge man's growling pronouncements, either, as most men were. Turning from the window, the big Ranger watched Carlow's eyes, searching for something.

"Aye, would there be a wee bit of wisdom in that Mick head along with the handsome?"

Kileen's voice was softer than anyone would have

thought his huge frame could deliver. Kileen loved what the little boy he raised had become. A Texas Ranger. He didn't like his apparent overconfidence—or lack of understanding of the situation.

"We'll see. Wish me luck." Carlow winked at the use of the word *luck* and rushed through the door.

Kileen's rifle opened fire and bullets snapped at the molding around the roof. Nothing moved there that he could see. A braggart wind pushed its way down the street at the same time as Carlow ran across it, catching the stretched-out kerchief that hung low across his once-blue collarless shirt and snapping at the fringe on his Kiowa leggings. A Comanche war knife rested in his right legging; its bone handle barely visible above the buckskin where it cleared his Levi's just below the knees. Gray vest pockets rattled with extra cartridges, hard candy, and an old silver watch. The Ranger badge on his shirt caught the light and glistened for an instant before disappearing in his dash to the Williams building.

Without breaking stride, Carlow slammed his shoulder against the locked door of the closed store. Smaller than his uncle, the young Ranger was deceptively strong, with a solidly built chest, arms heavy with hard-earned muscle, and a natural inclination to fight. The impact shattered the simple lock, sending splinters across his face and body. His hat bounced away from his head as he hit the dark store floor inside. With a life of its own, the hat slid until it hit a display case with the pushed-up front brim resting against the obstacle.

From a prone position, he studied the shadowy world of shelves laden with patent medicine bottles, simple remedies of quinine, paragoric, Epsom salts, castor oil, camphor, snakeroot, and cod-liver oil, as well as pressed soaps, apothecary containers, and packages of herbal concoctions. Farther away were showcases he couldn't make out for certain, but thought they contained jewelry and eyeglasses or perfume. Beyond was the area where Doc Williams, physician-pharmacist, had his clinic. The room swirled with intertwined aromas: sour, sweet, and strange. And everywhere was silence. And shadow.

Carlow stood, cursing at the jingle of his large-roweled Mexican spurs. Carlow's light-blue eyes could be cold or soft, depending on the situation, and definitely could see into a man's soul—or into a darkened store. He could hear boots scraping on the roof and muffled conversation.

His eyes adjusted to the darkness quickly and he spotted the wood staircase in the far corner, probably leading first to an attic storeroom, then the roof. He stepped forward and saw a polished human skull eerily staring at him from a shelf, next to a pill press, stone mortar and pestle, and a balance scale. Startled, he jumped back and bumped into a low wooden box holding umbrellas and canes. Four canes and an umbrella spilled onto the floor, sounding like someone dancing. There was no time to scold himself; heavy boots thundered down the stairs, accompanied by the rattle of spurs.

Had they heard him? No, they were continuing their descent. One was a stocky Mexican, judging by his sombrero, with cross-belted handguns; the other, a narrow-faced man in a smashed derby with a long scarf around his neck. Both carried rifles. Carlow waited until they cleared the last steps, yet were twenty feet from the back door.

"Find everything you needed, boys? There's some real pretty pills over here." Carlow's words were bullets to the two surprised outlaws.

The Mexican was the first to react, aiming his gun at the Ranger. Only his slitted eyes and clenched teeth were definable, along with the blurred flash of a rifle barrel. Three arrows of flame raced from Carlow's cut-down Winchester, firing it two-handed with the butt pushed against his hip

Shortened in stock and barrel, the weapon also had an enlarged circular lever for speed, replacing the standard narrow one. A Waco gunsmith had converted the Winchester for him, along with making the unusual holster. He could handle the weapon one-handed as fast as most could pull a handgun. With both hands he could lever shots faster than many could fan one.

The Mexican outlaw's body jerked as the bullets took control. His eyes rolled upward and his own rifle blast followed in that direction, pounding lead into the low ceiling. Not waiting to evaluate the result of his shooting, Carlow lunged, crashing into a showcase displaying cigars, tobacco sacks, and plugs. An opened box of cigars cascaded over him. Sensing an opportunity, the second outlaw fired wildly in Carlow's direction and raced for the back door. With his rifle in his left hand, he yanked it open and stutter-stepped to a halt. The doorway was filled by a man. Ranger Aaron "Old Thunder" Kileen. At his left side was his rifle. In his huge fist it looked like a toy.

Kileen's attire contrasted greatly to Carlow's. Dressed more like a businessman than a range rider, Kileen wore a trail-stained tweed suit. Spots on his vest were from tonight's supper. Massive arms and chest put great strains on the worn fabric. His own high-crowned black hat made him appear even bigger; a close look would find a bullet hole through the upper crease. Over his suit was strapped a bullet belt weighted with a holstered pistol and a sheathed bowie knife, both carried for his right hand. Even the badge on his vest looked huge.

"Would ye be goin' to greet Silver for us, laddie? What a fine gesture that be."

The carrot-faced outlaw hesitated, then swung his

rifle upward, grabbing it with his free hand. Kileen's right fist exploded into the man's face and everything stopped. The gun clattered against the floor as the outlaw's chin snapped backward and he folded to the ground. Kileen stared at the collapsed figure in front of him.

"Hopin', I was, not to kill him," Kileen said, shaking his head. "He might be willin' to tell us o' Silver's plan for the night. Since the other not be doin' much talkin', 'ceptin' to Saint Peter, bless me soul." He shook his opened right hand to rid it of the pain. "Maybe he be tellin' us what the black-hearted devil hisself be lookin' like."

No one could identify the leader, Silver Mallow, or wanted to, if they could, making things worse for the Rangers. So far, none of the captured outlaws were interested in talking about the gang's hideout or in describing their leader. In the cell a black outlaw with a long scar across his neck had announced brazenly that he was Silver Mallow, and the rest chimed in that they, too, were the infamous killer. But the Rangers, between them, knew enough of the gang members to know none was telling the truth.

Carlow finished reloading the cut-down Winchester, stood, and shoved the gun into its special holster on his right hip. Two rawhide bands held it in place against a thick leather backing tied to his leg. On the left side of his gunbelt, a short-barreled Colt was held in a tilted holster. The walnut-handle positioned butt-forward for a right-handed draw.

"I didn't have any choice, Thunder."

"I know, me son. I know."

Carlow looked back at the jail; at least the door was closed. "You shouldn't have left the jail. What if more of Mallow's men were waiting—for us to leave? I was doing all right."

Kileen knelt beside the downed outlaw and checked for breathing. "Dammit to bloody hell, I be tryin' not to do that. Looks like I be hittin' the lad a wee too hard." He ignored his nephew's observation until he stood again. "Thought ye be sayin' Silver's gang o' devils would not be comin'?"

He was worried, but that wasn't the reason for the tight-lipped grin. Actually, he never liked showing his jack-o'-lantern missing teeth, the effects of fisticuff battles and a drunken Mexican who said he was a dentist. Of course, the big Ranger was equally drunk at the time. Kileen also said it was his fault because he had dreamt about rattlesnakes the night before. Carlow could never figure what the dream had to do with it.

"Come on, Thunder, everybody in Bennett would see them sneaking in." Carlow was the only Ranger who dared to challenge the big Ranger's judgment.

"And who be seein' this pair o' Southern gentlemen—and be tellin' us about it? Me lad, the town will be helpin' them—or have you not been watchin'?" Kileen's heavy eyebrows arched, moving the flat scar at the edge of his right eyelid like the tail of a dog. "An' none o' us would know it was Silver Mallow, if his bleemin' self came a-walkin' in here to buy hisself a fine bit o' toothache powder."

Grinning, Carlow walked to the back door. Putting both hands alongside his face, he made an exaggerated attempt to look both ways. "I don't see him coming."

"Take a good look . . . at the fine Texas moon as she be risin' from the land," Kileen growled. "Some of us Rangers may not be seein' it again."

Thunder's statement brought Carlow's hands to his side. He looked at the senior Ranger as though Kileen had just entered the room.

"What do you mean, Thunder?" Carlow finally asked, his right hand resting on the butt of the holstered hand-carbine.

"Ye know well what I be meanin', me son." The answer slammed against the silence.

How could he convince his beloved nephew that the night would be a killing time? All the signs were there. A dead crow on the street earlier today. A certain omen of coming death. When no one was looking, he yanked a feather from the tail and stuck it in the ground. Sometimes, that created good luck by walking past it. He had done so three times. A few minutes before he left to help Carlow, the candle went out, then the flame returned. A signal of death being close to someone in the room. At least the flame hadn't turned blue, so there were no evil spirits in the room.

Carlow would have laughed if he told him. Worst of all, his ears had been ringing most of the day. His nephew would tell him it was from one too many blows from his prizefighting days. Kileen realized it was something else. The sound of a distant bell. A death peal. He had heard it before many battles. He had seen too much fighting not to know what was coming.

Kileen was proud of his nephew, anyone could see that, but the big man pushed further into the young Ranger's confidence. "These townsfolk don't want us here, lad. If they be choosin', t'is Silver they be sidin' with. Your heart an' your head must be votin' together on this." Kileen rubbed his unshaved chin and cocked his head to the side. "Silver Mallow won't come paradin' down the street—and, if he did, these townsfolk be cheerin' for hisself. They're afraid to do otherwise. Didn't ya feel it when ye boys went to eat?"

Carlow said nothing, but his eyes spoke clearly enough. He didn't believe him. Neither did the two other Rangers. In spite of the older man's battle-wise counsel, the three young warriors thought the gang would roar into view to intimidate the Rangers into surrendering their jailed associates or try to overwhelm them if they didn't. If Silver Mallow and his gang came at all. All three expected the men of Bennett to join in the battle against the outlaws at the right moment as well. If there was one. Together, they had decided—without discussing it with Kileen— that Mallow's lack of known identity was a sure indication the man was overrated. They had heard him described as everything from blond-headed to black-haired, from tall to short, even as a Mexican. One story had him looking a lot like Carlow himself. It didn't make any sense to believe he was anything but a figment of scared people's imaginations.

"By me sainted sister, Silver Mallow cannot let our arrest stand. Not an' be the king he wishes to be. Count on the bastird to know we are only four. Ye know that, don't ye, lad?" Kileen continued, speaking as gently as Time Carlow could remember. "Ye be expectin' the scoundrels themselves to be sneakin' into town. Aye, the shadows will be hateful this night."

For emphasis, he pointed the Henry in his thick hands like it was a stick toward the jail. Scars on huge knuckles whitened with his tight grip as he tapped the door frame with the rifle barrel three times for luck.

"I'm not afraid of Mallow, or the Holt brothers, or any of those peckerheads with him." Carlow grinned again, walking over to retrieve his hat and shove it back on his head. "We'll catch 'em in a cross fire if they come—and there'll be a lot of empty saddles when we're through. They've never had to deal with Rangers. Just scared rabbits like this town's excuse for lawmen."

"Aye, a wee touch o' fear can be makin' a man wise. Don't ye be looking for many when it might be only one opening the door for other rascals." Kileen's smile was again close-mouthed.

"You mean like these two?" Carlow's chiseled face, painted tan by Texas sun, wasn't hard to read. He didn't think the outlaws would come. Perhaps the hot supper had made him complacent. But he figured any bunch of outlaws charging into town would immediately draw the fire of every townsman with a gun, not to mention well-armed Rangers. And he didn't think the two would-be snipers were anything more than that. And likely they were all that Silver Mallow intended to do. Why would he challenge an entire town?

"Aye. Their hosses be out back. Ye be goin' back to the jail an' I'll strap 'em on an' send back a message to Silver." Kileen surveyed the room. "Me thinks we should clean up the store, too."

He strolled over to the spilled cigars, put half of them back in the display box, and shoved a fistful into his inside coat pocket. Carlow glimpsed the sprawled canes and walked over to return them to their place of honor. He was picking up the lone umbrella when he heard it. Heavy footsteps outside pounded both Rangers into a tense alert. Carlow's hand-carbine jumped into his hand and the umbrella fell again; Kileen dropped to one knee with his rifle readied.

At the opened front door Rangers Shannon Dornan and Noah Wilkins appeared, breathing heavily. White breath-smoke swirled around fearful faces. Long coats were buttoned and collars raised against their necks for warmth. Winchesters were levered and ready.

Dornan spoke first in halting phrases. "What the hell be goin' on? Time? Thunder? Ye be all right? We heard the shootin' an' came as fast as we could."

The tall, redheaded Ranger was Carlow's best friend and had been since their childhood days in Bennett. His hat had a pushed-up brim like Carlow's, and his leggings matched those covering Carlow's calves, except for the knife. Both men had been encouraging Wilkins to get a pair so they would look alike. "They're better than chaps—and sort of like a uniform," Dornan put it. Wilkins didn't understand why that would be a good idea.

Wrapped around the stock of Dornan's rifle was a leather strap holding bullets and tied with buckskin thongs, in addition to the mysterious symbol Kileen had cut into the walnut stock. At the end of each knotted thong was a blue bead to protect him from witches, something an old woman had once advised. Within each knot was a small eagle pin feather and a thin magpie feather, each decorated with a red circle. They came from a buffalo hunter who said he knew Comanche medicine. Dornan said the feathers would redirect his enemies' bullets, but he wasn't sure how. Dornan's red locks and hot temper were more than matched by his superstitious streak, nearly equal to Kileen's.

"Who are these two? Are they dead?" The stocky, blonde Wilkins twisted his sunburned face into concern. His mouth stayed open; spittle on his lower lip. He had been a state lawman for over three years and had been in a dozen scrapes with outlaws, but always seemed easily distracted. Right now his attention was on a stray cigar that had rolled against a long display case filled with bolts of cloth and sewing items. He strolled over and picked it up. After studying the cigar for a moment, he shoved it into his coat pocket. His interest in knowing who the dead men were, or why, was gone.

Dornan restated Wilkins's question: "Were these Silver's men? How'd you know they were here?"

Carlow started to explain, but was interrupted by Kileen. "Me boys, ye be goin' back to the jail now. Ranger Carlow be givin' ye the story o' it there." Without waiting for any response, Kileen lifted the dead Mexican to his shoulder like the body was a sack of beans. Blood dripped a thin line of red along the top of his coat. "Go on now, I be along as soon as I be puttin' these poor devils on their hosses—an' sendin' 'em back to Silver."

Wilkins blurted, "They won't be a-comin' anyways. It's too cold. Outlaws don't like the cold. Not even Texas cold. Too much work. They'll figure the whole town'll be waitin'. These two were just scouts. We'll have a quiet night—an' you boys'll get nothin' but the chills out there. On your watch. Should just stay in the jail."

He blinked and looked away from Carlow, as scarlet flooded Wilkins's neck. Carlow glanced past the embarrassed Ranger to Dornan. The tall redhead winked and grinned. Carlow listened and tried not to smile. He knew Wilkins's reasoning was colored by love, but wondered if Kileen knew it. Yesterday, Wilkins met a young woman who served drinks and sold favors at the Corao Saloon and hadn't been thinking or talking about much else since. It was obvious he had been with her again now.

"A little hot coffee would be real nice," Wilkins said, too casually.

"Well, Shannon, what do you think? Is Noah right?" Carlow glanced at Kileen, who hadn't moved, to remind him of his uncle's negative view of the coming night.

"Aye, 'twill be as cold as Ranger Wilkins says. Cold as a whore's heart. An' a bit o' hot coffee would be good." Dornan's mouth turned up at the corners. He laid a hand on Carlow's shoulder and walked past him to where Kileen stood with the body over his shoulder. "Old Thunder, we can help . . . with these."

"No, thank ye. Meself, I'd feel better knowin' ye be watchin' the jail," Kileen said. "An' Ranger Wilkins be needin' his coffee. Ye, too, Shannon."

Carlow thought his uncle was going to say more, but the big man headed for the back door with his load. Absentmindedly Wilkins picked up a wrapped bar of soap from a shelf and smelled it. He looked up to see both Carlow and Dornan staring at him. Red-faced, Wilkins returned the soap and walked away, toward the street. Carlow nudged Dornan on the arm and they left, with Carlow explaining the situation.

Kileen walked outside to the alley where two saddled horses were tied to a scrawny bush. Nightfall painted the town strange, yet familiar. As he threw the body over the saddle of a stocky bay, he blurted, "Step up an' fight, Silver Mallow, ye black-hearted devil. Ye an' me. Right now. Leave the lads out of it."

After lifting the second body onto a horse, tying

both in place with their own lariats, he slapped the mounts hard and watched them lope down the alley into the advancing night.

"That's what will be waitin' for ye, Silver Mallow, me darlin'." His hard voice echoed within the tight buildings.

Standing for a moment, his thoughts raced to places he didn't want them to go. His hand slipped into his pocket for a small silver flask of whiskey. Something else was there. He remembered. Acorns. Carrying an acorn would bring good luck. He'd gotten them from an old woman in town. Yes, he would give one to Carlow and the other young Rangers— even if it made them angry. How could it hurt? He pulled out the flask and took a long pull. Drinking was clearly against regulations, but no one ever said anything. Old Thunder could outfight any handful of Rangers—drunk or sober. He took another swig and returned the flask to his pocket, studying the back- side of a town he knew well, and expected the worst.

If the battle couldn't be settled man to man with Silver Mallow, he wished the whole gang would rush them now. His fist rattled the door three times. "Do ye hear me, spirits? Let it be me—an' Silver. An' be done with it."

Maybe the death signs were for the outlaws. But usually they came for friends—or family. His huge frame shivered, and he looked through the back door to the front, but that entrance was closed again or, at least, the door was propped in place. He must convince his young protégés that tonight's fight would be fierce. And unlike any they had been in. Before it was too late. They must expect the unexpected. How could he make them understand the town itself was against them? The town they grew up in! But they were Irish—that alone was enough for the townsfolk to hate them—and they had brought Silver Mallow outlaws into the very bosom of this settlement.

Wilkins's performance might be erratic, but Kileen knew both Carlow and Dornan would fight with courage and skill. Especially his nephew. His swift attack was typical. In fact, the outlaws in the cell had surrendered quickly after Carlow emptied two of their saddles. Kileen smiled to himself; he had never seen anyone—at any age—with Time Carlow's instincts for fighting. And there were a lot of great fighting men in this new Special Force of Rangers sent to southwest Texas. Their sole objective was to handle the out-of-control outlawry on the border.

The Rangers now prowled this savage frontier constantly; sometimes riding as one man, sometimes as two or three, occasionally as a unit in force. The numbers changed, but the purpose remained the same: to make Texas safe—for Texans. They functioned as a cross between lawmen and soldiers in a land that vomited any attempt to make it swallow law-abiding ways. Their justice was usually swift; execution on the spot was frequent, unless town or county authority was close at hand. This was more courtesy than requirement, for the Rangers were not subordinate to any other law enforcement. But so far, not even the Rangers had been able to stop Silver Mallow in any way. Until now.

Staying outside, he closed the back door, noticing for the first time that it had been broken. At least, Doc Williams hadn't let them in. That was good; Williams had been a friend. A long time ago. Kileen walked around the building, repeating his advance. One must return the way he came, everyone knew that. Out of the corner of his eye, he caught movement. In the alley. He tensed and studied the shadow figure. A boy. It was a small boy! *Wouldn't ye know a wee lad it would be, not afraid to roam these cold streets,* he said to himself with a laugh. His mind jolted to years earlier. Time Carlow could have been that boy. Alone and unafraid. Kileen blinked away the memory and yanked on his hat brim as the boy disappeared around a corner.

Nightfall lay thick on his massive shoulders as he reached the jail. " 'Tis me, Time, me son."

Carlow opened the door and immediately asked, "What's the plan, Thunder? Do we go take the watch—or stay here?" Carlow's eyes couldn't hide the fact the three younger Rangers had reassured themselves that the gang wouldn't attack tonight.

"We be takin' the watch, me son. They be coming, sure as me name is Kileen and the Isle is green. Already, there be more in town. The shadows should not be knowin' what ye think this night."

"What's that mean?" Noah Wilkins said as he fiddled with making a pot of fresh coffee on a cranky stove in the far corner.

Carlow answered for his uncle. "It means . . . don't make it easy for them to figure out what you're going to do, Noah."

"Oh. Why didn't you just say that?" Noah pouted. "Them two was jes' scoutin' 'round. That's the end of it."

Shaking his head, Kileen's sad eyes sought the feeble candle as he entered the jail. It was burning again. That was good. The jail itself was soon quiet again, except for some snoring from the cells and Kileen's own occasional slurp from his flask. Outside, the steady ping of a blacksmith's hammer meant Orville Frederick was working late. A large stoneware jar dangling from the overhang clanked against the wall, orchestrated by self-indulgent breezes.

Without any comment Carlow turned away to get his long coat. He loved his uncle. Even when he was wrong. And all the guard duty was going to cost was getting cold. They could argue about the wisdom of it in the morning. He glanced at Dornan as he picked up the garment from the corner of the desk. Sitting behind it, where Carlow had been earlier, the red-headed Ranger shook his head slightly and returned to reloading the Henry rifle in his lap.

On the desk's scratched surface was a circle of seventeen bullets. A prebattle loading ritual to avoid using any thirteenth bullets. His rifle was already fully loaded, but the young Ranger always made it a point to reload with fresh ammunition whenever possible. It made no sense, except to him—and Kileen. Ejected bullets bounced and rolled across the floor as he methodically levered them from the gun. Without paying any attention to the scattered ammunition, Dornan picked up a single new cartridge from the circle and slid it in the gun's loading tube. He counted out eleven more bullets, loaded them, skipped over the next, and finished loading the gun. The remaining cartridge was tossed into the sheriff's waste basket. Kileen had told him such bullets were bad luck for the shooter and considered it a sacred matter.

He looked up and Carlow thought Dornan was going to criticize the decision for the two Rangers to stand watch in the town; instead Dornan smiled and said, "Here's a toast to your enemies' enemies." It was an Irish cheer they'd heard Kileen give many times.

The lean-faced Ranger was quite serious about his

collection of beliefs and had well-developed repetitive steps he took to ready himself for the day and, particularly, a battle. It wasn't a sign of cowardice or indecision. He was fierce and unyielding when challenged, especially so after his rituals were completed. Carlow tried to step around the beliefs of his uncle and his best friend whenever possible, but couldn't resist teasing Dornan about some of his most arcane. Time Carlow was the only person who could do that without endangering himself to an instant verbal—or worse—reaction. Of course, Kileen would never criticize such behavior since he was known to embrace about every kind of superstition Carlow had ever heard of, and many he hadn't.

The coffeepot was finally beginning to boil and the minor success boosted Wilkins's confidence. He twisted his face to gather the courage to speak. Picking up a stoneware mug, he stared at the adobe wall behind the stove, and not at Kileen. Absentmindedly Wilkins spun the mug by its handle in his hand and finally turned toward Kileen. "Y'all think I kin see Daisy tomorry? She'll be a mite worried—with all them windies we bin a-hearin'."

"Aye, me lad, that you can. Tomorrow, that is," Kileen answered confidently. "Tonight, ye be keepin' your wee little mind on them bandits—an' not on her sweet bosoms. If I'm wrong, I'll buy dinner for ye an' the lass."

With one arm in his coat Time Carlow laughed and Dornan joined in, waking two of the captured Mallow gang who yelled for them to be quiet. Spinning the chair toward the cell, Dornan snapped back, "We can be startin' the hangin' right now if that be your wish." The banter from the cell ended.

Pouting, Wilkins said, "Ya shouldn'a be talkin' about her that way. Daisy's a real lady."

Neither Carlow nor Kileen responded to the observation.

"Aye, an' I be a black-and-white pinto," Dornan chipped. "Come on, Noah, you just like what she can do with her tongue."

Red-faced, Wilkins threw his coffee mug at the laughing Ranger. Dornan caught it with one hand as the cup clanked off the table, and threw it back at him, missing by a foot. The stoneware shattered into pieces against the stove. Carlow finished putting on his coat, glanced at his uncle, and smiled. But the response was forced and both knew it. There was silence and the old man realized his nephew wasn't in a mood to discuss further the gang's possible attack—or the town's reaction. When that realization settled within his head, Kileen drew a Smith & Wesson .44 revolver from his own coat pocket and held it out to the young Ranger.

"Aye, an' it's firepower you'll be needin' "—he paused and then continued with a suggestion—"an' maybe the wee edge of surprise. Put this iron in your pocket fer safe keepin'. Remember, move first, then be shootin'."

"I've already got a six-gun," Carlow responded and held open his long coat to remind his uncle of his second weapon, the short-barreled Colt holstered on the left side of his gunbelt. He was embarrassed by his uncle's attention and avoided looking at Dornan or Wilkins.

"Ye be takin' this, too, and be humorin' your kindly old uncle. An' be takin' this with ye besides."

Carlow accepted the gun and stared at the accompanying gift. "A nut?"

The older Ranger frowned. " 'Tis an acorn, Time. If you carry one, it will be givin' ye a long life."

"Where'd you get that idea?"

"Mrs. Jacobs."

"Who?"

"Don't ye remember that sweet lady who made hats an' ribbons an' stuff like that? Herself still be havin' a store down the street." Kileen turned toward the other two Rangers and tossed acorns in their direction. "Here, me lads. Long life to ye." He shoved his fat fist into his coat pocket. "I be carryin' one meself."

Wilkins tried to catch the nut, but it flew through his hands and banged off the stove. He picked up the acorn, blew on it to remove any dust, and shoved it in his pocket. Dornan casually caught the tossed acorn with his right hand, kissed it, and placed the charm in his shirt pocket. Nodding at Dornan and Wilkins, Carlow hoped they would understand it was better to honor his uncle's heightened concern than to argue with him when others were around. They also tried to accommodate the big man's superstitions, which seemed to grow daily. Some were pure Irish beliefs; many were imagined cause-and-effects, both acquired and made up. It was easy for Dornan, who had never heard a superstition he didn't believe.

"Do ye remember Mr. Jacobs—and his drawings?" Kileen asked, knowing the young men were merely humoring him with their acceptance of his good-luck charms. "She be havin' many o' them up on the walls in her place. Drawings of men and women around town. Barns an' dogs an' sech. Mr. Jacobs, bless his soul, passed on a few years back, ye know."

"Did you see any drawings of Daisy?" Wilkins stopped shoving the cup's pieces under the stove with his boot.

Kileen shook his head negatively and Dornan chuckled. After retrieving his friend's rejected bullets closest to him, Carlow glanced at Kileen's Henry rifle, then Dornan's. He couldn't resist saying what he felt. "When are the two of you going to put those Henrys away—and get Winchesters? My God, it's twice the weapon."

With a chuckle Kileen patted his rifle. "Ah, 'tis a sweet beauty, she is. Sixteen blessed shots."

"But it jams—and it's easier to load a Winchester, Thunder."

"Maybe it does in your hands. In mine a lady she be. Never a thirteenth bullet in her, do I be forcin'. Aye, that be the trick."

Dornan shook his head enthusiastically; the only reason he carried a Henry instead of the newer Winchester was because he was afraid it would bring him bad luck to change. He had purchased it with hard-earned money as a teenager. It had been blessed by both a Comanche medicine man and an Irish witch. One didn't tempt such magic.

Many in town remembered the two Ranger friends growing up in these now empty streets. In guarded whispers townspeople marveled that the two had lived this long with their many scrapes and wild escapades, and haughtily disapproved that both had become lawmen. As teenagers both had worked as men and fought for fun and money. Neither had parents; Dornan's died from a Kiowa raid when he was four, and he was raised by an immigrant family with eight children and little time to watch him. Neither realized the stigma of being Irish until they were teenagers. They had ridden in horse races for bookies until they got too big; that was twelve for Dornan, sixteen for Carlow. Old Thunder Kileen made more than his share betting on both young riders when he was around.

Dornan spun the blue beads on the thongs in front of him, then looked into the eyes of his best friend and asked, "Ye be carryin' your stone?"

Carlow didn't speak but touched the small, flat stone in his shirt pocket. It was always there.

" 'Tis a good thing, " Dornan said and repeated the motion on a smiliar stone he was wearing in his shirt pocket. A tribute to their own secret ceremony of friendship.

It was their own idea of an Indian blood-brother ceremony mixed with an ancient Gaelic rite. On Carlow's fourteenth birthday the two friends had conducted their version of *Lia Fail,* "the stone of destiny," upon which the ancient kings of Ireland took their oath of office. Carlow had heard the story from his mother. She said the stone actually came from biblical times and had been brought to Ireland by a prophet at the time of Moses. Both carried small stones with marks of their blood from that day.

Different in many ways, they were best friends and had been since childhood. Where Carlow was agile, Dornan was strong; where Carlow was quick to smile, Dornan was quicker to frown; where Carlow was ice in a fight, Dornan erupted into hot rage; where Carlow was instinctive, Dornan was locked into rituals and patterns.

Amused at the exchange, Kileen pulled the flask from his coat pocket and took another drink to end his concern about their realization of what the night might bring. Standing next to the blackened stove, Noah Wilkins frowned, not understanding the stone tribute exchange or, for that matter, any of the superstitions that flowed back and forth between the three Irishmen. He resumed his passionate hand-rubbing above the stove's warm lid, humming a tune to himself. He had already forgotten his second mug filled and now resting on the top ledge of the rifle rack on the wall.

"Are ye sure that's not a bird a-tryin' to get inside?" Shannon Dornan asked, referring to the thumping noise outside. His ruddy face squinted with concern. "You know a bird in a house is a sign of death."

"Any bird that comes into my house is a dead bird for sure," Time Carlow snapped. "An' you know damn well that's the water jar."

"That's not funny, Time—and ye be knowin' that."

Watching the two friends banter, Kileen wiped his mouth with the back of his fat hand. "You fine lads better be keepin' a sharp eye out for somethin' worse than birds. Meself will be keepin' the eye outside the fine Alamo drinkin' establishment."

The Alamo Saloon was one building away from the resumption of the open land on the west end of town. Kileen said it was a better location than the last building itself, the new hardware store. Carlow figured his uncle intended to catch a nip or two—for warmth—during the night's waiting, but said nothing. Carlow would stand guard at the other end of town. Whoever spotted the gang, if they came, was to slow them down with his gun, allowing the two Rangers watching the prisoners and the other Ranger on guard to create a cross fire. They decided it was better than all four of them holing up in the jail, waiting to be surrounded and burned out. Actually the idea was Kileen's and he said it without interest in discussing its merits. Even Carlow knew it was not something to argue about—with Old Thunder.

Remembering his coffee, Wilkins retrieved it from the rack. He sipped it cautiously, decided the hot liquid was sufficiently cooled, and took a large swallow. Then he surprised them all with his declaration, "I think all that stuff about Silver Mallow is bull. Jes' bull."

Carlow rubbed his chin and avoided Kileen's stare. Did Wilkins realize he was pushing the big man with this comment? What would Kileen do? Besides killing a man tonight with his fist, Carlow had seen him nearly behead another fellow Ranger with one punch, when the man foolishly challenged his judgment once too often. Carlow stepped away from the door, taking a cue from the big man's pause for another drink from his flask before responding.

"That's fool talk, Noah, and you know it," Carlow blurted. "Which part is 'bull'? The ranches he's burned? The innocent families he's killed? Or the women he's raped—and taken to trade with Comancheros? Or maybe it's the herds he rustled? Tell me, Ranger, I'd really like to know. Which part?" Carlow paused, knowing he should. His voice dropped in intensity. "I don't think Silver's men will come tonight, either. I really don't. But he might, Noah. And this old man has seen a helluva lot more fights than the three of us put together."

A knock on the door saved Wilkins from having to answer. Ranger Time Carlow was the first to react and asked for the visitor's identification.

A deep voice seeking to sound authoritative answered. "It's Mayor Pickenson. May I come in? Official town business."

Carlow glanced at Kileen, then Dornan, before opening the sturdy, plank-reinforced door. Rusty hinges squealed their discomfort as the greasy-haired, bespectacled mayor stepped into the opening. Carlow remembered him as a vain man with long, ponderous sideburns and an inclination to use religion like a club. Joshuah B. Pickenson owned a large general store in town and was also part-time minister of the Methodist church. He was also filled with pious phrases, arrogant judgments of other men's weaknesses, and a fondness for a particular widow with wealth.

Kileen didn't move, barely hiding his disgust for the leader of this border settlement of mostly second- and third-generation Texans with a small contingent of poor Irish and poorer Mexicans. Neither of the latter were accepted by the majority. It was also clear they considered Kileen and the two young Irish Rangers to be among the lesser souls, growing up poor among them. Kileen had lived mostly above the Corao Saloon, with young Time Carlow and his mother, until he joined the Rangers and stayed at the barracks. After his mother died, Carlow shared his time with ranchers who hired him; initially out of pity, then for his hard work and fast gun. Every time Carlow heard Ranger Wilkins mention the Corao, he saw his mother there and realized what she was and did. So far, he hadn't brought it up to Kileen because he knew his uncle would be terribly hurt; first, to be reminded, and second, to know his nephew knew.

"We be mighty busy ourselves now, Pickenson. What do you be wantin'?" Kileen snarled.

Even Carlow was surprised at his uncle's curt question. The words hit the mayor like a slap, and he instinctively recoiled from them. Swallowing away his nervousness, Pickenson cleared his throat and spoke in the most officious voice he could muster. "I am instructed by the Bennett town council to demand that you leave now—and take your prisoners with you. We have seen no proof of their lawbreaking. And if such criminal acts were done, it was not within our city limits and, therefore, beyond our jurisdiction and responsibility."

None of the Rangers responded. Wilkins poured himself more coffee in a third cup, sipped the liquid, and shook his head at its too-hot condition. Only then did he notice the second cup was back on the rifle rack, then looked again at the floor to see if all the pieces of his first cup were out of sight. He pushed the half dozen remaining chips under the stove's front legs.

Nonchalantly, Dornan leaned over to make sure his bullet hadn't moved from the sheriff's wastebasket. Carlow just stared at the man, the young Ranger's fists tightening so hard that his knuckles turned white. Kileen took another swig from his small flask and merely acted annoyed by the interruption. He would have given a horsefly more attention.

Unnerved by the lack of reaction, Pickenson hesitated. He knew three of these men: Kileen, Carlow, and Dornan. The two young Rangers were Irish street urchins only a few years ago. The other was a drunken fistfighter of horrible reputation. What had law enforcement in Texas become when men like these were welcomed into the brotherhood of state militia, he thought, but dared not express. Something inside his mind kept trying to tell him that this was not going as he and his friends had laughingly discussed earlier. His ego found its balance and he spoke again, his words coming quicker this time, hastened by an undefined sense of fear.

"Rangers, we do not want you in Bennett. There is nothing here for you. We will not protect you from your enemies. They are not our enemies." He spoke loudly, hoping the Mallow gang prisoners might also catch his words. "As the Good Book teaches, 'Love your enemies, bless them that curse you, do good to them that hate you.' "

From the cell rang out encouragement. "Right purty words, Mayor. Smart o' ya, too. Ya jes' mighta saved your town. Tell these bastards to let us go. We dun nothin'. We're jes't honest cowhands, tryin' to do a day's wages. They upped an' grabbed us fer no reason."

Wilkins threw the coffee from his mug in the direction of the comment and a string of curses immediately followed from the cell. Dornan laughed and stood, shoving the chair back as he did. His words came from anger always close.

"Pickenson, ye be gettin' your sorry ass outta here. I haven't forgotten the time you called us Irish trash—an' ya did it from your poor excuse of a pulpit. There be no God worth having who'd have the likes o' ye speakin' for Himself."

Kileen crossed himself.

Pickenson's face erupted into crimson; his eyes widened and he spluttered to find something to say. "L-Lord almighty! Don't you know that I-I am a m-man of G-God? I will not take such blasphemy from . . . from . . ."

"An Irishman," Time Carlow finished the sentence. His face was tanned slate and he added, "Get out, Pickenson. Go tell your buddies we aren't going anywhere. We're going to bring law and order to this territory. Although you don't deserve, either. Go crawl back under the rock you came from and stay out of our way. Say an 'Amen' when you do."

Pickenson's jaw pushed forward and tilted upward. His eyes were black and beady. "You Irish trash have no right to come back to our town and bring such danger upon us. I will inform the council—and we will be informing your superiors of this intolerable situation. You will rue the day you came back, I assure you.'Repent ye, for the Kingdom of Heaven is at hand.' " He stepped toward the jail entrance at the summation of his statement.

Old Thunder Kileen's move was so fast not even Carlow could believe the big man could react so quickly. Kileen lunged forward and placed his outstretched arm against the door just as the mayor pulled on the latch. Pickenson attempted to open it, but nothing gave way. A tear bubbled in his eye, then scurried down his cheek. He dared not face Kileen, staring instead at the scarred wood frame. His breath was heavy, close to gasping for air that wouldn't come fast enough. A slight tremble gave away his state of mind.

"Pickenson, ye be out of me sight when this is over," Kileen growled, then slid his hand to the latch and yanked it open. With his other hand he shoved the mayor out the door and slammed it shut.

Dornan's words trailed the exchange. "Be sure an' be givin' our best regards to Widow Snyder!" Laughter followed.

A few minutes later Carlow looked outside. Streets and sidewalks were deserted. Only wild rumors of pending doom swept through the rows of unpainted buildings like unseen birds of prey. Of course, no offers came to help the Rangers stand against the gang, even though many of the menfolk had served in the War of Northern Aggression.

It also didn't matter that three of the Rangers were from the town; they were Irish, so they weren't really looked upon as their own kind. Nothing more than eastern shanty Irish come west. Townsmen, huddled mostly in the handful of saloons, told each other that it would be different if these Rangers were actually part of someone's family. In fact, they had no right whatsoever to bring this danger to their town. It wasn't like these returning Irish were welcomed back. Hadn't that already been made clear—to every Irishman? Every Negro? Every Mexican? None was welcome. But the Irish families, for the most part, had hung on anyway. Why in the world would the Rangers let such lowlife join the force anyway? It was easy at such times to ignore the fact that the fearless Captain McNelly was himself an Irishman.

Where the rumors of gang retaliation first started was impossible to tell. All indications were that the outlaw gang remained camped somewhere to the northwest, but that was only speculation. So far, Rangers hadn't found any of their camps, at least none with outlaws still in them. Carlow's scouting ride beyond the outskirts of town yesterday and today hadn't produced any reason to believe they were close. On top of that, last night had gone quietly, like this one until now. Kileen expected orders from Captain McNelly—in the field somewhere to the north—tomorrow. Likely it would be to proceed with hanging. McNelly wasn't known for waiting for things like judges, especially local ones. Carlow didn't say it, neither did Dornan; but both felt Kileen was overreacting. After all, the Mallow gang had only run when Rangers got close, never staying to fight.

Kileen studied each younger Ranger's face and knew they didn't share his concern. He pursed his lips and tried one last time, "I never seen an outlaw who wouldn't talk—if it meant savin' his bleeming self from a hangin' rope. None back there be talkin'. Do ye get the meanin'?" He waved his arm in the direction of the cell. Only Wilkins turned toward the prisoners in response to the motion. "They be certain freedom be comin' soon."

After a stilted response from Wilkins about no one really being free until they found love, Carlow couldn't think of anything else to keep him from the cold and lonely watch. He walked to the front door, smiled confidently, and opened the door. The flame of the lone candle, sitting in a wax-bloated candle-holder, wiggled and went out. Dornan stared at the smoking wick as if it were evil personified. Kileen frowned but quickly said, " 'Tis only a bad sign if it be comin' back on. Ye be wantin' to put out all the lights anyway—when we leave." He didn't mention the candle flame going out and returning earlier.

Dornan started to remind Carlow about not using the thirteenth bullet, but instead called out, "Wait, Time!" He pushed himself away from the desk and hurried to Carlow, his rifle in his right hand at his side.

Carlow waited, watching his lanky friend skip toward him. Dornan stopped a foot away and whispered, "You be rememberin' what I said about makin' a circle and standin' in it. The evil spirits can't get to you when you're inside a circle, me friend."

"Sure, I remember," Carlow answered, equally soft-voiced. He was the one who had told Dornan about the superstition, but this wasn't the moment to remind him.

"You be doin' that, right?" Dornan said and held out his hand.

Smiling, Carlow shook his friend's hand and left. Outside a nipping wind greeted him harshly, and he yanked up his collar around his neck. Hunching his shoulders to further lessen the exposure, he strode toward the predetermined sentry spot.

From a darkened building came a harsh cry, "Get out of here, Mick! You're bringing Hell down on us!"

Carlow stopped. It was impossible to tell from which building the challenge came. He shrugged his shoulders and yelled back, in his best imitation of his uncle, "Top o' the evenin' to ye, too, sir."

He waited. Nothing more came, so he walked on. A dozen steps slower, the huge Kileen told the remaining two Rangers to recheck all the rifles in the rack, shut the jail door behind him, and douse the oil lamp. Tapping the door three times with his rifle, he paused just outside to hear the sounds of the planked reinforcement on the inside being shoved in place. He watched his young nephew push against the biting air, his jingling spurs a reminder of the young man's confidence. Kileen hoped Carlow would turn around and wave, but he didn't.

The big Ranger shrugged and headed in the other direction. His right hand shoved its way into his pocket to reassure him the acorn was still there and brushed against a tiny pouch, containing earth from the Green Isle itself. He had carried the tribute since his sister brought it with her from Ireland. "As the big hound is, so will the pup be," he muttered to himself and glanced back but couldn't see Carlow. "Time, me son, may the acorn be strong with ye tonight."

His wide shoulders rising and falling to release the worry, he was glad to see his own shadow had a head; a shadow without one meant death within the year. Did Carlow's shadow have a head? Yes, he assured himself, then wasn't certain. His distraction didn't keep him from stepping between the cracks in the planked sidewalk. He was headed to the saloon, slowly and loudly, pausing at each store window, hoping to draw Mallow's men to him and not his nephew. That was a ploy he had decided on some time ago. The big Ranger was certain the gang was already here. The two they had killed in Williams's store were just the beginning.

He didn't blame the first two Rangers for being careless on patrol; they just didn't understand how the gang was going to infiltrate the town—and the town was going to help. "Be careful, me son. They be coming, " he muttered and hoped the outlaws came for him. Loudly, he began to sing an Irish ballad.

At the other end of town Carlow's back straightened from leaning against the last storefront before the dark sky took sole possession of the land. Standing watch was an odd mixture of daydreams, alertness, and boredom. Heavy shadows controlled the split-board sidewalk where he stood or occasionally walked to accelerate the night's passage. For something to do, and to keep awake, he walked to the end of the boardwalk, down and across the alley, up to the remaining piece of sidewalk, then back again.

It would be difficult for anyone passing on the other side of the street to see him, even when he was moving. That was by design. From this position he could see anyone who might ride into town from this end of the small but sturdy main street. He could barely read the small sign in the store window across the street: "No Irish. No Coloreds. No Mex." Carlow shook his head and shoved away memories that were crowding into his mind. The young Ranger had grown up in this dusty, raw settlement, barefoot and laughing, never realizing how poor he and his mother were until his teen years. Or how they were looked down upon by the town's chosen elite. As a young lad, he played games on these same streets, fought for love and honor with his friends, worked at nearby ranches, and was in awe of his uncle and his two-fisted ways. Only gradually did he realize the rejection his Irish ancestry automatically brought him—and with that awareness came an anger he found difficult to seal off, at times.

Kileen was watching the other end but had told his nephew to expect a few men sneaking into position and not to look for the whole outlaw gang to come riding boldly into town. In spite of his reaction in the jail, Carlow knew his uncle was rarely wrong about fighting. With that in mind the young Ranger had spent most of his watch, wondering when, where, how—or if—the Mallow gang would come—

when he wasn't thinking about something else. Led by the half-crazed killer Silver Mallow, his gang of outlaws had been ravishing the territory for the better part of two years, enjoying whatever they wanted in the small settlements or lonely ranches. Without fear of reprisal or law enforcement. Except now, the Rangers had come to this part of Texas with the assignment to rid the state of scourges like the Mallow gang.

He shook his head, recalling Wilkins's foolish challenge in the jail. It was a wonder Kileen didn't strangle him. *That's what happens when a man thinks too much about a woman,* Carlow decided. He shook off the thought that followed of the two Mallow outlaws on the Williams store roof.

Night made it easy to understand why Kileen and Dornan—like many Irish men and women he knew growing up—placed great stock in fairies, druids, banshees, and leprechauns. The shadows always seemed alive with otherworldly activity. Both his uncle and his mother had told him fascinating tales of Gaelic myths that he usually tried to relay to Dornan when they were together. She was a sweet, naive woman filled with romantic notions about Celtic warriors, noble kings, and magical fairies, a direct contrast to her life of poverty, loneliness, and hard work.

Sometimes he thought he did see something that

had to be from the otherworld and didn't know whether to curse or praise her memory for the notion. Of course, it was Shannon Dornan doing guard duty last night who proclaimed he was certain he had seen a *puca*, a spirit who often appeared as a black horse. When he told Kileen, the broken-nosed brawler asked, "By Jesus, lad, will she be running in the sixth race tomorrow?" Then he laughed hard and long, deep within his throat. But Carlow knew his uncle was intrigued as always about things mystical and magic.

Carlow observed that his friend had probably just seen a loose black horse. After all, a *puca* was usually described as a "water horse," coming and going from bodies of water, and there wasn't much of that around. The Rio Grande was miles away. Dornan reminded him that the *puca* was a November spirit and could roam wherever it wanted. Kileen asked if he was certain it was a horse because the spirit could also take the form of a bull, or a goat, or even an eagle. Carlow finally shook his head and walked away, leaving the two to continue their conversation about what Dornan had actually experienced. There was no way to convince either man of the silliness of superstitions and the like.

His mind shifted back again to the Mallow gang. Ironically, Carlow knew three of the nastiest members of the gang, having played with the youngest,

Lee, as kids. The three Holt brothers were wanted for a long list of crimes, including blinding an older man and woman with a white-hot iron before ransacking their home and running off with their small herd. Carlow realized that, if it wasn't for Old Thunder, he might be one of the Mallow gang himself today. His father died on shipboard to the New World, leaving a pregnant young wife with no money or hope.

Her brother, Old Thunder Kileen, took in his younger sister and helped raise her son as if he were his own. They made their way west with Kileen funding their journey from prizefighting money won in city contests, county fairs, and other gatherings where a purse could be wagered to have him fight the local hero. Their dream was to own a small farm. Actually that was Carlow's mother's dream. Kileen leaned toward owning a saloon. The plow held little fascination for him.

Both made certain the lad learned America's way of speaking. Unlike Dornan, Carlow carried barely a hint of Irish in his voice. Well covered by Texas drawl, none of his uncle's rich, rolling brogue took hold. Once in Texas, they had continued to drift, never quite finding a place that was home. Carlow's mother died from the fevers five years ago. Now there was a huge wall separating Carlow and the Mallow outlaws he had known as a child, a wall of integrity and honor. Maybe the realization of how close he came to a life of crime stirred his anger more.

He'd never seen Silver Mallow nor known any-one—alive—who had. In all, the Mallow gang thrived on the intimidation and fear they generated within the region. And some of that came from the mystery of Silver Mallow himself. This arrest was a symbol Mallow couldn't afford: someone had stood up to his gang and won. Maybe the young Ranger was letting his imagination get the best of him again. Night had a way of doing that.

He yawned and stretched. Out of the corner of his eye he saw something. Maybe. Moonlight had flickered off something inside the alley between the two buildings to his left. It blinked again and disappeared into the cold night as he stepped to his right, more out of instinct than design. Texas Ranger Time Carlow stiffened and silently cursed the frost-breath that surrounded his face. Was the Mallow gang coming?

To himself, Carlow muttered calming advice, "Don't be so jumpy, Time. It might not be the gang at all. Just some ranny looking for an easy target. How would he know I was a Ranger? Dornan would never let me live it down if I got them all in a stir over one damn thief."

But he knew. One of the Mallow outlaw gang was closing in to kill him. His thoughts ran skittishly toward Kileen, wondering if his uncle was facing the same situation, then to Dornan's suggestion of making a circle and standing in it. For a moment he wished he'd done that. Sweat glistened from Carlow's forehead in spite of the rawness of the black hours before dawn. He was nervous. Opening his coat, he thought for an instant about repinning the Ranger badge on his long coat instead of his vest. Instead, he holstered the sawed-off rifle and drew the Colt revolver.

His hand trembled as his gloved fist wrapped around the weapon. Just the gripping was comforting. He always preferred the shortened Winchester over a handgun, but the pistol would be the better weapon in this situation. Something else was there, too. The acorn from Kileen. His uncle said carrying an acorn would ensure a long life. *Where did he get this stuff?* Carlow thought but left the nut where it was. Slowly he placed his left hand over his mouth to dissipate the blossom of frosty expelled air that came with his long exhalation of tension. His right hand held the Colt at his side.

A thin moon of ice, desiring rest from the long night, offered no additional light. He couldn't see any shape within the darkened space. *Was there one man or was there a second?* He couldn't tell for certain. Probably just one man. The strained words to himself reformed into strings of white frost, slipping through his gloved fingers, as he tried to learn more about the black shadow through the corner of his eyes.

Surely, a hidden assailant was waiting for him to repeat his pacing toward the alley and then attack. *A knife or a club, that's what the assailant would use,* he decided. He wouldn't want to alert the other Rangers. *Was the Mallow gang closing in? How could they have spotted me in the darkness?* It angered the young Ranger that his imagination was running wildly when danger was so close.

Dornan and Wilkins were inside the jail, safe and warm; athough the building itself was nothing more than an abandoned storefront with some hastily built cells, a reinforced door, and two barred windows. Kileen was probably telling stories about fast horses and long-ago fights in the saloon. Carlow wished Kileen was here right now. What would he do? The savvy old street fighter would move, that's what. Make his enemy make a mistake.

That's what Kileen, the former prizefighter, always said. "Me lad, be fakin' the jab, fakin' the jab—and movin', always movin', then when he's come to expect your journey—boom, ye let 'im have it with your bloomin' right. From the tips o' your toes, it does come. Oh, 'tis not a sight for the women or the troubled, aye, 'tis not." Then he would laugh that fierce, lionlike growl of a laugh and imitate the action.

Carlow made up his mind quickly; hesitation was

the first step to defeat. His uncle had taught that principle well and often. He wouldn't assume it was the gang; he would deal with his hidden adversaries first and then decide what to do. A plan settled in his mind, and the young Ranger switched the pistol to his left hand and drew again his sawed-off Winchester. He didn't worry about the indecisive appearance of duplicating his actions. It might serve to make whoever was out there feel more confident.

To create a lack of concern, he propped the Winchester against the building and left it, walking swiftly toward the next building, closest to the menacing alley.

At the last moment he ducked behind a rickety outside staircase, as if intending to relieve himself. Long shadows embraced him immediately. He would wait for the man to become curious about his suddenly disappearing prey and come out to see what had happened.

4

After a prolonged jaunt across town, Old Thunder Kileen closed the saloon door behind him unaware his nephew was being cornered by Mallow outlaws at that very moment. All saloons smelled the same, he thought. A strange mixture of tobacco, whiskey, and sweat, mixed with the thick smoky odor of oil lamps. An aroma he always found most inviting. Tonight, however, there was an added smell—fear.

Before entering, he decided that if the first man he saw was dark-haired, the night would go well; if the first was light-haired, it would be a hard time. As he thudded into the smoke-thick room, he avoided looking at anyone until he was certain the man had dark hair, then he stared at him and smiled. His rifle was casually laid against the wall next to the door, beside several others. He tapped the barrel three times before releasing it.

His appearance brought instant recognition from

the men crowded in the saloon—and, equally instant, disdain. Timid moonlight tiptoed through two angular windows, crossed the big Ranger's war map of a face, and danced with the yellow light of the oil lamps hanging from the walls. It was impossible to read his mind from his stone square visage. He knew many of these men from his own days here. He learned the hard way not to trust them—or few of them, anyway. Angry stares couldn't hide what the tough Ranger already knew. This was a room afraid the Mallow gang wouldn't be satisfied with just killing four Rangers.

Kileen rolled his heavy shoulders again to relieve the cold from outside. If another Ranger had left his post this way, Kileen would've been furious. But this wasn't about whiskey, although the brown liquid always tasted sweet to an Irishman. He was certain three Mallow gang members were sneaking up on him and was satisfied his ploy had worked. Going inside now might be the edge he needed. Always keep moving, that's what he told his nephew. At the far corner of his thought was the possibility that one of them might be Silver Mallow himself. Who would know? Kileen thought he would. A true Irishman would know, he assured himself, not bothering to question himself about why such an observation would be true.

Kileen walked straight to the bar, ignoring the

stares that ranged from alarm to hate. None of these men were worth the lives of his young Rangers, but that option wasn't in the oath any of them had taken. That oath was to Texas—and this was Texas, too. He eased his massive frame onto a bar stool, then drew a circle in the dust around his position with his outstretched boot toe. Behind him in close order came three shadowy men. He pretended not to notice. The first wandered toward the back of the smoke-filled room; the other two headed nonchalantly toward the bar. The taller went to Kileen's left and the other, a man with a full beard and hooded eyes, slid into an open place on his right.

"Bartender, a fine glass o' rye would ye be pourin'," Kileen said, waving his hand in the direction of the busy bartender, a thin man of indeterminate age. He turned to the man on his left and said, "Aye, 'tis a wee nippy out there. Be goin' right through a man, it does."

Pleased at their apparent deception, the tall man supported the comment. "Yeah, it's colder'n hell out thar. Bring the bottle!" The other man watched Kileen from the corner of his eye and only motioned with his left hand. The bartender nodded his awareness of the requests and headed toward them.

Kileen took out a cigar from his coat, rolled it in his fat fingers, and struck a match on his belt buckle. White smoke began to curl around his shaggy head as the bartender spun three glasses in front of them with practiced ease and poured the brown liquid without splashing a drop.

Silver Mallow's reputation as a cold-blooded killer and arsonist was well established. Even though no lawman knew for certain what he looked like. Some of the tales told about the outlaw leader were hard to swallow, like his supposed fascination with music. Hard to imagine a killer of his reputation with an interest in songs and bands.

Of course, everyone knew about his love of silver jewelry. Silver rings on each finger and a heavy chain necklace with a solid silver cross had earned him the nickname Texas knew him by. Mallow's real name was Paul Sedrick Mallow. He was the son of a Methodist circuit preacher and was himself once a town sheriff in Ohio. Those who had met him, and lived to tell about it, thought he was deranged; some said it was due to a head wound in childhood; others thought it was due to syphilis obtained during the war; more than a few claimed he was Satan incarnate. Most of these firsthand observations also said he was dark-haired, blue-eyed, and handsome. Kileen had never met Silver Mallow, but he knew the Holt brothers who rode with him. If Silver Mallow was worse, Heaven help Texas.

It dawned on Kileen that the outlaw leader could actually walk up to him right now and he wouldn't

know the man, if he wasn't wearing all those rings.
That brought a shiver and the recollection of a
rancher to the south who had described Silver Mallow to Carlow a month ago. Basically, the rancher
said, Mallow looked a lot like Carlow. Same build,
same dark hair, same light blue eyes, same cut to
their jaws. Only Mallow was clean shaven, unlike
Carlow with a mustache. The man had glimpsed the
silver chain under Carlow's shirt when he told him.
That was probably what triggered it, Carlow had told
Kileen.

Still, it made him even more curious to see what
this outlaw leader looked like. Was he really dark-
haired like Carlow—or blond-headed like he'd
heard? The big Ranger chuckled to himself and decided he'd just have to shoot the next man who
showed up fitting the description. Unless it was his
nephew, of course. But it wasn't funny. Silver Mallow
was elusive and clever, whatever else he was. There
was also Ranger talk of an inclination to use disguises. That would make the various different descriptions of him make some sense. That also made a
Ranger's job tougher. And more dangerous.

Meanwhile, Time Carlow waited beneath the
staircase. His legs cramped with the awkward squat-
ting, his mind frustrated by his natural impatience.
Attacking was a much preferred action. A straying

breeze forced the old railing to whine and he jumped. Waiting cut at his courage and made him hesitant. He hated the fear rising within him. Timidity was for others, for victims, not for Time Carlow. What would his uncle think if he told him he was scared? Was that someone coming out? No, no one was coming. Had he overreacted? Maybe it was just the night's way of teasing him.

Carlow watched the silent alley and tried to focus his attention—and his patience. Was he seeing things because of all the talk about the gang coming? Maybe they had decided to clear out of the county. Maybe they hadn't even heard the news of Rangers arresting some of the gang. Maybe it had been nothing more than a reflection off of a bottle. Carlow's hands inside his gloves were wet with the sweat of anticipation. But the streets remained innocent and so was the ramshackle sidewalk.

Five minutes crawled by—seemed like an hour— before there was movement at the alley's entrance. Carlow held his breath, cursing the cold night air that would turn it into visible frost-smoke. He exhaled down into the opening of his overcoat. A man slithered around the edge of the alley and stared into the darkness for his prey. He took three more careful steps, then motioned toward the alley. A second man! Carlow was right.

He could see the first man's frown of confusion

about the Ranger's longer-than-expected disappearance. Both men were now in the open. Both held long knives. He gasped in spite of himself. The first was one of the Holt brothers; it was Lee, the youngest. Carlow would know him anywhere, even though childhood, when they were together, had long passed. With greasy hair brushing against his shoulders, Lee Holt swung his head in an agitated half circle, searching for a target. Carlow couldn't make out the second man's face; his hat was pulled low over his eyes, but he was taller.

"Ye be lookin' for a Texas Ranger, me lads?" Carlow called into the night, imitating his uncle's rhythmic brogue. His grin matched his devilish question. A distinctive *click-click* as he cocked his Colt's hammer into readiness turned his mischievous question into a hard challenge. The two men froze. Kileen would have advised against such a warning, no matter how it was spoken. Dornan would have been angry at their creeping around and started shooting; Wilkins would have asked who they were and if they knew Daisy. Carlow knew he gave the warning only because it was a childhood acquaintance waiting.

"Drop your knives or you will die this night. I can see you fine as an Irish morn," he continued, certain his uncle would be proud of the analogy.

The two outlaws looked at each other, silently trying to determine if the other saw Carlow clearly enough to attack first. Slowly two bone-handled blades skittered along the hard ground; a finger of moonlight tested their sharp edges. Carlow stood, trying not to show the stiffness his wait had brought on. He silently urged his hands not to tremble. "Good, now toss your pistols into the street."

The response was quicker this time. Two long-nosed revolvers thudded in front of the outlaws.

"Glad to see you're showing a bit of wisdom. Saves me the trouble of dealing with two dead bodies," Carlow said with more bravado than he felt. "Where're the rest of your friends?" He wasn't certain, but there might have been a silent nod of agreement between the two men as he approached.

Agility saved his life. Sensing the attack before realizing what it was, he jumped sideways as the stocky Lee Holt leaped at him, swinging a hidden bowie knife. Darkness made the deception easy. Lee's blow missed and Carlow fired. A scream followed and Lee Holt fell to his knees. Carlow whirled and fired again in the direction of the second assailant, whose blow with a second hidden knife was a breath behind Lee's.

Carlow's bullet found only air. The second man's blade caught Carlow's right shoulder as he tried to duck, moving to his left. Lightning pain straightened the young Ranger's fingers, and the gun dropped from his opened hand. Before the outlaw could strike again, Carlow drove his other fist into the taller man's exposed rib cage. He followed with an overhand right that splattered the bandit's nose, spraying blood everywhere. The blow dislodged the knife from the outlaw's hand and tore away his valor. Half of his face was encased in dripping crimson. The outlaw froze in horror for an instant at his own situation, then looked up into Carlow's face. Recognition by both men stopped their attacks. Years ago they had been friends. Lee Holt he had only known; Mickey Houlihan he had liked.

Clutching his ribs, the taller man took a long, halting breath, then turned and ran. Carlow let him go, uncertain of his feelings about having another boyhood friend try to kill him. Mickey Houlihan was a member of the Mallow gang. Carlow had heard that, but knowing its likely truth and having old friends try to kill him were two very different things. For a moment he was trapped in yesterday and forgot about the first assailant. But the corner of his eye caught movement toward his dropped gun.

Quickly retrieving the revolver with his throbbing right hand, Carlow commanded, "Lay flat, Lee. Move wrong and your head is a bloody pumpkin."

"My arm's busted," Lee Holt groaned, struggling to comply with the order, "I'm bleeding bad. Come on, this is no way to treat an old friend."

Ignoring his complaint and his comment, Carlow

retrieved the outlaws' surrendered pistols and shoved them into his belt with his own. He kicked the knives toward the street, then checked the wounded acquaintance for other weapons. Another pistol soon took its place in Carlow's belt.

"Carlow, you—and your stupid drunk of an uncle—should know better than to mess with Silver Mallow," Lee growled through clenched teeth, holding his wounded arm against his stomach with the other. Blood had blossomed along the upper coat sleeve, turning the cloth into a dark pattern of its own.

Carlow stared at the outlaw and couldn't help recalling yesterdays. A blurry time when Mickey Houlihan played tricks on town merchants and Lee Holt was an ornery kid with a burning need to impress his older brothers. The young Texas Ranger wondered if the same motivation had led him to the bandit trail. He had no idea about Houlihan and rolled his shoulders to let a shiver find its own way out. With it came the realization that he could just as easily been riding there, too.

"Thank your blessed mother, Lee, that I'm in a good mood or you'd never get up," Carlow spat. "Where are your brothers? Under some rock out there?"

"My brothers, they're waiting. Outside of town. Mickey'll bring 'em. They're going to run over this crappy little town—and you. Ohh, it hurts, it hurts."

Dawn was trying to flirt with the leaden sky. One pale star remained, not yet convinced the night was over and unaware of Ranger Carlow's fight. His body drained of battle energy; his mind sagged from the release of fearful tension; shock from his shoulder wound was only beginning to seep into his mind. Stepping back to look toward the gray prairie that rested beyond the edge of town, he was mildly surprised none of the noise had brought any response, not even a lighted lamp from some window.

"How many?" Carlow didn't expect a truthful answer but the question came out anyway. He avoided grasping his shoulder so that Lee wouldn't realize he was hurt.

"Thirty riders. They're going to tear you and your fool friends apart."

Carlow was uncertain what he should do. Stay where he was? Head back to the jail? He doubted the number, but not the intent.

"Get up, we're going to the jail," Carlow commanded and yanked on Lee's coat. "Get up." The young Ranger made up his mind as the words came out.

He would drop off the wounded outlaw. The two Rangers there would be wondering about the gunshots, as would Old Thunder. As soon as Lee was behind bars, Carlow would find and talk to his uncle before retaking a new guard position. In the back of

Carlow's thinking was the worry that he might pass out. The knife wound was still bleeding.

"I-I'm . . . damn, ohhh, that hurts . . . I'm gettin' up," Lee Holt expressed what Time Carlow felt.

"Walk in front of me," Carlow ordered. "Stop when I say or I'll stop you with a bullet."

"You haven't changed any, Carlow. Still an asshole who has to win every time. How bad did Mickey get you . . . Ranger?" The question crawled from Lee's mouth, each word smiling.

"I've been scratched worse ridin' through sagebrush. Get movin'," Carlow said, biting the inside of his cheek to keep the pain of his stabbed shoulder from showing in his face.

"I see you haven't gotten any smarter, *Time*," Lee snarled, emphasizing Carlow's first name.

His first name, "Time," was the result of his mother knowing little English at the time of his birth and thinking *time* meant something like "eternal." She could think of no better description for her child, so "Time Carlow," it became. Many a fistfight had been started over being teased about his name. "Time Lucent Carlow," to be exact. "Lucent" was his mother's maiden name. Whenever he thought of her, his hand went instinctively to the silver chain and Celtic cross worn under his shirt. It was the only thing that remained of her, besides his memories. She told him the chain and cross had been his father's.

"How's your momma these days? Still doin' pokes for gold?" Lee said. "My brothers always thought she was a fine lay."

Carlow's fury rose, but the pounding pain made him cautious. This was no time to waste precious energy on an attempt to force him into a mistake. "I said, move, Holt, or do you want to stay in the street?"

Inside the saloon, Carlow's gunshots were unwanted jolts through "Old Thunder" Kileen's huge frame. He straightened at the bar and grabbed its planked edges with both hands, a grip so tight that his scarred knuckles turned snow-white. In the massive Ranger's eyes was fear. Not for himself, but for his nephew. His mouth was a locked thin line of anxiousness.

The tall Mallow outlaw standing beside him on his left chuckled and said, "Those damn cowboys! They can't come to town without shootin' at the moon or somethin'." He downed his whiskey and yelled at the bartender for another. The bearded man on the other side of Kileen laughed and slid his right hand toward the pistol under his coat.

Kileen knew differently and his ears longed for more gunfire, as if it would mean Carlow was alive and fighting back. His attention to the sound made him less aware than he would have been. But his eyes caught the odd movement of the bartender, a hurried jerk toward the far end of the bar that spilled beer from the glasses in his hands.

"Here's to the cowboys!" the tall outlaw said and held up his refilled glass with his left hand.

"Aye, to the cowlads," Kileen responded appreciatively. "An' to the blessed Green Isle."

His right hand reached for the whiskey glass in front of him. Halfway there it suddenly became a giant fist and slammed against the face of the salute-giving Mallow outlaw reaching for his holstered pistol, smashing his jaw. Cracking bone shattered the still, smoky room. Teeth and blood spewed across the bar, and the man's glass of whiskey followed, spinning wildly in the air and spreading the fiery brown liquid across the staggering body. The outlaw's pistol thudded to the ground as he fell unseeing into a table behind him.

In a second move, actually a smooth extension of the first, Kileen spun and grabbed the arm of the man to his right as the second outlaw's hand brought a belt pistol into play. A fierce yank straightened the outlaw's arm, pointing the gun toward the back wall of the bar. Kileen's right fist delivered an uppercut that drove through the man's elbow and snapped his arm. The pistol exploded and its bullet rammed harmlessly into the plastered wall. A scream of maddening pain loosed itself into the room, bouncing off the grimy walls like a crazed cougar.

The big Ranger released the man's dangling arm and followed with a punch that broke the man's jaw. As the outlaw collapsed, a bullet too hastily fired clipped the top of the bar next to Kileen. Yells trailed the gunfire as men scurried for any kind of cover they could find, overturning chairs and tables. One man escaped through the back door and his terrifying yell into the night was a long echo.

Kileen's dark eyes followed the attack and saw the third Mallow outlaw across the room, recocking his pistol for another attempt. Kileen made no attempt to draw his own gun. Instead, he roared a Gaelic curse that rattled the courage of the huddling customers beneath chairs and overturned tables. The Mallow outlaw's eyes widened in fear as he hurriedly cocked his pistol and fired again. A businessman in a suit under a table screamed in pain.

Witnesses said they had never seen a man receive so many vicious blows in so few seconds. Kileen drove his fists into the outlaw's stomach and face again and again, pounding him senseless. Nearly unconscious, the outlaw was held up by Kileen's left-handed grasp while his right fist continued to tear up the man's insides. Kileen's fury was unquenchable and everyone in the saloon feared that he would seek more flesh when he finally released his adversary to crumple on the floor.

Instead, the big Ranger turned back to the scared

bartender and commanded, "Be givin' me that scattergun under the bar. Do it now or I'll be killin' ye with me bare hands. An' a box o' shells. There be good Rangers in need o' help tonight. If one o' me laddies dies, this pissant town be answerin' for it from meself."

From under the closest table a cowboy in a long trail coat said, "Ranger, I'd like to help, if you'll have me."

A shorter cowhand supported the offer, "Me, too. I kin handle myself with a gun. Those Mallow bastards dun kilt a friend o' mine."

Grabbing the shotgun from the white-faced bartender, Kileen nodded toward the two cowboys, then picked up his own rifle and handed it to the first to reach him. Without waiting to see what they would do, he rushed through the saloon door and into the troubled night. Both men followed. The second cowboy grabbed another rifle resting against the wall. Two other cowhands slowly stood, looked at each other, yanked handguns from their belts, and ran to join the fight.

At the other end of town Carlow shivered at the sounds of shooting from the direction where his uncle was stationed. Thunder!

The youngest Holt smiled savagely. "We just kilt that damn big Ranger."

"Don't bet against the acorn."

"What?"

"Forget it. Keep moving."

Carlow knew the key was to stay focused as he pushed his prisoner ahead of him through the gray neighborhood. Lack of sleep was tearing at his alertness; his bloody arm, at his courage; the possibility of Kileen being ambushed, at his heart. He mustn't let his mind wander onto worrying where the rest of the Mallow gang might be, or to the sweetness of catching a nap at the jail, or if Thunder survived. *Concentrate on the now. Stay alert.* It was as simple as that.

Without turning his back, he retreated to the wall, holstered his Colt, and retrieved the shortened carbine. Cocking it by twirling the lever and the weapon in his hand, the gun popped back into his fist with the hammer readied for firing. But the movement shot pain through his shoulder so furious he thought he would drop the gun. Instead, he gripped it tightly and didn't move, allowing the wave of nausea to subside.

Passing the gun and ammunition store, Carlow thought he saw movement on the far side. He grabbed Lee and pulled him into a thin shadow lining the building's south side. Carlow held the outlaw against the wall while he waited to see if there was anyone hiding. His fists held the hand-carbine, cocked and ready, although his right arm was numb from shoulder to fingers. Lee chuckled at Carlow's reaction; the young Ranger's response was to jab him in the stomach with the nose of the gun. Carlow's stab wound was throbbing at its source and trying to weaken his resolve.

"If you even breathe too hard, you're going down with my bullet in your ugly heart," he whispered into Lee's ear and concentrated on the silent house ahead.

Suddenly a pencil-thin shadow appeared where Carlow had sensed movement earlier. Its needle-shaped head fattened into a body. There was a man hidden there, probably kneeling! Carlow ordered Lee Holt to lie flat on the ground with his arms and legs widely spread. Then he turned his attention to the hidden assailant ahead.

"Step out slow with your hands where I can see them," Time Carlow commanded. The shadow retreated somewhat and he called out again. Still no answer.

"Answer or I'll shoot," Carlow warned.

He swung his gun toward Lee to let the outlaw know he wasn't forgotten. The youngest Holt only groaned and muttered something about his arm hurting. Carlow was about to spring into the street and shoot back toward the side of the building, when he heard the whimper, followed by a soft growl.

5

A dog! It was a dog. He had been scared by nothing but a stray dog! *It was a good thing he was headed back*, Time Carlow muttered sarcastically to himself, *or he might hurt some innocent person*. Carlow leaned over to pet the tentative black terrier, letting his emotions dissolve in a long sigh that covered his face with a white smoke.

"Next time, present yourself when called upon," Carlow said with a smile. The dog eagerly accepted the attention and licked his gloved hand.

"Looks like you're a bit shaky, Carlow. Next, you'll be shootin' at old women with that fancy gun of yours," Lee tormented. "I reckon Mickey cut ya good. Can you move that shoulder? Bet I could take you right now."

Weakened by the loss of blood, Carlow stared at Lee Holt without speaking. Lee blinked and looked down at the cold ground. Carlow growled for the broken-armed man to stand, and the outlaw gathered himself and got to his feet without further expressions of bravado. They resumed their walk to the jail, now only a block away, with the dog strutting alongside Carlow, a few steps behind Lee. The young Ranger grinned at the animal's bouncy walk and looked for signs of Dornan or Wilkins at the jail.

Carlow worked his shoulder easily, trying to keep it from stiffening, but the pain stopped his exercise and almost made him vomit. A glance at his coat showed a long rip in the cloth surrounded by a dark crimson circle. He swallowed hard, decided not to look further, and refocused on the outlaw walking ahead of him. He tried to ignore the faintness filling his head.

Soft dots of yellow were slowly bringing the crowded buildings and surrounding houses back to their drab reality from the fanciful silver and black images of the night. At times like this, he wondered what Ireland must look like in the early morning, with all the thatched-roof houses scattered about the green countryside his mother used to praise and his uncle still loved to talk about. There wasn't much to sing about here, just a land in which a man could lose himself—or find his soul.

Ahead, he saw a woman sweeping the sidewalk in front of her small millinery store. Obviously, she was getting an early start on her day and seemed oblivous to the gunfight minutes before. Her crinkly pale face was a familiar one. He had known Mrs. Jacobs since boyhood. It had never occurred to him before that she, too, had endured the nastiness of discrimination all these years because she was Jewish. How had she handled it so well? He shook away the question. Now wasn't the time to be concerned about such a matter.

"Mornin', Mrs. Jacobs," Carlow greeted the old woman and added, "It might be best for you to stay inside a bit longer. We're expecting trouble from a gang of outlaws. You know we've got eight of them locked up in the jail."

"Bless you, son, but a woman feels safe with you Rangers around," she responded with a craggy-toothed smile and huge wrinkles around her eyes. "May I ask if you are carrying an acorn . . . for luck? I gave some to your uncle, the fine rascal, bless his great strength. Did he give you one? He was supposed to, but I have the feeling he was, well, drinking. I have more inside." Her voice trailed into a softness-layered shyness. Carlow guessed she had something of a crush on Kileen.

"Yes, ma'am, I do—and I thank you for thinking of us," he said proudly and glanced at Lee, who snickered.

She nodded and held out a scrap of bread from her apron pocket for the dog, which he swallowed in one gulp. Carlow touched the brim of his hat, chuckled, and walked on, proud of the small metal badge under his coat. Her warm greeting turned back the chill inside him. It felt good to be appreciated for a change in this town.

For a moment it was like the first days as a Ranger when he thrilled to the image of being one of the protectors of his Texas. He was sorry his mother hadn't lived long enough to see him take the oath. Her death from pneumonia had twisted him into a teenager seeking trouble to pound away the ache in his soul. By that time Kileen had left them to become a Texas Ranger. Carlow's mind returned him to a room above the saloon where Carlow's mother worked as a waitress. A comely lady even to the end, she had likely sold herself to keep her family fed. Even now, his mind didn't want to settle long on that probability.

After her death he lived wherever a ranch provided a bed along with meals and a little day pay. Then Kileen learned Carlow was going alone to town and picking fights in saloons. Shortly after that, Ranger Captain McNelly invited Carlow—and Dornan—to join the force. When Carlow realized the captain was an old friend of his uncle's, he confronted Kileen about the matter.

Kileen's answer was brusque. " 'Twas a wee past time for ye to become a real man, Time. Your sweet mither—me sainted sister—God bless her soul, she didn't raise ye to become a barroom thug. An' besides, me heart went out to those poor cowlads who were left to fend for theirselves against the likes of ye."

As Carlow walked away from the old woman, pushing Lee Holt ahead of him with his hand-carbine, she called out, *"Dia's Muire dhuit."* The young Ranger stopped, turned around, and repeated the Irish blessing with a wide smile. He knew few smatterings of the old tongue, besides the magnificent curses Kileen could deliver so eloquently, but the sweet blessing of "God and Mary be with you" was one. It was especially nice coming from her, a Jew. The old woman put her hand to her mouth gratefully and nodded. Lee spat and swore. Carlow jabbed him in the side with the nose of his gun, and the movement sent a jolt of pain through Carlow's shoulder and arm. He cringed and looked away so his childhood acquaintance wouldn't see the tears that pushed themselves to the corners of his eyes.

"You know, Holt, I'd put in a good word for you—with the judge," Carlow said through clenched teeth, "if you told me where Mallow's gang hid out—and what Silver looks like. Might keep you from hanging."

"Hard to put in a good word when you're dead, Carlow," Holt shot back. "Besides, you wouldn't believe me if I told you."

"Try me."

"Naw, forget it. You'll be cold by this hour tomorrow."

Overhead the dull sky was brightening with a touch of rose blossoming on its edges, but adding no warmth. After covering the remaining distance to the corner, Carlow saw a familiar silhouette in the jail doorway across the street. Carlow waved and Shannon Dornan waved back. The sudden movement triggered another shrill pain that flew through his body. Carlow shivered and ground his teeth together to hold it off.

"Hey, Time! Glad your face has appeared. Gettin' worried, I was!" Dornan yelled to his friend, bringing Carlow back to the morning. "I've been alone here since Wilkins left to help that fool mayor. Screamin' all bejesus Pickenson was, something about a man breaking into his store. Wilkins hasn't come back yet, probably stopped to see that Daisy girl." Dornan chuckled, paused, and continued, "Have you seen Old Thunder? I heard gunfire down by the Alamo awhile back. Not long after I heard shots your way."

"No. I know where he is, though. I'll give you Lee Holt here and go see how he's doing," Carlow yelled back as he cleared the sidewalk and entered the quiet street.

"Lee Holt? Oh, yeah, the youngest skunk. How are ye, Lee, still as full of it as ever?" Dornan shouted into the still morning as he tossed something small in his hand, catching and flipping it into the air. After several tosses Carlow realized it was the acorn from Kileen.

Lee sneered and Carlow said, "That's not a nice way to greet an old friend. Try again. Do it now."

"Ah, ah, g-good mornin', Sh-Shannon."

"That's much better," Carlow said and grinned, in spite of the weak feeling that washed over him.

Nearly a block away a young prostitute in a dark blue coat and hat walked toward Dornan and interrupted the Rangers' long-distance conversation. She smiled a greeting to him; her eyes moved to Carlow, and her expression was a warm invitation. He smiled back, as did Dornan. Ten feet behind her, three drunks struggled to keep each other from falling off the earth as they walked together toward the jail. Their heads were covered with dirty, misshapen hats; a torn blanket was wrapped half around one man to keep off the chill while another wore what once was a tweed suitcoat. The third drunk was swallowed up in a much-too-large overcoat.

Dornan watched the drunks with casual interest for a moment, and then the woman with personal interest for a moment more. The tossed acorn caught the back of his palm and bounced onto the street. Glancing at it, Dornan returned his attention to Carlow crossing the street.

"I see ye have some company, Time," Dornan said,

referring to the black dog trotting beside the young Ranger. "Where'd you find the black laddie there? 'Twould be good luck, I reckon, to have a stray dog join you in the night. Say, are you hurt, Time?"

"No, Shannon, I'm fine. This bastard and Mickey Houlihan, remember him? They jumped me."

"Where's Mickey?"

"Left for his mother's table, I suppose," Carlow responded, his grin widening.

"Did ya see the *puca* this night?" Dornan asked very seriously. "There be one about, you know. Your uncle agrees with meself on that."

Carlow grinned and shook his head negatively. Much of his response was simply relief from the tension of the night. It hurt to laugh and made him a little dizzy. He was glad the ordeal was over but would admit it to no one, especially not Old Thunder. Every shadow, every noise, had been the Mallow gang coming for him. A soft chuckle was his self-rebuke for being so intimidated by the very darkness itself. In response to his good luck, he touched the small, flat stone in his shirt pocket with his left hand. It was always there. He saw Dornan repeat the motion on his own shirt.

"When this is over, I'm goin' to my cousin's," Dornan said happily, waving a letter he had read regularly for a month, "And you know he wants you to come, too."

For months Dornan had been talking about leaving Texas and going north to Saint Louis, Missouri. Dornan's older cousin had built a large general store there and had invited him to come and work. Dornan wanted Carlow to come with him and talked about it almost daily. But Carlow couldn't imagine life elsewhere. Kileen had helped raise him, and the young Ranger couldn't just leave him behind. It wasn't the same for Dornan, who had no relatives near at all.

"Right, and the mayor has invited us to tea," Carlow answered.

A buggy turned the corner at a disjointed trot and headed down the street where Carlow, the stray dog, and the arrested outlaw were crossing. *It's awfully early—or awfully late—for that kind of travel*, Carlow thought. *Even the freighters haven't started yet*. Carlow was alert, forcing his mind away from the pain of his shoulder. Lee Holt took a step to his left as they paused to let the advancing carriage pass. Carlow caught the man's furtive glance toward the buggy's driver.

Of course! Ranger Wilkins had been drawn away to leave his friend alone while Carlow and Kileen were ambushed at their posts. The gang hadn't expected him to get this far! They hadn't expected him to be alive! Without hesitation, Carlow dived in front of the trotting horse, throwing his hand-carbine at the animal's nose as he moved. Startled, the animal reared just as the dark-bearded, evil-faced Willie Holt raised a hidden shotgun from within the buggy.

Carlow rolled away from the prancing hooves, yanked two outlaw pistols from his belt, and fired, still on his back, at the off-balanced Willie. Bullets from both guns caught the oldest brother before he could regain control of the horse or aim. Willie's shotgun blasted into the cold morning sky as lead struck the outlaw's stomach three times and hurled him backward from the buggy seat. The broken-armed Lee Holt looked on in total disbelief, shouted at his wounded brother, and ran back toward the opposite row of buildings. Barking fiercely, the black terrier took off after him.

Carlow's head was swimming in pain from reopening his knife wound. He fired twice at the fleeing Lee, missed with both shots, and yelled over his head, "Shannon! Get inside!"

His warning was too late as the three Mallow gang members, who were masquerading as drunks, opened fire at Dornan. Horrified, the young whore on the sidewalk screamed and ran into the street. She paused long enough to retch before scurrying away. Dornan hesitated and reached for his holstered gun. One shot clipped the planked sidewalk where he stood and another whined into the still air. A third bullet thudded into his right shoulder, spinning him sideways. Two more slugs slammed into his chest and threw him halfway through the open doorway.

Carlow fired again with the revolver in his right hand, more carefully this time, and Willie Holt disappeared inside the buggy. The terrified horse bolted, uncontrolled, down the street. Without standing, Carlow flipped over on his stomach and emptied both guns at the drunks. A bullet ripped into his left arm, leaving a growing path of blood on his overcoat. He dropped the smoking empty pistols in front of him and grabbed his holstered pistol and the remaining outlaw gun from his belt. Lying in the street, his hand-carbine was forgotten.

From behind him a solitary shot searched for Carlow's head. Only its fleeting orange flame told him of the source as the bullet spat venom into the frozen, clotted earth to his right. He was surrounded! Carlow pulled himself up and raced for the jail. Bullets sang death songs past his face and arms as he ran. A shot from behind drove into his lower right leg as he stepped onto the sidewalk. He crumpled with the sickening impact, and the outlaw gun in his left hand went sailing into the street.

Three more shots smashed into him and two slammed into the planked sidewalk beside him. He was going to die! Right here, right now. He tried to think, remembered the Smith & Wesson revolver from Kileen and shifted his Colt to his left hand.

Yanking it free of his pocket with his right, he fired both guns in the direction of his assailants behind him and knew he must move or be killed. The shock of his wounds hadn't yet registered but weakness and pain were draining away his ability to react. He knew he was already badly wounded. Glancing at his blood-soaked clothes, he forced himself to crawl.

Finally he managed to get behind the post that had once held a wooden railing in front of the jail. Another train of bullets cut at the post, his sole protection from both the masquerading drunks and the hidden shooter across the street. Wood slivers scattered onto his back. One shot clipped the top of his left shoulder. Behind him, lying still and facedown, was the unmoving body of his best friend, Shannon Dornan. The sidewalk under him was seeping with red pools. A foot from his still hand was a crumpled letter. Carlow would not allow himself to look. This could not be happening!

The disguised outlaws were hidden somewhere down the street and shooting at his position, but doing it carefully so as not to expose themselves. As far as he knew, only one was down. The outlaw's body was sprawled across the sidewalk. Across the street must be at least one outlaw and the broken-armed Lee Holt. There would be more, if the whole gang had sneaked into town. Where was Kileen?

Where was Wilkins? Probably both were already dead. Just like they tried to get him earlier.

He was in the fight of his life, and apparently no one in town intended to raise a hand. His breath was coming in short gasps, not nearly fast enough. The thought slid through him about what they would do when he was dead and the gang was free to go as it pleased. Carlow took a deep breath to calm himself; he had to get inside. Kileen had pounded into him the need to think; only animals reacted.

First, he must set up a covering fire. Firing as rapidly as he could work the hammers of his pistols, he drove bullets toward the hidden gang down the sidewalk and across the street. Then coiling his body into a tight knot, he sprang on one leg, through the open doorway, landing on his friend's body. Bullets challenged his flight. Three hit Dornan's body, delivering puffs of white smoke from the back of his shirt. A fourth sliced along Carlow's stomach. Another nicked the doorframe and a flying chunk of wood cut his cheek.

He scrambled to get over the unmoving Dornan and inside. The pain throughout his body was excruciating, yanking away what thinning breath he had. Finally inside, Carlow lay flat on his stomach, gasping for air, unable to move farther. A bullet searched for his head and dug itself into the floor.

"Well, look here, Raul. Look at what the cat has

drug to the party. We got us another scared Ranger," came the sarcastic voice of the balding outlaw from behind the bars of his cell.

"*Sí*, ees bloody one, too," the flat-nosed Mexican beside him answered. Laughter followed from the other captured gang members, mixed with swearing and sarcastic challenges for Carlow to go back outside.

"You're gonna die like your friend there. Unless you're smart enough to let us be on our way," said another outlaw, a short, portly man with a fancy leather vest under a gray coat. He spat for emphasis.

Carlow didn't look at the prisoners but took strength from their taunts. Wobbling to his feet, he grabbed Dornan's shirt and dragged the body into the jail. One bullet drove a furrow in his overcoat sleeve but missed his arm, another slammed against the door. He pushed it shut with his left shoulder. The impact made his chest vibrate with a searing ache that grabbed at his courage. Two more bullets hit against the oak door as it closed. With great effort he lifted the support plank beside the door frame and placed it into position.

Moving as fast as he could drag his stiffening leg, Carlow went to a wall rack of loaded rifles and shotguns. Leaving his empty pistols on the adjacent desk, he grabbed a Henry breech-loading rifle and returned to the small front window. His chest heaving, he fired six times rapidly at shapes slipping in and out of the shadows toward him from the left. He couldn't tell if he was accurate, but the shapes quit advancing. He was dizzy and held out his arm against the wall to keep from falling. Blood strings covered his supporting hand.

As his gunshots died, the street turned menacingly quiet. Where were his enemies? How many were left? Were they sneaking closer? The window gave him a good field of fire for the street and some of the sidewalk. But a man could crawl close to the wall and come up from under the window. Or they could sneak around the jail and come from both sides of the sidewalk at once.

At least he had been able to get his friend out of the line of fire. He glanced over at Dornan's still body and blinked back the tears that wanted out. A glance at the back door told him it was bolted shut and reinforced with a nailed support board. It would sustain heavy pounding, he thought.

"Silver's gonna git ya, Carlow. He's got too many guns." A strangely friendly voice came from among the prisoners. "Why in hell die in this godforsaken place? This town won't be helpin' any Irishman—an' you know it. Get out of here, now—while you still can."

Without turning from the window, Carlow responded, "If your friends rush this place, you'll never know how it turns out. I'll kill all of you first."

There was silence, then the first prisoner said with a quiver in his voice, "Goddamn, man, you can't do that! That'd be murder. Y-You're a Ranger!"

"Not since your friends killed my friend Shannon I'm not," he said. Reaching inside his coat, he ripped the small shield from his shirt. He threw it toward the far wall and pain followed, rippling through his entire body.

Across the street the unmistakable sound of a shotgun blast ripped through the morning. It was too far away to reach him, and he wondered why they shot from there. Other shots followed, but nothing rattled against the building. He heard scuffling down the street where the drunks apparently were hidden. He shook his head to clear it from the dizziness that sought what alertness remained. Wounds clawed at his stamina. He shut his eyes just for an instant. Was he dying?

Did he just see Mrs. Jacobs with a shotgun? Did he glimpse the grocer Sampson with a rifle? He saw the wounded Lee Holt race from his hiding place across the street. Behind him orange flame roared. Lee stopped, spun, and collapsed into the street. A voice like no other cut into his fuzzy brain. Thunder! It was his uncle out there! Time Carlow let the dizziness take him away.

Suddenly the front door of the jail splintered open, and a huge bear of a man stood there, a smoking shotgun in his hands. Behind him came the sounds of other men shouting, shooting at shadows, and yelling orders. Carlow heard none of it. Old Thunder Kileen glanced at the silent form of Shannon Dornan. In the big man's fist was the acorn dropped in the street outside the jail. He fell to his knees beside the unconscious Carlow.

"Time! Time, me son. It's gonna be all right. The Mallow gang is gone. They got Wilkins. But me an' some fightin' cowlads . . . look outside," Old Thunder said, holding Carlow's head in his huge hands. "Do ye be havin' the acorn, me son?" He reached into Carlow's pocket and felt for the tiny tribute and bit his lower lip as his fingers touched it.

He looked back at the unmoving shape of Shannon Dornan. Silently he reminded himself that all windows should be opened at the moment of death so the soul could leave. The big Ranger stood and went to the three windows in the jail and released the wooden shutters. He glanced at the front door to reassure himself that it, too, was open.

As he returned to his unconscious nephew, Kileen glared at the Mallow outlaws inside the cell; his face contracted into a sight that made each man cringe. "By the saints, 'tis a shame your own lads killed ye— all o' ye—with stray bullets."

Sweating in spite of the cold morning air, Mickey Houlihan worked his way along a narrow and steeply banked creek bed, one of the gang's established trails to their hideout. Morning haze was being pushed aside by an increasingly confident sun. Little water remained from autumn rains, but the rock lining removed tracks, except in the eyes of an accomplished scout. He told himself Ranger Kileen wouldn't get down from his horse to look at clicks on rocks and tried to laugh. His forced gaiety came in white puffs of air-smoke. It was a way to fool himself into thinking he wasn't scared. He glanced at his back trail again and was comforted by the absence of any sign of riders following.

His clothes were damp with battle sweat, and his empty holster flopped against his thigh as he rode. Shivering, he tried to forget he had surrendered his pistol to Carlow—without a fight. His hat was also gone, but he remembered it flying off as he galloped away from the big Ranger and some cowhands chasing him. The sheathed Winchester beneath his right leg felt good. It was Lee's. So was the bay under him. He couldn't find his sorrel in his frightened rush to escape Kileen's wrath. He turned in the saddle and squinted. Nothing. He spurred his tiring horse into a lope.

The ache in his ribs was all too familiar; they were cracked. His nose was broken, again, but he had straightened it and felt the loosened cartilage ripple in his fingers. Dried blood was caked to his freckled cheeks and thin mustache. His leg ached from buckshot that had ripped his pants and tore across flesh, but he had been lucky. Irish lucky. As far as he knew, the other members of the gang were dead, dying, or arrested.

Time Carlow. Time Carlow. His mind wouldn't let go of seeing him. It had been years since they played together. The little boy had grown up into a tough man—with a devastating punch. He should have known, having Kileen to raise him. He didn't like to think about it, but he was sure both Time Carlow and Shannon Dornan were dead. They had to be with all the lead coming at them. Two friends, they were, from another time, a time long forgotten and best kept that way, he reassured himself. From what Jesse Wilson told him before he rattled and ran, they had killed the third Ranger, too.

Old Thunder Kileen was another matter. Houli-han knew he escaped from the big man's wrath by seconds—and only because Jesse lost his nerve and started running, and that had caught the attention of their adversaries. What happened? Silver Mallow had told him—and the others—that the whole thing was set up. The mayor would let them into town through the back door of his store. Pickenson had told them where each Ranger could be found. The Rangers wouldn't know they were around until it was too late. What happened to the three who were sup-posed to kill Kileen? And where the hell did those cowboys come from? Wasn't everyone in town sup-posed to stay out of sight while they overran the Rangers? Wasn't that what Pickenson guaranteed? He shivered when he recalled Mrs. Jacobs with a shotgun. That old witch had fired both barrels at him. He glanced at his leg and shivered.

Ahead was a small ranch. A hideout for Silver Mallow and his gang. *They would be there, having enjoyed a good night's sleep and a hot breakfast,* he thought bitterly. Down through a shallow arroyo he eased the spent horse. This was the only way into the cabin area from the north. Annoyed shadows within the ravine fretted at their plight below his horse's feet. Minutes later he rose out of a dry creek bed that served as an open spoon inside the stretch of clustered trees. The gray day felt as if it had grown even colder against his perspiring skin as he rode slowly toward the main ranch building. He wasn't sure of time, but it had to be mid-morning, although it looked earlier.

Familiar outlines took shape of a ramshackle barn, a narrow bunkhouse, a small stone shed for keeping meat and butter cool, an outhouse, and a corral attached to the barn. A thin line of smoke rising from the main house indicated the breakfast fire was still alive, if barely. In the corral a dozen horses stirred as he approached. Whinnies sought his own horse, and the tired animal responded gratefully. Houlihan patted the horse's sticky neck; it had brought him far and fast. He rolled his tongue across his lips. Whoever was standing guard should have seen him by now.

Where were they? Usually Silver had two sentries in place day and night. There was no way to hide a ranch, especially out here. Silver had arranged it so the apparent owner was an elderly Mexican couple. If strangers came, they were the ones who came out to greet them. There hadn't been any serious mistakes in the three years Silver had operated from here, and it wasn't going to change now. It was the ultimate disguise, the outlaw leader proclaimed often.

There was always a posse sent out, or a bunch of angry cowhands; nothing different about that. Only this time the gang had failed. That was different and

Houlihan didn't like it. He believed Silver Mallow was invincible; it made him feel stronger. For one thing, just the way Mallow came up with various disguises to make himself look different. It was something to see, all right. He didn't like the thought of this powerful man being capable of mistakes. *Insane at times, yes, and cruel, but not like the rest of us,* he thought. Of course, Silver Mallow didn't know much about "Old Thunder" Kileen—or his nephew, either, for that matter. Houlihan did because he grew up with them. He winced, not relishing the idea of telling Houston Holt that his two brothers were dead.

He made the horse move slowly toward the corral. The horse was nearing exhaustion but the sight and smell of other horses had revived it somewhat. From the main house, yellow light seeped through the edges of the closed window shutters and out of the small watch holes in the center of each shutter. One solitary ray touched the rock-lined bed surrounding three scrawny bushes on the side of the wooden porch.

Casually he pulled the Bull Durham pouch from his vest pocket. Both hands were kept in sight. Slowly the paper was unfolded and tobacco sprinkled into the crease. It was all right to smoke. He was safe. After rolling it tightly, he placed the cigarette in his mouth, letting his eyes search the ranch buildings for movement or the glimmer of gun metal. He popped life into the match on the pommel and drew deeply from the cigarette, finding calmness as he let the smoke curl in front of his chiseled face. A trickle of sweat skidded down his cheek, leaving a trail through dried blood.

"Hey, the house! It's meself, Mickey!" he yelled from fifty yards out, his hands held away from his sides to further indicate his nonaggressive intentions.

He tried to keep his voice low, a practiced hard growl he favored but hadn't quite perfected. It was a little like Silver's voice, he thought—and hoped. At least, that was his goal. No one was quite like Silver Mallow. No one. His eyes stopped at the bushes, one of Mallow's fetishes. Houlihan thought the man cared more about those pathetic bushes than he did any of his men. Only silence reached his examination. From under his hat another sweat trickle followed the first. He blotted it carefully with his shirtsleeve and took another drag on his cigarette. Could Ranger Kileen have gotten in front of him? No, that couldn't be.

"Hey, inside! I be alone, hungry—and would be fightin' hell for a wee cup of coffee. I be hit. Ourselves ran into trouble!" he yelled, breath-smoke trailing his words. Astride his horse, he sat, unmoving, fifteen yards from the barn's planked door with the leather strap hinges.

"Hey, Mickey, how are you, man? Where are the

others? How come you're ridin' Lee's bay? Where's that sorrel o' yurn?"

Houlihan jumped in the saddle, even as he recognized the voice. It was Joe Benson. The bulldog-faced outlaw had a head that looked as if it connected to his shoulders without benefit of a neck. A flat rock for a nose and a thick, droopy mustache added to his rather comical appearance. A cigar stub grew from the corner of his mouth, which was cocked in a smile that was part fear and part relief.

"Dead—or gonna be. Bless their souls." Houlihan flipped the cigarette toward the dirt and swung down. "My horse, he were shot."

"What? Take his hoss, will ya, Lemmie? Looks like it's gonna fall down." Benson half-turned into the barn, his face partially hidden by his own frosty breathe. "You ran an awful good hoss into the ground, Mickey. Better be a good reason."

The silhouette of a one-armed man filled the space beside Benson. Lemmie Truitt's empty left sleeve pinned at his shoulder wiggled as he stepped toward Houlihan. He had lost his left arm in the war. It was said he shot the Union surgeon who did it, right in the field hospital, as soon as he was conscious. His weapon of choice was a Smith & Wesson double-action .44 revolver. It rested in a flapped holster on his left hip, positioned with the butt forward, for a right-hand draw, his only hand.

"Lemmie, it be mighty fine seein' you. Didn't think meself would be seein' anything but the devil hisself. The night's been full o' lead." Houlihan tried to keep his voice low and growling, moving to shake the man's hand.

Truitt received Houlihan's hand with a strong grip and smiled thinly. "Sounds like you've got bad news for the boss. You boys botched it, huh? Damn, Silver'll be fit to be tied. Say, you won't tell him we was inside, will ya? Damn cold out here."

"I thought it was all set up—with that fool of a mayor." Benson eyed the lanky Irishman suspiciously. "What the hell happened, Mickey? Lopez and Abbie came back last night, tied to their saddles. Dead as the day. Are there Rangers headed our way?"

"Naw, no way they be trailin' me," Houlihan responded. He rolled another cigarette and put the thought of Old Thunder Kileen out of his mind. He told the two outlaws what had happened, including the deaths of the three Rangers, and ended with his near-death escape. The woman's shotgun became one fired by Kileen himself; Jesse Wilson's death became a desperate attempt on his part to save the outlaw's life before being forced to flee.

"Are you sayin' they got both Lee—and Willie?" Benson questioned.

"Aye, early on, it be. That bloody bastird Ranger

Time Carlow, he be killin' Willie." Houlihan couldn't help feeling a sense of pride about the way his childhood friend had battled.

"In a fair fight?"

"Fact 'tis, Willie be sneakin' up on him, came driving by in a fine buggy. Like we planned. But ourselves, we got Carlow—an' his friend, Dornan—an' the other'n, too."

Benson didn't ask about Houlihan's familiarity with the Rangers' names, focusing, instead, on the status of the gang members who had ridden with him. "Damn. An' you're sure they were all dead—when you left? Houston'll want every detail—and it better not change with the tellin'. He's not as mean as Willie, but I wouldn't push him nohow."

Houlihan scuffed his boot in the dirt, avoiding Benson's intense stare. "They be lookin' mighty dead to meself, Joe. But I didn't be gettin' down to check on their fine souls. By that time, bullets were comin' from everywhere. I tried to be savin' Jesse, but—"

"So you left their bodies."

Houlihan swallowed hard. "Aye, reckon I be doin' that."

"So, it's just you that got away." Benson cocked his head to the side. "How about our boys—in the jail?"

"They still be stayin' there, I reckon. Bless 'em all."

"How'd you do all that shootin'—without your

Colt?" Benson pointed at the empy holster on Houlihan's hip.

Houlihan followed Benson's hand. His shoulders
rose and fell before answering. "The blasted thing
musta come out when I be ridin'. Didn't have time
fer no reloadin' anyway."

"Here, let me have your hoss. I'll rub him down
and give him some grain while you go in an' see the
boss." Truitt reached out for the reins in Houlihan's
hand. "You hurt bad, Mickey?"

"No, just hurts." He patted the horse's slick neck.
"I be thankin' ye, Lemmie. I be ridin' hisself awful
hard."

"Yeah, appears that way."

"Better walk 'im first, Lemmie," Benson advised.
"No water 'til he cools down."

Inside the log-lined ranch house a blackened and
cracked stone fireplace held a simmering fire. Mickey
Houlihan stepped into the familiar main room; it
reeked of fried food, urine, tobacco, and sweat. Setting on the fire's edge was a coffeepot, mixing its tan-
talizing aroma with the other smells. Four cups lay
next to the pot; one half-filled. Left over from breakfast, he figured. A single oil lamp was doing its best to
push the shadows into the corners. Unrolled bedrolls
lay in the far corner of the packed clay floor. Next to
them was a pile of flour-sack masks with eyeholes cut
in them, the gang's basic disguise, when they weren't

wearing something more elaborate. In the far northwest corner was a stack of Winchesters.

Around a long, gray table sat four hard-looking
men. Houlihan expected to see them; they were Silver's lieutenants. The rest were in the bunkhouse,
sleeping or playing cards. Silver Mallow—the only
one that really mattered—wasn't in sight. His was
the bedroom to the right. *Surely he was up by now*,
Houlihan thought. *Of course, the man liked his privacy.* The Mexican man and wife were in their small
bedroom with a torn blanket across the doorway for
privacy.

Besides Silver Mallow, the one man he didn't
want to face was there. But Houlihan knew he would
be. Whiskey-eyed Houston Holt was a skinny man
with odd, yellowish skin and a haughty face that
stared at the world through thick spectacles. Resemblance to his older and younger brothers was slight.
Only their meanness seemed familial. His dark coat
and short-brimmed hat were streaked with old trail
dust. Although Holt was seated, Houlihan could see
two revolvers, butts forward, at the outlaw's waist,
and the flat handle of a large knife. He thought again
of his empty holster and cursed himself for losing his
pistol. Holt's only greeting was movement of his eyes
to see who was coming behind him.

Leering at the tired Irishman, like a one-eyed
jack-o'-lantern, was Jesus. The Mexican bandit's head

was covered by a tied bandanna; his sombrero, nowhere in sight. A filthy black eye patch covered his left eye, taken years ago in a knife fight. Across his chest were crossed bandoliers. In front of him, on the table, was a full cup of coffee and a crumpled map. He was tracing a route with his fingers, more for his own consideration than anyone else's. Next to him was William Terrell, dressed in a full Confederate officer's uniform. He liked being called "General," but it was common knowledge among the gang that the uniform was stolen and he had been a deserter. A blackened and frayed bullet hole in the back of the jacket was an indication of what happened to its real owner. Terrell said something to Jesus, and the Mexican's hard eye immediately went to the empty holster, then Houlihan's blooded leg. Jesus's laugh followed.

Only Manuel Santos smiled warmly. He was a gentle soul, in Houlihan's estimation, a man given to following others without much thought of the consequences. The Mexican outlaw should have been a schoolteacher or a store clerk, Houlihan often thought. Wearing a scruffy coat, fringed leather leggings, and a sombrero that was too large for his head, the diminutive man was little more than a slave, cooking, packing, and doing chores.

"Well, me boys, 'tis a fine sight you are for this Irishman's tired eyes." Houlihan's words started off low in his throat but ended with a nervous whine to them. He bit the inside of his cheek to end his nervousness.

"What happened to you, Mickey?" Manuel Santos asked as he looked at the Irishman's bloody condition. "Did you know Lopez—and Abbie—are dead?"

"Oh, not bad, I be. Ourselves, we . . . ah, we ran into the devil's own," Houlihan explained, holding his arm with his other and wishing he were somewhere else. He told the four men what had happened in town. Joe Benson slid into the room behind him. The room got smaller as silence slithered up the walls and surrounded the men inside.

Houston Holt was the first to respond. His hands gripped the table in disbelief. Crimson crawled up his neck to his balding forehead. "Are you saying my brothers are dead?"

With his head down, Santos offered, "You was lucky to git 'way. Mickey. That's fer sure."

"You left them? Their bodies?" Houston Holt stood, his eyes darting through the heavy spectacles and daring Houlihan to say the wrong thing.

Houlihan stared at the floor. He scuffed his boot at an unseen spot near where he stood. Finally he answered, "Aye. I be havin' no choice, Houston. On me dear mither's grave. Really. They be pourin' lead at us."

"Bet they killed Lee's purty bay, too," Santos said, a tear edging into the corner of his right eye.

"No, he came ridin' in on Lee's hoss," Benson advised, examining the cups for one not yet used.

"Shut up, Santos, you fool," Holt snarled. "You're sure my brothers are dead?"

"Aye, sure as the sun be risin'," Houlihan reaffirmed.

"Did you run off like some woman—with them needin' help?" Holt asked, his eyes narrowing. He already knew the answer.

Houlihan glanced at Jesus. The evil Mexican's giggling was scary and making him even more nervous. His solitary eye seemed to glow. A frown slipped over the Irish outlaw's face, then disappeared as soon as he realized it might be misunderstood. Ignoring the discussion, "General" Terrell rose and headed toward Benson to refill his own cup. The bulldog outlaw poured him fresh coffee, and Terrell patted him on the back and returned to the table.

"No, Houston, I swear on me mither's grave, I sure 'nuff didn't be leavin' them in need. I-I-I'm sorry. We just, well . . ."

"Shut up, you stupid Irish bastard! I don't give a damn about your whore of a mother."

Houlihan's lower lip gave away his fear. "I-I'm s-sorry, Houston. There be nuthin' I could do, I tell ya."

"What couldn't you do, Houlihan?" The question snapped against the room like a bullwhip. Silver Mallow stood in the doorway of his bedroom.

7

Silver Mallow's handsome face spoke of a late-morning nap; his six-foot frame appeared stiff; a full dark beard matched his thick black hair. A white shirt with a ruffled front was only halfway buttoned with a silver chain and cross wandering along the seam. His suspenders hung at the sides of pants stuck in knee-high black boots. A pearl-handled revolver was barely visible from its position in his waistband. As always, he carried himself like an elegant Southern gentleman.

He smiled warmly and his pale blue eyes sparkled friendliness. "I asked you a question, Mickey." The voice was almost syrupy.

"Silver, ah, Boss, I be bringin' bad news." Houlihan's voice had lost its attempt to sound like Mallow; it was more like that of a child seeking forgiveness. He tried not to stare at Mallow's beard, but it was a disguise he hadn't seen before. *Why was Mallow wearing something like that now?* he asked himself silently. *Can't he see I'm hurt?*

"Has anyone asked if you would like some coffee? Have you eaten?" Mallow motioned toward the coffeepot. Yellowed light scurried across the four silver rings on his right hand. Without looking up, Santos hurried to pour cups for Houlihan and Mallow. Benson stepped aside to let him have the pot.

"Oh, thank ye, Silver. Coffee an' food would taste mighty good. An awful night, it be. We got three Rangers, but we didn't get our friends busted loose—and they got Lee, an' Willie. All . . . but me."

Mallow's light blue eyes measured Houlihan curiously; his mouth twisting into a half-smile. Vain and supremely confident, his fingers found his fake beard and stroked it. Houlihan swallowed and tried to shut out remembrances of his fellow gang members' whisperings about their leader being a psychotic killer; one said a Confederate army medical report listed him as deranged, bordering on a split personality.

After two drinks Jesse Wilson had related one particularly disturbing story about how Mallow had decapitated a lynching victim somewhere in Texas and walked around showing off the head and singing some Italian song nobody could understand. General Terrell was the only one who seemed to appreciate how much Silver enjoyed his mysterious presence with the law. Mallow liked presenting himself as "Mr. Beethoven," even occasionally sneaking into a town to play a cornet or guitar with the local band undetected—and took great pride in the fact that no wanted poster carried anything about him except a description that could fit a thousand men. Terrell advised any of the gang who wanted to listen that this meant Silver Mallow could walk away from arrest when they couldn't. He reminded them of the large trunk in Mallow's room that held all manner of disguises.

Santos handed Houlihan the filled cup, and the Irishman excessively thanked him. The small outlaw smiled and walked over to give a cup to Mallow. The six-foot Southerner thanked him graciously, and Santos backed away so he wouldn't turn his back on Mallow out of respect, eventually retaking his position beside the far wall.

"Isn't anyone going to ask me about my new beard?" Mallow smiled and stroked the fake covering again. "I woke up thinking about it—and thought I'd see how it looked. Bought it off that traveling actor troupe. Remember the ones that came through Bennett a few months back?"

Laughter and compliments about the beard followed.

"There was a black-haired woman with them you-all thought quite worthy." That brought more vigorous response and a few crude remarks that generated a frown from Mallow.

Benson smiled widely and said, "Damn. Makes you look like one o' them senators, Boss."

"I like that yeller wig the best. I don't think your own momma would know ya in that one," Terrell added.

Jesus howled at that response and said something in Spanish that no one, except Santos, understood. The little Mexican nodded and grinned.

Mallow sipped the coffee and turned his attention to the Irishman as Houlihan nervously began reciting what had happened in town, gulping his coffee as he spoke to help hold his nerves in place. Mallow listened without interrupting. Only his heavy black eyebrows showed any signs of emotion, arching occasionally as Houlihan recounted some failed detail of the attack.

When Houlihan finished, Mallow's first question surprised everyone but Terrell. "I don't suppose you had time to hear that new singer in town? What's her name . . . Anna something . . . ah, yes, Anna Nalene."

Houlihan's face was a question mark. He glanced at Jesus, who was laughing again, then at Santos, who appeared to be on the verge of crying.

Rubbing his chin, Houlihan finally answered, "No, Silver, we were too busy."

"A shame, Mickey. A shame. I understand she has an excellent voice. Trained back East. We all must go hear her one of these days," Mallow said, taking another sip of his coffee. "No one would know us."

Terrell glanced at Jesus, but the Mexican outlaw was staring at his map.

"Aye, that we must," Houlihan agreed enthusiastically.

That brought laughter from everyone in the room, except Holt.

"So you killed three Rangers out of four." Mallow took a sip of his coffee without taking his gaze from the nervous Irishman. His tone remained gentle, almost soft. "You were stopped by one man?"

Houlihan waved his arms as if swatting away the statement before answering. "Oh, no, Silver, the whole town be shootin' at us. The big Ranger had a dozen men with him all by hisself."

"You let them kill both of my brothers, you Irish bastard!" Holt interrupted.

"Come off it, Houston," Terrell said. "Enough about last night. I think we need to drink to our fallen comrades." He stood and went to the cupboard, gingerly touched the one door barely hanging in place, and grabbed a bottle.

"A worthy idea, General," Mallow responded, without a trace of sarcasm in his use of the title.

As the bottle was passed from man to man, Manuel Santos grew more agitated. "*Sí*, are we safe here?" he finally asked, his eyes wide and blinking. Santos bit his lip before speaking; it wasn't like the small outlaw to question anything they did. Terrell was watching Mallow, who appeared not to be listening, just staring at the fire. He was now in control of the bottle and adding enough whiskey to refill his cup.

"Manuel, everything'll be fine. Won't she be, Silver?" Houlihan said, his tongue pushing against the side of his mouth before speaking. "Ourselves are doin' a smart job, we are. 'Ceptin' this one wee time. An' there be three Rangers who won't be ridin' ag'in us no more." He glanced at Mallow for approval, but their leader was preoccupied with whatever was on his mind.

Unconvinced that the ranch remained a safe haven, Santos turned pale and began to swallow over and over, like a man who was going to vomit. He put his hand over his mouth and breathed deeply. Glancing at the agitated outlaw, Jesus saw his expression and slid his chair back from the table. In Spanish he told Santos to go outside. The frail outlaw stumbled for the door, opened it, and made a loud gurgling noise into the cool day.

"Don't throw up on my bushes." Mallow's voice was gentle but firm.

Jesus glanced at Mallow, snorted, and said, "*Sí*, Silver, eet weel be *bueno* . . . how you say . . . fer-tee-lie-zeer."

"That's not funny, Jesus, and you know it." Mallow turned away from the fire.

"Lo siento." Jesus's face was suddenly tense. "Jesus ees sorry, El Silver."

Mallow raised his cup in tribute as if nothing had happened. "To our fallen friends, warriors to the end. May we ride with them again in the next life. And may our enemies quiver at that thought."

"To Lee . . . and Willie," Houston Holt growled and downed his mixture of whiskey and coffee in one large gulp, leaving dribbles on his chin.

Holt wrinkled his yellowish forehead, pushed his glasses back to the bridge of his nose, and asked, "Silver, what do you think happened? Did that Pickenson crawfish on us? Can we go get their bodies? I'd like to give 'em a proper burial. Maw an' Paw would've favored that."

Mallow examined his cup, stirring it with his ringed first finger. "No, Houston, I don't think so. Joshuah B. Pickenson is a man of God. He preaches on Sundays. Methodist church. My father was a Methodist minister, you know."

Holt wanted to ask what that had to do with anything, but he noticed Mallow perked up whenever he talked about religion, music, or jewelry. They weren't subjects to push Mallow on. Holt had never known any man interested in such things, but the outlaw leader's intensity surfaced in unusual ways. Incensed at his own fear of arguing with Mallow, especially bringing up the burial of his brothers again,

Holt slammed his empty cup on the table. "God-dammit, Houlihan, what happened?" Holt screamed in an agitated voice, "If Pickenson did his job, why did I lose my two brothers? Tell me . . . again. An' none o' that Irish gibberish this time."

"Let it go, Houston, " Mallow said. "He's already answered that." Smiling broadly as he spoke, Mallow walked over to the table and grabbed Holt by the front of his shirt, pulling him from his seat in one swift motion. The sudden violence surprised everyone in the room, except Jesus, who only grinned.

"Question a man of God again and I'll kill you," Mallow snarled into the surprised man's face. Holt's yellow cheeks drained, his thin eyebrows arched, his glasses slid halfway down his nose; both hands clenched and opened at his side. Mallow released the shirt and stepped back.

Like the crack of a whip, Holt reached for his holstered pistol. As his hand settled around the butt, Mallow's pearl-handled revolver was staring at Holt's nose four feet away. The room grew small; it felt no bigger than the dark hole at the barrel's end of Mallow's gun.

Manuel Santos returned to the house, smiling grimly and wiping his mouth with his shirtsleeve. He was greeted by Benson, looking for a way to ease the tension. "Say, Santos, how 'bout fixin' some grub? Silver? Houston? Bin awhile since breakfast. Ol' Manuel is mighty good with a skillet."

The diminutive outlaw glanced eagerly at Mallow for a friendly response, not yet comprehending the gun in Mallow's fist. Holt's face was shattered yellow pastry as he moved his right hand slowly up and away from the unmoved gun. Gingerly both hands finally touched the tabletop; one pushed his glasses into place, then returned to lie beside the other. His eyes blinked twice, then averted Mallow's glare, bracing for the shot that would follow. Mallow uncocked his gun and returned it to his waistband. Benson's sigh of relief sounded like a rusty water handle.

"Don't mind Houston none, Boss," the bulldog-necked outlaw said, his coiled body belying the words, "He don't mean nuthin'. He's jes' feelin' bad about his brothers, that's all."

"Shut up!" Holt snapped. "I'll decide what I mean." He didn't want to look down at his groin for the wetness he knew was there.

Mallow ignored both remarks and walked over to the nervous Santos rapidly laying strips of salt pork into a large frying pan. After filling it, the little outlaw took the iron handle with both hands, partly because of its weight but mostly to keep the nervousness from upsetting his display, and placed it on the edge of the fire. As the meat began to sizzle, Santos stood over it and cut chunks of raw potato and peppers, letting them drop into the pan. A handful of wild onions and Indian root lay nearby to be added later.

"Mickey, how good is this big Ranger . . . what did you call him? Old Thunder?" Mallow asked casually, taking a small bite of potato from the skillet.

"Well, hisself was a fine bare-knuckle fighter. O' course, that were days past, it were. Most agreeable fella, like you 'n' me, 'cept when he be roused. Fierce as a lion, he be then."

Without commenting, Mallow watched Santos prepare breakfast in his jerky manner.

"Mind you, lads, if Old Thunder Kileen be leadin' a posse, we be havin' plenty of time. No tracker, he be. Not unless it's in a saloon or a whorehouse." Houlihan chuckled at his joke and Mallow did, too. Benson didn't know what to do or say, so he headed for the coffeepot.

"You say three Rangers were killed?" Mallow asked. Santos watched him, disappointment growing on his face that Mallow evidently didn't comment as he usually did about food.

"Aye. Time Carlow, Shannon Dornan—and an-other'n I not be knowin'."

Pouring coffee, Benson observed, "I hear Kileen ain't much with a gun."

"Aye, Old Thunder's more likely to be beatin' ya to death with his fists or a gun butt. He's hard, Silver. Don't mess with hisself." Houlihan eyed the coffee and motioned for Benson to pour him some more. "Time Carlow, he's the hand with a gun. Somethin' fierce, as I recall."

"You seem to know these Irishmen well." Mallow probed and took another bite of potato. "Who broke your nose? One of them? Who hit you with the scattergun?"

"Aye, Carlow did both, before I shot him. We be lads in Bennett."

"I see." Mallow turned toward Santos. "Tastes very good, Manuel."

The small outlaw beamed and looked at Jesus, who snorted.

General Terrell entered the conversation to remind the others that eight of their colleagues were still in jail and that now only one Ranger stood between them and their release.

With his back to the table and Mickey Houlihan, Mallow picked up an onion and examined it. Suddenly the onion fell from his hand and a single peeling fluttered downward in a feeble chase to catch its core. He drew his gun and fired before either hit the ground. No one saw his hand move; the falling onion was the only movement that registered with anyone's eyes.

Houlihan's chest exploded with a crimson circle where his heart was. A second shot was an eye-blink behind, slamming a hole in his forehead. A third bullet hit the Irish outlaw again in the chest. The combined impact tore his body from the chair like giant, invisible hands had grabbed it and tossed the bloody shape onto the floor. The three rapid gunshots were followed by acrid gunsmoke sucking all of the sound from the room.

Frozen by the violent suddenness, the other outlaws watched Houlihan's body heave and sag as life fled and blood seeped into the clay floor. Instinctively Benson's peripheral vision was on Jesus. He should have expected something like this from Mallow. The hard-faced Mexican was the only one who hadn't reacted to the gunfight. His drinking continued during the gunshots, as if nothing was out of the ordinary. Houston Holt was crouched with a pistol in his fat fist, his walrus face barely clearing the tabletop. Manuel Santos lay flat on the floor, his eyes closed, clutching an uncut portion of the potato with both hands under him. Next to him was a whole pepper. Terrell was slowly moving his hand away from his own holstered revolver, his face drawn with intensity.

Mallow stared at his smoking revolver, looked up at the men frozen at the table, and stroked his fake beard. "There's no place at our table for a coward. He left good men to die." Looking around for a plate, he asked Santos, as if nothing had occurred, "How's the food comin'? I'm certain everyone here is starving. It's been a long morning."

The diminutive outlaw stood and smiled, visibly proud to be noticed by Mallow. It was almost ready.

Mallow took only passing notice of the chopped greens that Santos was working into the cooking meat and potato slices. His focus was now on Benson. "Joe, do you have any cigars? A cigar would taste good right now."

"I-I-I think there's some in my saddlebags."

"That's a shame."

"Oh, no problem, I'll go get them—after I get . . . Houlihan outta here." Benson responded, trying to catch Jesus's attention to help him with the body. Jesus was deliberately ignoring his attempts, pretending to study the map again.

As Benson headed urgently toward the unmoving body, five men appeared at the door, each armed and worried. "What's the shootin' about?" the one-armed Truitt asked, a pistol in his lone hand. At his side was "Shorty" Beathard in long johns and boots and holding a long-barreled Colt. He barely came to Truitt's shoulders. Behind them were three other men in long johns, carrying guns.

"Mornin', boys," Mallow said cheerfully. "Thanks for coming. It's nothing. Mickey didn't understand how I feel about not leaving any of us behind, that's all." He gestured in the direction of the dead outlaw. "You're welcome to stay for some chow. We won't be heading for the Bar Six range until this afternoon. Billy is already there, right, General?"

"Yes, sir."

Santos grimaced at the thought of cooking enough for five more men, then tried to smile. It was best around Mallow.

Shorty Beathard was the first to respond. "Thanks, Boss, I'm headin' back to the game. Got a nice streak goin'. We's jes' worried ya was in trouble, that's all."

"I appreciate your concern a great deal, Shorty. I really do," Mallow said. The others nodded and followed Beathard back to the bunkhouse. One of the outlaws advised Beathard that he better not be dealing from the bottom. Truitt lingered a moment, hoping for a special invitation. Benson motioned for him to help with carrying out Houlihan. Santos turned toward Benson and said gently, "Chow's ready, Joe." His statement was really a question.

General Terrell heard the comment and roared, "Let's eat, by God!" He hiccupped, then again. His third hiccup bothered him, like the reason for it was a force somewhere in the room, not inside his body. He looked around as if to find the reason and hiccupped once more.

Mallow nodded agreement to Santos, and the small man immediately began shoving the hot food onto stoneware plates. By the time Truitt and Joe Benson returned, holding a fistful of cigars, the others were eating. Mallow was talking about an orchestra he had heard in Waco that had really moved him. He explained in detail how the violins seemed to lift the audience to another place and time, then hummed a passage and became angry when he couldn't recall more of it. No one attempted to interrupt or change the subject. Benson glanced at Terrell and noticed a pistol was in his lap. With Silver Mallow, that was smart.

"One of these days we'll ride over to Waco—and listen to them again. Maybe I'll take my cornet and sit in with them. They liked that before," Mallow continued. "They do an exceptional Beethoven. Do you like Beethoven, Houston?"

Houston Holt was surprised to be asked the question. "Ah, Silver, well . . . I don't know. I don't know if I've ever heard him."

Mallow smiled and General Terrell chuckled. Unsure of what to do, Benson walked toward Mallow and handed him a cigar while Truitt took a seat next to Jesus. Taking a second to focus, Mallow snatched the fistful from Benson's other hand, leaving the offered smoke. Then he took that cigar, placed it in his mouth, and shoved the others into his shirt pocket. One slid out his hand to the floor. Mallow stared at the fallen cigar, then stared at the scared Benson. The bulldog-framed outlaw bent over and retrieved the cigar, offering it with a trembling hand. Mallow took it and placed the cigar in his pocket with the rest.

From his place on the other side of the table,

Jesus struck a match on the tabletop and lit his cigar, returning Mallow's attention to the conversation. Terrell noticed that Jesus's right hand remained in his lap. The outlaw leader rattled on about Beethoven's gift for counter melody, blowing white smoke across the table. Only Jesus attempted to wipe it away from his face before he swallowed the rest of his coffee. He looked up at Santos for more, and the little man jumped to comply.

Holt finally managed to say, "I kinda like 'Dixie'— an' 'Camptown Ladies'—an' 'Bury Me Not on the Lone Prairie." He smiled widely at his contribution to the conversation.

"Good, Houston, good. I think you'd like Beethoven, too." Mallow finished bringing the food to his mouth, chewed it slowly, and swallowed. "Joe, you are the best tracker I know. I want this Kileen dead—an' our men out of that Bennett jail. I want to know if this stupid Irishman was right about the other Rangers. Take four men and go after that big Ranger. Find him and kill him, wherever he is, in town or in camp. I've also got a hunch Houlihan is wrong about how many Rangers made it. If any are alive, they'll be wherever he is."

A wide smile on his face, Benson jumped to his feet. "I'll git 'er done, Silver."

"I know you will, Joe. You could outtrack a Comanche," Mallow responded and turned toward

Benson. "Manuel, water my bushes today, will you? I thought they looked a bit peaked last evening, didn't you?" He took another puff on his cigar. "Houston, I think it's time we took a little more interest in music, don't you?"

Holt bit his lower lip. Why were the tough questions always aimed at him? "Ah, sure, Boss, what do you want us to do?"

"After we get through with the Bar Six, let's go to Bennett and hear that Anna what's-her-name. What do you think, Houston?"

Holt swallowed and avoided Jesus's eyes. "Ah, yes, Boss, I'd like that. Does she do Beethoven?"

Without waiting for another response, Mallow turned toward the terrified Manuel Santos. "Manuel, please ask Señor Valdez and his wife to join us. Tell him to bring his guitar. I am in the mood for some music." He rubbed his beard and said, "Oh, and bring my guitar, too, will you, please?" Santos scurried away and Mallow asked the one-eyed Mexican outlaw, "Jesus, you're confident we can move the Bar Six herd across the Rio Grande during the night?"

Jesus ran his finger over the route on the map. Slowly he looked up at Mallow and grinned. "*Sí.*"

"Excellent." Mallow began to sing, " 'Beautiful dreamer, wake unto me, Starlight and dew drops are waiting for thee . . .' "

Three days later a lone buckboard wagon rattled across the prairie toward a predetermined destination: the *hacienda* of an old Mexican bandit queen named Angel Balta. Trailing the wagon on lead ropes were three Ranger horses. Besides being the Rangers' primary possessions, the animals served the practical purpose of walking over tracks the wagon made in the hard ground. Kileen was worried Silver Mallow would send men to follow him and finish the job, and he had lived too long not to be careful.

His route included several side trips into timber to further deceive any possible followers, keeping close to cottonwood, stunted post oak, and hickory trees where he could, and using underbrush and curled mesquite to further obliterate his purpose. Taking advantage of a wall of thick-growing juniper, he backtracked a quarter mile and brushed away the markings with a tree branch. Any Comanche warrior could have followed it without slowing down, but he hoped none of the Mallow outlaws were that good at tracking.

Besides, it gave him time to think—and to drink enough not to think. About what had happened. Fading light brought texture to three large burlap sacks containing supplies and a feverish Time Carlow, wrapped in tight bandages and covered with heavy blankets. As the wagon passed, shadows shivered in the cold still air and reached out to touch them in mournful reverence.

On the other side of the horizon behind him was the numbed town, trying to recover from the Mallow gang attack. None of the Mallow outlaws were arrested; all were killed, even the three who attempted to ambush Kileen. Several Alamo patrons remembered the big Ranger dragging them out of the saloon after the fighting was over. None knew anything about them showing up dead in the jail. There was also a disagreement about how many had sneaked into town or if any had escaped. Kileen told a town councilman he thought stray bullets from the gang had killed all of the prisoners, including the three he hauled in from the Alamo. Mayor Pickenson was livid about the dead prisoners, but offered nothing about the two dead Rangers, except the observation that they should never have come to town.

Before leaving Bennett, Kileen had sent a

telegram to Captain McNelly apprising him of the situation; the death of thirteen of Silver Mallow's outlaws; the death of two Rangers and the near death of a third. He expressed disappointment in not arresting Mallow or the rest of his gang, or even knowing what the outlaw leader looked like, or the location of his hideout. But asked for a leave of absence for himself and Carlow to give him time to heal before going after Mallow again. Silver Mallow's continued attacks on the region's ranchers was stated as likely, even though his numbers were considerably decreased.

Captain McNelly's responding telegram was hard; he informed Kileen that he would be expected in Brownsville by June 1 or would no longer be a Ranger. Carlow was not an active Ranger as of the Mallow gang fight and, therefore, would not be paid by the state, nor expected to rejoin the unit. The entire Special Force was headed toward El Paso to squelch another cattle-rustling ring. Silver Mallow would have to wait. The response angered Kileen and he burned it before leaving town.

That wasn't the worst of it. Two ranchers confronted him while he was loading his buckboard and asked when the Rangers would stop Silver Mallow completely. They didn't expect the failed ambush and loss of men to keep the gang from stealing their herds and moving them across the border. Kileen said he would return with more Rangers soon. The ranchers walked away with the impression Kileen was as fearful of the gang as the local sheriff. Leaving quickly with his wagon of supplies, Kileen felt the skeptical looks on the ranchers' faces followed him.

Overhead, a gloomy horizon held only the promise of winter. Red-eyed, Old Thunder Kileen snapped the reins of the two-horse hitch and yelled a drunken curse at the brown horse nipping at the bay on the left side. Ahead he could see a line of cottonwood trees standing sentry along a creek. Nearby was a worn adobe house that belonged to Angel Balta, once feared by both sides of the border, now old and living alone. There was a brief rumor, at least a year back, about a Mexican woman running with the Mallow gang, but he was certain it wasn't Angel.

The small house stood resigned and gaunt in the cold dusk; weather had wounded the outer walls of sun-dried alluvial clay and straw, leaving long streaks of discoloration and crumbling mud. A tired sunset tried to soften the appearance, giving it a distinctive red texture, along with every rock, bush, and tree one could see. The house had stood empty for years, except for an occasional passing traveler, until Angel moved in. He thought she'd been there, by herself, for at least three years, maybe more. He and Carlow discovered it by accident one day searching for three bank robbers. They found them later in San Antonio.

Angel's *hacienda* was miles outside of town and not convenient to the settlement's offerings or its trails. Years ago the first owner had raised crops of corn and oats, but the fields adjacent to the home had not felt the edge of a plow since their passing. Weeds and randy bushes had retaken command of the soil. Kileen intended to stay there with Carlow until the young man healed. If he lived. It was the only place that came to his mind. He hadn't asked her. Angel Balta owed him a favor from years back when the Ranger helped her escape from a wild bunch of vigilantes. He hoped she would remember it favorably, as well as that summer they spent in Mexico together. He did and it stirred him.

The old Ranger's mind rode in yesterday's flickering memories as he snapped the reins over stable-fat horses that came along with the wagon from one of the town stables. The owner, at first, attempted to bargain, but something in Kileen's eyes made him wary. Wagon and horses became a gift.

While Carlow was fighting outside the jail, the old Ranger himself had mounted a surprise counterattack against the Mallow gang with the help of four gun-savvy cowhands from the saloon. They thought only one outlaw escaped. People who saw Kileen said he would have killed his mother that morning if she had been in his way. Rumors of the old Ranger killing the prisoners himself slipped into saloon conversations but were said carefully to make sure the speaker couldn't be singled out for the statement. Kileen himself remembered little of the situation, only that his heart collapsed when he saw Carlow and Dornan lying in the jail.

He had already removed the bullets from Carlow's weakened body, rather Doc Williams had—under Kileen's gun. It wasn't conducive to good operating procedure, but Kileen simply told the man he would die if Carlow did. That seemed to provide all the motivation required.

As soon as the battle was over, townspeople appeared from everywhere to thank Kileen and to express their sorrow about the two dead Rangers and the badly wounded one. But it didn't matter what anyone said; they had spoken clearly by not helping. Only two townspeople had lent a hand during the battle, plus the four cowboys. Mrs. Jacobs had wounded one outlaw with her double-barreled shotgun just outside her store, but he had escaped. Kileen thought the outlaw looked familiar but wasn't certain.

The town's fear of retaliation by the gang was understandable to a point, but they had allowed two fine young Rangers to die and another to be severely wounded. Ten extra riflemen, easily achieved in a settlement filled with former Civil War combatants, would have wiped out the gang completely and probably saved the lives of both young lawmen. The bitter realization of that fact chewed on Kileen's mind and wouldn't release itself, even when the whiskey tried to wash it away.

What made it worse for him was the hateful recognition that he still didn't have the faintest idea of what Silver Mallow looked like. No Ranger did. He knew many of his henchmen; they were wanted for all manner of crimes. Jesus had lost his eye to Kileen in a wild fight four years ago; and he knew that Confederate army runaway they called General, and, of course, he knew the Holt brothers. He crossed himself in memory of two of them. There was a one-armed outlaw named Truitt, or something like that, who ran with them, and a fat, obnoxious man named Barat. And he would recognize bulldog-faced Joe Benson anywhere. He knew the worst of them—but not Silver Mallow. Maybe there really wasn't a Silver Mallow and it was just the figment of some newspaperman's imagination, but he didn't believe that. His examination of their attackers convinced him that none was the infamous Silver Mallow.

He cursed that he couldn't identify the man. Oh, there had been descriptions—of all kinds. One put him seven feet tall with horns under his hat. Another said he was blond, handsome, and dapper, an accomplished guitarist and cornet player who loved music of all kinds, popular and classical. Kileen dismissed this report as idle fantasy. Still, another said the man was totally unbalanced. That Kileen believed. A mad killer who cared about no one, not even his own men. Yet an apparent genius for rustling and raiding. But the fact was, while Silver Mallow's reputation was well established, his face wasn't. That wasn't unusual. Kileen had never met the great Mexican outlaw king General Juan Flores, either. Yet his bandit army had taken thousands of Texas cattle across the Rio Grande.

After the fighting was over and Carlow tended, Kileen decided he wouldn't let the town soil the memory of Shannon Dornan or touch the young man who was a son in his soul. He declined the town's free offer of a "boot hill" cemetery burial. Mayor Pickenson himself didn't come forward, remembering well Kileen's parting threat. Instead, a town councilman presented the cemetery offer to Kileen, bestowing the opportunity as if it were a precious gift to a child who might not understand the value. To the councilman's surprise, Old Thunder told him to bury the dead outlaws there but added that he actually thought they were too good for the town's cemetery.

Shannon Dornan's body he had buried beneath trees where he and Carlow had played and laughed as children. It was two hours north of town where

Dornan's parents had once lived. As the day's light settled along dark branches, he recalled seeing them climb the trees, laughing and shouting. Sometimes jumping into the creek. Sometimes shooting at each other with stick guns. Sometimes chasing Indians and outlaws that rode only in their imagination. Dornan would like that, the big man decided.

Not far away under a gnarled cottonwood tree was a small headstone, where Carlow and Dornan had buried Carlow's mother years before. Kileen had studied the dead wildflowers and buffalo grass imposing on the stone tribute after caring for Dornan's resting place. It pleased him to see the flowers, even though they were now dead from the changing season. He knew the presence of flowers growing on a grave meant the person buried there had lived a good life. If weeds grew, it meant the life had been evil.

Of course, Dornan would criticize him if the mound wasn't shaped right or the shadow from the tree didn't fully cover the grave. *That would be bad luck, the lad would hisself say*, Kileen thought, pushed the imagined conversation away, and took a long swig from a bottle held in place by his feet. He had left the unmarked grave knowing the mound was shaped right. Come spring, he would add a headstone that he ordered from the cheerful undertaker who also ran a barbershop and a bathhouse. He had stood quietly by the grave for a moment before leaving, hoping to hear a ripple of thunder, proof that Dornan's soul had reached heaven. He didn't hear any but decided his hearing wasn't as good as it used to be.

Kileen was certain Carlow and Dornan first met at a church social. He had only attended two of those in his life, so they were easy to remember. Both times his attendance—with Carlow—was the result of the prizefighter's attraction to a young woman who considered the church an important part of her life. Their affair was brief, but he still recalled that the prim woman was absolutely devilish in her bedroom.

Ranger Noah Wilkins was also killed during the gang's attack; Mayor Pickenson had led him into an ambush. Kileen knew his family and telegraphed them in Houston, advising of the death and asking what they would like to do with his remains and his horse. The return message advised they would come for his body and take him home to Houston for burial. The dead Ranger was left with the undertaker; Kileen paid the cheery man in gold to handle the readiness and warned him that if the Wilkins family was unhappy about any detail he would come back and stuff the man in one of his caskets. Kileen left Wilkins's horse with the stable owner, a fine blue roan that could run all day. With a toothy smile the undertaker assured him all such matters would be painstakingly handled and the mount would be turned over only to the family.

Pulling up in front of the house at last, Kileen waited until Angel Balta came out. He said nothing but blew into his cupped hands to warm them and to keep them where they could easily be seen. The big-breasted Mexican woman came to the doorway and stood for a minute studying the massive Ranger in the wagon. Like Old Thunder, she was an aging warrior who asked for no quarter of any man and gave none over three decades of banditry. She had ridden with different gangs and alone, robbing, stealing, and killing.

Once a stunning woman of considerable sensuality, Angelina Balta had reportedly bedded a hundred men, young and old. In her younger days she could outshoot and outdrink most of them. Saloon talk had it that "Angel Balta'll either kiss ya or kill ya." What lead and steel couldn't do, age achieved. Uneven eyesight, slower reflexes, and cranky bones were relentless enemies she'd never faced before. Still, she was a formidable-looking woman, and a sensuous one.

A bullet-hole-infested sombrero sat cockeyed on Angel Balta's head, setting off long, mostly gray hair that curled about her shoulders. She wore a faded shirt with billowy sleeves connected to dark leather cuffs. The cloth had worn thin trying to cover her enormous bosom, and the buttons were straining to hold their places. A tan leather skirt flared wide about her knees. A row of tiny bells was sewn around the bottom edge of the skirt. Heavy boots covered her calves and nearly reached her knees. They carried an inset design of green, red, and gold, now mostly gray and worn to bare rawhide.

Although she rode rarely these days and didn't own a horse, Angel Balta continued to wear large-roweled spurs that clanked in the cold air. Her brown hands held two pearl-handled, silver-plated revolvers as if they had been born there. A wide grin slowly took over her wrinkled brown face. Across her high cheekbones and wide nose was a long scar from Federal steel, a reminder of a guerilla fight after the war. Dark eyes sparkled happily. She batted her eyelashes and looked into Kileen's face. Both guns were quickly shoved into her waist belt, and she held out her arms to welome him.

"*Buenas tardes,* Señor Beeg Thunder, eet ees you! I thought eet was you, maybe, I hope," Angel said. "Bring your *compadre* into my *hacienda.* I hear of beeg fight. Two riders come this way yesterday. *Por favor,* you are most welcome. *Pronto,* bring the young warrior inside."

"I do thank ye, Angel, didn't know where else to be goin'."

"*De nada*, you ees *mucho* welcome, Señor Beeg Thunder."

Kileen jumped down and stood for a moment to let the wagon's rocking leave him. He turned into her waiting arms, and they held each other so long it took away their breath. He kissed her on the cheek.

"Cannot Beeg Thunder do better than that?" she teased and placed her opened mouth full on his. Her hands raced about his huge frame and ended at his groin. "*Sí*, just as Angel remembers. Beeg Thunder. Maybe later we can see some of that, maybe. Me have missed you *mucho*."

Kileen grinned from ear to ear and said, "Well, me fine lass, 'tis no secret I am most glad to see ye." He looked down at the bulge in his pants and laughed.

She chuckled deep in her throat and rubbed his groin. " Ees not good to keep thees buttoned."

"I-I've got to take care of me nephew."

"Of course you do, mi love," Angel said. "I am so glad to see you. I am sorry eet has to be thees way. How bad ees he hurt?"

Spinning away from her released embrace, Kileen lifted his nephew into his arms and carried the heavy load into the house. He explained Carlow's wounds but didn't ask more about the two riders' description of the fight. He didn't want to replay it again in his mind. The thought occurred to him that they came for sex and paid for it.

"Hisself, my nephew, is hit bad. Lost hisself a lot o' blood," Kileen said, grunting under the uncooperating weight of the unconscious Time Carlow. "The Mallow gang theirselves came for us. Many they be and four Rangers we be. Now only two, him an' me, but the outlaws lay about the town, dead. My laddie here, he got the oldest Holt brother hisself, Willie Holt, and wounded his brother Lee. I be helpin' Lee along to hell."

Angel nodded and her face curled into a sneer. "I hear of Silver Mallow—an' Jesus. Coyotes. No honor in their stealing. They keel women an' chil'run. You were lucky to get out alive, Beeg Thunder." She touched his face with fingers surprisingly gentle.

"Dammit all to hell! The stinking town wouldn't lift a finger to help us, except for an old lady, a grocer, and four cowlads," Kileen continued. "On me sister's grave, I swear I should've burned down the whole bleemin' town. Time Carlow and Shannon Dornan, they be lads there." It was a long speech for the old Ranger, helped along by anguish and whiskey.

"Sí, Beeg Thunder, but they ees Irish an' not welcome," Angel said and held open the door for Kileen to move through it. "No Mehican. No colored. No Mick."

Angel directed Kileen to lay Carlow on a bed with a straw mattress, her own bed. Kileen hesitated, but she insisted, then he asked if she would mind if the bed was moved to an east-west position, since its current angle, north-south, could bring misfortune. She grinned, remembering the big man's dependence on superstition, and shoved the bed in the other direction before he could help.

"Let's not be placing his hat on the wee bed, all right, Angel?" Kileen observed as he pushed the bed a bit farther in the right direction.

"*Sí, mucho* bad luck." Angel bit her lower lip to keep a second smile away. She helped Kileen pull back Carlow's thick woolly blankets to check his bandaging, leaving him naked. His chest and shoulders were tightly wrapped, as was his upper right arm. His right leg was strapped with rigid splints, and his cheek carried a small padded bandage. With false shyness, she avoided looking at Carlow's manhood, except for one glance that brought a sparkle to her eyes. Kileen examined the wrapping, more to comfort himself than to achieve any medical advance. Smiling, Angel stood quietly while Kileen drew a circle on the floor's dust around the bed with his finger.

A confident fire in a massive fireplace with a split-log mantel had already shoved the cold into one shivering corner of the one-room house and wouldn't let it move from there. Both returned to the wagon, unhitched the tired horses, and led them to the sagging lean-to that served as a stable. Pleased to be working with horses again, Angel began rubbing down their sweaty backs with handfuls of straw while Kileen brought around the three Ranger horses tied to the back of the wagon. He turned them loose in the adjacent corral. It looked like the sturdiest thing on the place, he mused to himself. Angel brought a sack of grain for each horse.

"Hell, these darlin' beasts not be knowin' what grain be, Angel, me lass," Kileen said with gusto. "They been a-eatin' sagebrush and weed—an' happy to get a wee of buffalo grass."

"Bueno hosses. You care for theem," Angel said and pointed at a stout bay. "That ees a fine one. Reminds me of *mi Cuchillo.*"

"Aye, that's the laddie's hoss. He named it Shadow. Could outrun one if'n the thought be occurrin'." Kileen observed and added, "Your *Cuchillo* would've been runnin' ri't with 'im."

Angel grinned and listened to a long story about Time Carlow riding that horse and running down two outlaws trying to escape from a bank robbery. Not to be outdone, the old Mexican bandit told a tale of her own about outracing a U. S. cavalry division to the Rio Grande. After settling the horses into the new quarters, they went to the wagon for Kileen's food sacks.

"Ees eet *Americano* pipe tobacco?" Angel asked eagerly.

"Ye damn betcha," Kileen chortled. "I remembered ye liked a good pipe—and I brought a whole can. Good stuff, it be." He lifted the can of tobacco from his sack and handed the container to her as if he were presenting a silver necklace.

Her eyes dropped shyly and then sought his gaze for something only she understood.

"Oh, an' I be bringin' somethin' fer your picture makin'," Kileen announced proudly. "Ye be drawin' those pretty things still, don't ye? Trees an' horses an' fine flowers, ye be bringin' to life on the papers?"

Angel smiled and acknowledged she still like to draw.

"Be shuttin' your eyes, then." Carefully he laid a pad of papers on the ground in front of her, along with wooden pencils, ink pens, and a small bag of salt.

She opened her eyes and her toothy smile was followed by a jump, then a wet kiss on Kileen's mouth. He told her the bag of salt was a symbol that abundance would always be found in her home. She kissed him again. He held up his finger and showed her a decorative glass ink bottle filled with black liquid. It couldn't have been more significant to her than receiving a piece of jewelry. As she took the ink bottle with both hands and held it to her, Angel happily explained that she hadn't been drawing much lately because of a lack of supplies. Implicit in the statement was the lack of funds to buy them. She was surprised that he found them in town, and he said they came from the old lady who ran the millinery store.

"I couldn't find the picture-drawin' things at Pickenson's store." His face flared with anger. "Hisself, the mayor, was in cahoots with Silver. Of that, meself is sure."

"So, you went to hees store to keel him, *sí?*"

"Yeah, I suppose I did. But I was after all these supplies, too," Kileen said. "Guess I figured on shootin' the bastard, then loadin' me wagon. But he wasn't there. Wasn't at his home, either. Hidin' until I left, he be. Only some yellow-haired helper was at the store. Goin' back to find Pickenson, I be. After the lad is well an' runnin' again. Then I will kill Silver Mallow—and any of his bunch that want to stand against us. Captain McNelly can damn wait."

A shadow crossed Angel's face as he talked about Mallow, then it disappeared. Her eyes began to tease his big face and her fingers ran across his unshaven cheek. "Was ze yellow-haired helper *señor*—or *señorita?*"

Kileen rubbed his chin. "Ah, he were a man."

"Oh, how nice, Beeg Thunder." Angel's smile pushed against deep dimples. "Please take thees and I weel get ze other presents."

"Ye let me, Angel." Kileen took the ink bottle and

leaned over to begin picking up his gifts. She leaned over, too, then looked up, pleased to see he was staring at her nearly exposed breasts. She took the pencils, pens, and bag of salt and stood, unable to stop grinning.

"Why does ze lady who make ze hats have theese theengs?"

"Aye, 'tis strange, indeed. I be askin' her where I might find picture-drawin' stuff since none be in the general store." Kileen held the papers and ink jar and was quiet for a moment. "Bless his soul, her late husband—the beloved Mr. Jacobs—was himself a man of drawings. His pictures are all about her store. She be glad for these things to be goin' to you."

"Did you tell her where you go?"

"Nay, jes' that I had meself a lady friend who be fond o' the drawin'."

Angel lowered her eyes.

Soon the small house smelled of aromatic pipe tobacco as Angel puffed on an old scratched pipe, seated in a rocking chair close to the fire. Kileen continued to remove food and supplies from the burlap sacks, stacking them into a cabinet that once had a door. He ignored nagging cobwebs but stopped when he saw a family of raccoons huddled under a chair next to the south wall.

"Angel, what be these lads? Breakfast on the hoof?"

"Aiie, they ees *mi amigos.*" She laughed and showed him a bent paper with a charcoal drawing of the racoons. "*Bueno*, how you say, they ees company for thees old woman. Angel also keep them from me chickens an' me eggs this way, *comprende?* Federales keel me three sons, so Angel ees alone."

"Aye, when they were killed, I be rememberin'. I shoulda shot them vigilantes right then an' there. Meself be mighty sorry, Angel." He couldn't remember any mention of a husband. Ever.

"Ees not your fault, Beeg Thunder. You help Angel *vamose.* You bury *mi* sons. Thees I know an' never forget. Do you ever marry?"

"Meself be marryin'?" Kileen repeated the question, shaking his head before the answer came. "No, me lass. Far as meself is concerned, the lad over there be as close to me son as the good Lord wants it to be. He be a fine one, Angel. Got a good head on his shoulders an'—oh, Lord a mercy—can he fight!"

"*Sí*, I tell so from Beeg Thunder's strong words. Weel he live?" The question came as easily as if she were asking about the weather.

Kileen bit his lower lip and answered tersely, "He will."

But a hard fever was challenging the young man's right to life. After making a broth for Carlow, Kileen applied small spoonfuls to his tongue, gently closing his mouth each time to encourage swallowing. He repeated the technique with a tin cup full of water from an *olla*. The clay jug sat cockeyed on a table with a leg wrapped in burlap strips to hold its broken piece in place. Then he laid a wet cloth on Carlow's forehead, hesitated, withdrew the acorn from his pocket, and placed it next to Carlow's feverish body.

The young Ranger's trembling hand reached out for Kileen. "M-My gun . . . w-where's my . . ." Carlow tried to rise, his head jerking left and right in a half-crazed search for the weapon. The cloth slid from his forehead to the bed.

"Easy, me son, easy. Old Thunder be gettin' it fer ye. All be well. The battlin' be over." Kileen patted Carlow's hand and pushed gently on his nephew's chest, avoiding his silver chain and cross.

After finding the hand-carbine and laying it across Carlow's stomach, Kileen guided the young man's right hand to the engraved stock. "There it be, me son. There it be." He started to remind him what the strange hand-carved design meant about being victorious, then saw the wet compress and returned it to Carlow's head. He watched the young man relax his tensed frame as the sensation of touching the weapon soothed his mind. Carlow's mind suddenly recalled something and he tensed once more. "M-My *L-Lia Fail,* w-where is . . ."

"Aye, me son, I'll be gettin' it. Ye be restin' now." Grimacing, the older Ranger knew what Carlow wanted and went quickly to the pile of his clothes beside the bed and retrieved the flat pebble from the shirt pocket. Fresh markings of dark crimson were layered over bloodstains from years long past.

"Here, me son. 'Tis your blood stone. Ye be holdin' it in your hand." Kileen placed the pebble in Carlow's opened palm and closed his weak fingers around it. Next to Carlow's head he laid the discarded Ranger badge. Withdrawing the tiny pouch of dirt, brought by Carlow's mother from Ireland, he shoved it alongside the other tributes. "By your mither's love, ye will be safe."

He stepped back, remembered something, and went to the counter. Grabbing an onion, he cut it in half and placed the pieces under Carlow's bed. Angel watched with a frown. Sensing her presence, he turned toward her. "A large onion me could not be findin', so it will be takin' more time to draw out the fever," he explained seriously.

Angel decided not to comment about the raccoons getting it. Finally the old Ranger sank into a second rocking chair, only this one had been splinted with supporting planks to hold the rocker arms in place. He produced a new flask of whiskey, took a long swig, and handed it to Angel, who accepted it eagerly.

"*Sí*, hot whiskey—on a cold night."

"Any time," Kileen said and chuckled.

"*Sí*. Like making love."

Kileen laughed loudly and said, "Ah, 'tis me same wonderful Angelina. Aye, like making love."

Night rushed at them as the two shared stories of battle, of love, and of grief. She showed him a stack of drawings, some curled with age. A number of sketches were of men; several of the same man playing a guitar. Kileen noted to himself that the man looked somewhat like his nephew, only without a mustache, but knew that couldn't be so and hurried past them to pictures of horses. Cuddled together, he and Angel slept on blankets on the dirt floor in front of the fire, warmed by whiskey, remembrance, and passionate lovemaking that left Kileen gasping for breath and Angel shouting lustily for more.

Just before false dawn, Kileen rose and went over to Carlow. His fever had broken, and Kileen's smile was as wide as his face. He stood over the sleeping young man and held his fingers near Carlow's nose to make certain he was breathing. Satisfied, he walked slowly to the *olla*. After wetting a rag from water in the clay jug, he placed it on Carlow's forehead, removing the old one. Next, water went into a tin cup. He held open the young man's mouth and gently poured several drops on Carlow's tongue, then pushed his mouth closed and repeated the process until the water was gone.

He talked quietly to the young Ranger as he

worked. "Time, me lad, you are going to be fine as an Irish mornin'. Aye, 'tis so. Would your ol' uncle be a-lyin' to ye? Aye, never so, never so. Ye rest now, me son, and get the panther back inside ye." Ten feet away Angel Balta watched her old lover and smiled, but a question was in her eyes.

When he finally returned to the blankets, she touched his hard face and said softly, "Tell me one theeng, Beeg Thunder, *por favor.* Eef your Time Carlow was not *mucho* hurt, would you have come to Angel?"

Kileen's eyes answered first. "No, me lady, I would have been afraid. Me lad's being hurt so bad—it gave me . . . a bloody excuse to see you. I . . . I . . . missed you, Angel me lady . . . an' I . . ."

She put her finger to his lips and hushed him to silence.

Angel Balta was up before dawn was barely a suggestion on the cold horizon, slipping quietly from the blankets to allow Kileen to continue sleeping. Soon a pot of hot coffee filled the room with its delicious aroma. Balta pushed the coals around to clear a place for a blackened skillet holding slices of salt pork. Her few scrawny chickens, kept in a strange-looking coop out back, had produced eight eggs, and she planned on adding all of them to their breakfast.

Before cooking, she went to Carlow and was pleased to discover him sleeping easily. For that good sign, she prayed, letting her flowing Spanish take her thoughts to her God. To herself, she muttered, "Time Carlow, you would be the same years as my oldest son. Hees name was Miguel and he was very brave, like you. I not be able to save heem. I weel save you. You weel be my son. *Mi hijo*." A single tear fought its way down her brown cheek.

Expertly she dressed each wound with a concoction she kept in a tightly capped jar. Something a Kiowa medicine man had given her. It always worked on her bullet wounds, and there had been more than a few over the years. She rebandaged him and was careful not to disturb the collection of things around his bed; the shortened Winchester, acorn, stained pebble, and a pouch filled with what appeared to be dirt. Knowing Kileen, she was certain they were some kind of superstitious ritual he felt was important.

"You ees lucky one, Señor Time Carlow," she muttered. "You have Beeg Thunder to care for you, to love you. Balta tell you about heem one day. *Sí*, you ees lucky. So ees Balta to have heem one more time. And Balta has you, *mi hijo*. Eet ees *bueno*. Balta ees *mucho* lucky."

Behind her came the unmistakable sounds of an awakening Kileen. He groaned to a standing position beside the bed, rolled his shoulders to relieve ever-increasing stiffness, growling and coughing as he moved. Awake enough to comprehend his actions, he glanced around the bed to assure himself that he had gotten out of the bed from the same side he had gone in. Satisfied his body would take another day of abuse and that he hadn't created bad luck, he lumbered toward Carlow's bed like a hibernating bear disturbed from his winter's sleep.

"By the saints, Angel, me love, 'tis early for you be up an' around," Kileen said. "How is the lad this fine morn?"

"Ees same, me theenk. Balta put Kiowa medicine on hees wounds. Medicine make bullet holes go away. Many times it work for Angel, for me sons." She wanted to express her feelings about Carlow but bit her lip to keep them to herself. It might frighten the big man into thinking she was pressuring him.

"Aye, I do be appreciatin' that, me Angel lass," Kileen said, kissed her cheek, and felt Carlow's forehead with his hand. "Is his fever still gone?"

"*Sí*, eet vamose. He rests good now."

"Aye, the onion has done its work."

Angel glanced under the bed and was surprised the raccoons had left the onion halves alone. "We must keep heem filled with ze water. To build hees strength," Angel responded and pointed at the *olla* on the far table. She decided not to comment on the onion.

Kileen's response was to return to the earthen jug, pour water into the same cup, and begin giving drops to Carlow as he'd done before. The unconscious Ranger showed no signs of accepting the tiny amounts of liquid reaching his tongue. Kileen studied the slow dripping and looked up at Angel for advice.

"Don't be lookin' like much to be givin' the lad strength, Angel. What should meself be doin'?"

"You are doing *bueno*. More would make heem choke. Drown heem even. You must be like ze love-making. Take long, long time." She winked.

After watching Kileen for a few minutes, Angel said, "Beeg Thunder, you keep doin' that. I weel fix our breakfast. Eggs 'n' salt pork 'n' tamales. I weel make more broth for Time."

"Sounds great, Angel. I be starvin'—an' me boy be needin' his strength."

"Then we go check on your hosses. Water for theem ees needed also."

"Aye, done it should be."

"An' then?" She smiled seductively.

Kileen measured her happy face and returned the greeting with a wide, warm smile. He took the cloth from Carlow's feverish head, wet and refolded it, and returned the damp compress to his forehead, then continued feeding Carlow small measures of water. Singing to herself, Angel pulled a skillet from her cupboard and sought the eggs she had set aside from last night. Soon wonderful smells of coffee and frying salt pork invaded the crowded house.

With his chin upraised, Kileen drew in the aroma and said, "Aye, 'tis, indeed, a blessed Irish morn."

Angel laughed.

After breakfast Angel Balta stepped to the opened doorway, stretching and yawning. A struggling sun had found some confidence in the gray sky and was gaining color. Kileen sat at the heavy oak table, finishing his coffee and eating the remainder of the breakfast from the skillet she set in front of him, after his third helping. Her own stomach was filled with hot food and her head was filled with the return of her old lover. She considered drawing a picture of one of Kileen's horses. It would be good to sketch again.

Yet her practiced eyes, dulled by the years, still caught movement where there shouldn't have been any on a gray ridge fifty feet to her right. With a warrior's instinct, she threw herself to the ground as two rifle shots ripped where she'd been a moment before. Angel scrambled back inside as Kileen rushed beside her, slammed shut the door, and lifted the heavy beam into place to bolt it.

Gasping for breath, Angel exclaimed, "Beeg Thunder, men weeth guns are coming! I see three. Maybe more, I theenk."

"Damn, it must be Silver's men. I'm sorry, Angel," Kileen said, studying the ridge as he spoke. "I thought they wouldn't be able to track me here. On me sainted mither's soul, I am sorry."

"No matter who. Eet may be banditos looking for food and gold," Angel said. "You fire from here, Balta weel go out back an' see eef we can get theem where they do not want to be."

"All right, but careful ye be, me love."

Angel frowned as she shoved a sheathed machete into her belt and threw a bandolier of bullets over her shoulder. "Balta theenks you believe thees ol' woman cannot fight no more."

"By the saints, I be sayin' no such thing, Angel," Kileen snapped and added, "There be no gun-fighter—lad or lass—that can be touchin' ye in this territory. Unless it be my fine lad a-lyin' thar."

"That ees more like eet. Give me cover when I go." Balta grabbed her two revolvers from atop a dilapidated dresser, then slipped out the back door. Removing the wood brace and barely reopening the door, Kileen swept the ridge with his Henry, firing at shadows and shapes. A groan indicated he had struck flesh.

The big Ranger moved to another tiny window, more of a gun portal than an open space in the wall. He could study the surrounding land and it appeared deceivingly peaceful. A winter morning with sunshine dancing across the land. A shadow shifted behind a large boulder and he fired three times into the dark shape. Screaming followed. *How many?* he wondered, and glanced at his young nephew, oblivious to the growing battle. Kileen slipped new cartridges into his rifle and eased back to the front door, opening it a crack. Six shots splintered the frame in response, and he jammed it shut again.

Outside of the *hacienda,* to his right, he heard a

strange thudding noise and decided it was Angel's machete at work. He heard the same noise again, followed by a scream that sounded more like an animal's cry than a man's moan. Gunfire trailed the sound, then silence. After tapping his rifle against the door three times, Kileen moved away from the entrance. Out of impulse he began climbing upon the dinner table, near the middle of the room. It was a sturdy piece of handmade furniture, but he hoped it wouldn't crash under his weight.

He paused only a moment to consider the superstition that putting one's shoes or boots on a table was bad luck. He decided to risk it. There wasn't time to remove his boots. Grunting, he stepped from the chair to the tabletop itself. There, he stood, cocked his rifle, and waited. He tried to keep from thinking about Angel. He had heard nothing since those initial sounds.

His thoughts were jerked back to the room as a shadow grabbed the thin line of sunlight at the base of the door. Still Kileen waited.

With a hard push, the door swung open and a crouching bulldog-faced man with a rifle burst into the room. His eyes sought the front window where Kileen had been. He never saw the big Ranger until it was too late as the old Irishman's bullets drove the intruder into the wall. He gasped and slid down the adobe structure, leaving a streak of blood. His rifle quivered in his hands and tumbled forward as the dead outlaw came to a sitting position with his legs sprawled apart and his head lying against his unmoving chest.

Kileen jumped to the floor, limping for several steps to ease the pain of the shock and cursing his decision to get down that way. His mind told him that was the bad luck for getting on the table with his boots on. He kicked the leg of the unmoving body to assure himself there was no longer a threat, then kicked the man's rifle toward the table. Grabbing the man's collar, he dragged the dead outlaw toward the opened door. He knew immediately who it was: Joe Benson. *Damn, Mallow's men are better trackers than me be thinking,* he told himself.

With one hand gripping Benson's collar and the other holding the dead outlaw's belt, Kileen held the body in place, keeping himself hidden. After one shot, the firing stopped as the remaining outlaws realized who was at the door. An energetic yell followed, "Come on, Joe got the big sonvabitch!"

Swearing loudly in Irish, Kileen shoved the body forward and slammed the door shut.

In the corner Time Carlow awoke, the first time he had been fully conscious since the attack in town. Disoriented, he had no idea of where he was, or what day it was, or what was going on. Carlow felt disconnected from his body, from the room, from the gunfire that had awakened him. He was wrapped so tightly it was difficult to move. Hunger clawed at his stomach. He saw the racooons huddling in the corner and thought he was in a cave. Shaking his head to clear it, he glanced toward the door and saw his uncle slamming it shut, a fierce grin on his rugged face. Carlow's hand touched the cold steel of his hand-carbine, finding it reassuring. His fingers explored further and found the acorn, then the pouch, and, finally, the blood stone. He tried to squeeze it, but his hand wouldn't quite close and the pebble bounced out of his hand to the floor.

Clouded contemplation followed as he finally determined the house was not one he was familiar with. His body began to shake uncontrollably and he struggled to retain his consciousness. He leaned back to alleviate the awful trembling. When he awoke a few seconds later, he was cold.

For several minutes he sat up staring at the room without comprehending. Carlow's vision blurred and his father put his hand on Carlow's shoulder to show the boy something in their house. His mother smiled at him from the kitchen; she was making stew in a huge kettle. All of the windows were open, and sunlight made the small house bright. His father disappeared before Carlow could turn to see what he wanted to show him. His mother held her hand to her mouth to hold back tears. His dreaming was disjointed, violent, and dark. He screamed out Shannon Dornan's name and it jolted him awake again.

Kileen was still standing at the doorway, peering outside to determine how many outlaws remained and where they were. His Henry was a toy in his huge hands. If he heard Carlow's yell, he didn't respond. Carlow's attention was drawn to two raccoons snarling beside the back wall. A third lay unmoving, the victim of a stray bullet. At the lopsided window above them, Carlow glimpsed a face he didn't know. What had been a shutter, hung by a solitary nail that refused to give up its responsibility. He blinked his eyes to make it go away, but the face remained. Carlow was certain he was delirious. He shut his eyes to squeeze away the deception.

He opened them and the man was still there, studying the house to assess where everyone was. Satisfied that Kileen was the only combatant, he pushed his revolver through the window and into position to fire at Kileen. Carlow saw a fist holding a long-barreled Colt revolver. It was already cocked as the man steadied the weapon with his hand braced against the windowsill and took aim.

Wildly Carlow yelled, "Look out, Thunder!" But the big man was concentrating on the ridge outside and didn't hear his thin voice. The wounded Ranger grabbed for the hand-carbine and almost pushed it off the bed. Frantically he levered the gun with the stock braced against his leg and fired without aiming. Startled, the outlaw's pistol went off as Carlow's bullet slammed into the wall next to him. The outlaw's shot thumped into the door and Kileen spun around. Two shots from the big Ranger's rifle followed like one long sound and the outlaw's face disappeared.

Carlow's gun slipped from his hands. His head was throbbing again. Throbbing like the roar of a great train. Pain shot across his chest and he grabbed for the feeling. The sudden motion brought nausea. He retched, but nothing came out. Dizzy. So dizzy. He was going to die. It would be peaceful. So easy. So easy. Over there, see? His mother was smiling at him. Now she was coming toward him. Oh, how he missed her. He would join her now. It would be good again. But she disappeared in the growing mist. Something had changed about the clearing that held him safe. Knots of thick fog took birth from the silent ground beneath the encircling rocks. Guardian trees held the billows close. He tried to peer into their hazy whiteness but could see nothing.

Wait! A flicker of light! Then another, and another, and another! Tiny campfires. Hundreds of them in a big circle, all around him! All around the opening where he lay dying. Hundreds of fires! No, thousands! The campfires looked endless. As far as he could see into the haze, there were twinkles of campfire light. This couldn't be. No one even knew where he was! He was surrounded by outlaws! A huge army! How could they have sneaked up on him so quietly? He must go and tell them to leave. But their campfires were not on the ground anymore. Below them, and him, was the dark endless sky.

"Time. Time. Are you all right?" It was Kileen talking to him.

How did he get up here with the campfires? Carlow thought. *Will he help me fight them? They are too many. Where is Shannon? He needs to be here, too.*

"Wake up, me son, ye be savin' Old Thunder's life, aye, it be so."

Carlow blinked his eyes and tried to remove himself from the thickening fog. Campfires faded and he was again on earth, in his bed. He sat up, his body soaked in sweat.

"Aye, 'tis Time Carlow. Awake he be, Angel." Kileen felt Carlow's forehead and glanced over his shoulder at the smiling Mexican woman who was putting her reloaded revolvers back on top of her dresser. Her machete was once again sheathed and lay on the table.

Kileen glanced back at her guns, then at Angel. "No thirteenth bullets did ye be loadin', me colleen?"

She shook her head, holding back a smile, and walked over to the bed. The bandolier of bullets over her shoulder brushed against his bandaged chest as she leaned over to feel Carlow's neck and cheeks. She whispered, *"Mi hijo."* Carlow's eyes fluttered open and he smiled thinly. Pleased at his attention, she kissed his cheek before standing and identifying herself, "I am Balta, Ranger Time Carlow."

"I-I am very h-happy . . . to m-meet you, m-ma'am. T-Thank you." Carlow barely finished before his eyes were shut again.

Angel advised through clenched teeth. "All *desparadoes* that come are dead. *Muerte. Cinco.* Five horses. Five dead hombres. I keel ze last one— with *pistola*. He ees with only one arm—before I keel heem. He lie near their hosses, Beeg Thunder." She acted as if she was going to say more but licked her lips instead and said, "Young Carlow weel need some . . . water, I theenk. Maybe more broth."

Kileen patted her softly on the back. "I'm goin' to look at the dead bastirds out there. Could be one is Silver hisself, the glorious devil. Will ye be givin me Time Carlow a bit o' water—or comin' with me?"

Angel's jaw tightened and a vein above her right eye throbbed. "May be they jes' *banditos.* Balta's *hacienda* ees, how you say, awk-ci-dent."

"No, me lass, they not be road agents. 'Tis Mallow's men, for certain. That one jes' outside the door be Joe Benson. An' the one-armed fella sounds like Truitt." Kileen's forehead collected in a heavy frown.

"By me sainted sister's grave, I wouldn't be knowin' Silver Mallow if he come up and introduced hisself."

"I-I hear Silver Mallow wears *mucho* silver. *Mucho* rings on hees hands." Managing a thin smile, Angel shrugged and suggested they should check the bodies for rings; she would give Carlow water and then join him. For the next half hour the two wandered from body to body with Kileen studying them while Angel watched. He identified only one more as a Mallow outlaw. Angel observed that Mallow was no longer a threat since he was nearly alone, pointing out the outlaw leader had lost eighteen men between the Bennett fight and today. She suggested he might even leave the region on his own.

Kileen stood after examining the last dead outlaw, a heavily bearded Mexican with a derby hat, unknown to the Ranger. Angel avoided looking at the man, watching the horizon, she said, for possible other ambushers. The big Ranger rubbed his chin. "Well, General Terrell an' Jesus be alive an' kickin'. They weren't here or there. None o' these bastirds has rings—so at least three devils are about, as sure as the raven brings bad luck." He imitated her study of the dulled sky as if trying to recall something else. "The last Ranger report from the captain hisself put Mallow's numbers at thirty men. He ain't alone, Angel—an' he ain't through."

"*Sí*, I guess not," she responded quietly, then

became animated. "Let's geet away from here, Beeg Thunder. Let's take your horses an' *vamose*. Anywhere. We can start over. You an'—"

"Ye be forgettin' about my nephew? There be no way he can take ridin', lass. We'll just have to keep a close watch." Kileen took her arm.

"Put theem on their horses and send ze bastards back to Silver. That should send heem a warning. Make heem leave."

"Aye, a good idea. Maybe me be followin' them beasts—and find Silver's hiding place itself." Kileen's eyes sparkled with the idea, and his grasp of her arm grew tighter.

She pulled on his fingers to release the pressure. "Ze ground ees too hard for tracking." She stomped her boot heel halfheartedly against the earth to make her point.

"Old Thunder can track a leaf in a storm," Kileen said, looking at his hand in surprise. "Ye be sayin' they are better trackers than meself?"

Her response was tactical. "Tie ze bodies on strong. Lead their hosses to ze crooked creek. Remember eet? Run theem in thees water, then send theem . . . *vamose!*"

He nodded and they returned to the small house in silence, both lost in separate thoughts. Kileen went immediately to the sleeping Carlow. With care, the big Ranger straightened the blankets around

Carlow, then picked up the fallen stone and Ranger badge beside the bed, and the dropped hand-carbine, and laid them next to the young Ranger. His only concern was not seeing the acorn, then he noticed it was nestled under the folded blankets. Seeing the pouch of Irish earth, he picked it up and returned it to his coat pocket, muttering, "Ye did well, me sis."

Angel watched him arrange the bed, letting her eyes stray twice toward Carlow's face, but the young Ranger had already closed his eyes. Finished with his adjustments, he turned back to Angel and held her to him. They studied each other's faces and kissed gently, then passionately. Angel's eyes were bright from battle and the twinge of love refound. Something else was there, too, a secret she couldn't decide what to do with.

"I'm gonna follow the Mallow hosses—back to the devil's own lair," Kileen said, his eyes narrowing. " 'Tis one edge he'll no longer be havin'.' "

Her face blossomed with fear. "No, Beeg Thunder. No, *por favor*. Do not follow theem. What eef you do find where Silver stays? Eet weel be one man against many. You weel be killed. *Por favor*, do not go."

"Lass, I be gettin' the feelin' ye don't want me findin' the wolf's lair."

She shook her hand vigorously and waved her

arms. "No, that ees not so! But Balta no want you een with ze wolves."

"Now who's short-changin' who?"

"Stay here—with me. Balta make you *mucho* happy."

"That you do, me lady, that you do. But I be a Ranger and this I must do. If I can track them hosses, I must."

Releasing her embrace, Kileen headed for the door, grabbed his rifle, and tapped it three times against the door. He stopped in the doorway and turned back. "If ye be cleanin' around the young lad's bed, the onions can go, but be not disturbin' the circle—and don't be leavin' the broom against the bed. Evil spirits be in the broom an' they be castin' a spell on the bed, if they be touchin' it." He paused and continued, "Aye, an' ye be knowin' not to be sweepin' the dirt out the door, don't ye? 'Twill empty the house o' good luck, it will."

"There weel be no good luck in thees place . . . our ho . . . no good luck eef you ride out to be killed." Angel folded her arms and tears began to finger her face.

He swallowed and blurted, "I-I'll only see if the hosses will take me to their hideout. No farther, me Angel. Old Thunder is no fool. 'Ceptin' 'round you, lass." His smile was wide and he forgot about his missing teeth. "But if'n we know where Satan be, we can lead the Rangers to him easy like on a fine Irish morn . . . a few months from now. All right?"

"H-He weel have guards . . . to w-watch ze road."

"Aye, reckon so." Kileen turned back and headed for the barn.

"I weel pack food for you," she said loudly. To herself, she choked, "I know where Silver ees, my love."

10

Nearly five months later a weak and pale Time Carlow walked from Angel Balta's rundown *hacienda* by himself. It was the third day in a row he had done so without aid from either Kileen or Angel. His exercise had steadily grown from uneven wobbles around the small house to walks with Angel to the barn, to short horseback rides, and recently she insisted he help with the mucking of the stalls. The work exhausted him quickly, but he understood its value. The young Ranger had become fond of the Mexican woman and was pleased to see his uncle so happy with her.

Gentle spring breezes welcomed him to the reborn land, but he barely noticed. He squinted against the early morning sun and turned away from its glorious light, squeezed his eyes for a long moment, then looked again into the new day. Hesitating, he took two more steps, like the land was shifting under him. Around his waist was his gunbelt for the first time. He drew the Colt, spun it uneasily in his hand, cocked and aimed, then released the hammer and returned the gun to his holster. As the gun hit leather, he pulled the hand-carbine from its special holster, tried to spin the lever in his hand, and dropped it.

His eyes widened with surprise and he stared down at the gun as if his arm had just fallen off. He knelt but, instead of picking up the hand-carbine, grabbed a handful of dirt. Fine dust fled as his fingers parted, quickly seeking the ground. Twice more he repeated the action before returning to the gun. He lifted it from the ground and ran his fingers over the engraved stock.

Behind him came Old Thunder Kileen. Winter months with Angel had been the most enjoyable season he could remember, and he found himself no longer feeling guilty about not going after Silver Mallow. Angel reinforced his inaction with much attention and reminders that he didn't owe Texas his life. Her sketches of both Kileen and Carlow were highlights of their sweet time together as the couple helped the young Ranger return to health.

Two house raccoons followed the big Ranger to the doorway, decided the journey didn't involve food, and returned to the hearth. Angel was in the backyard, feeding her chickens. Kileen stopped in the doorway and watched his nephew with eyes that saw more than a young man recovering from bullet wounds. A dullness in Carlow's eyes worried him far more than any scar on the young man's body. It was the look of a man without a reason to return.

During the long winter recovery, the big Ranger Kileen had finally told him of his best friend's death, as well the death of Ranger Noah Wilkins and McNelly's telegram. Actually the information came only after Carlow had asked. The old Ranger had told himself that he wasn't putting it off, only waiting until his nephew was ready. His descripton of the jailed prisoners all dying indicated it had been from stray bullets; Carlow had been surprised at the heavy toll but didn't challenge the observation. Kileen had also shared the attempted ambush at Angel's house; Carlow had no recollection of it. After acknowledging he wasn't the best tracker to begin with, the big Ranger admitted he lost the trail of the dead outlaws' horses a few miles beyond the creek where he started them running. Carlow's stoic reaction to the information was troubling, but Angel advised Kileen that her youngest son had reacted the same way when recovering from bad wounds the first time.

Carlow had heard news about the outlaw gang—as did Kileen—when an old friend of Angel's came to visit one day, almost a month ago. To be safe, she insisted Kileen hide under Carlow's bed. Both men heard the white-haired Mexican tell about the

Rangers leaving the area for good and that Silver Mallow had added new gunmen to his gang and was freely moving cattle across the border again. He told her Mallow's men were even showing up in Bennett from time to time, strutting around town. After the old Mexican left, Angel talked for an hour to keep Kileen from riding into Bennett by himself.

Watching his nephew, Kileen's wide hand gripped the adobe doorway hard, as if he wanted to yank a piece of hardened clay away. Carlow's eyes said the young Ranger was reliving the gunfight and his friend's death. Kileen was sure of it. Carlow's second—and successful—attempt to cock the carbine by spinning its circular lever brought Kileen back to the front yard of the hacienda.

" 'Tis a day made for the Irish. Almost as pretty as the Isle itself, bless her green soul," Kileen said tentatively, trying to sound enthusiastic.

"Yeah, I guess so," Carlow answered slowly without looking at his uncle.

The young Ranger pointed the gun in the direction of a small rock twenty feet away and fired. His bullet spit dirt into the air. Carlow frowned and fired again. This time his lead shattered the rock. He held the gun against his thigh and levered it rapidly, firing six more times. Satisfied, he pulled cartridges from his belt and silently added them to the gun as if Kileen were no longer there.

"Skip over that one, me son. That be a thirteenth bullet."

Without hesitation Carlow shoved it into his hand-carbine. Kileen grimaced and changed the subject. "Look, me lad. There be a white butterfly. 'Tis the first butterfly o' the spring. 'Tis white. Good luck it be, lad. All year."

Kileen made no comment about the shooting. It was the first Carlow had done since the gunfight, but silently the old Ranger marveled at his nephew's dexterity. He knew men who were good with a gun. Dangerous men like Clay Allison, Bill Longley, John Wesley Hardin, and Kid Antrim. Time Carlow was in that group. Maybe Silver Mallow was, too. Both thoughts scared him. Kileen watched him wobble slightly when he reholstered the hand-carbine.

Looking up at Kileen, Carlow said, "I want to see Shannon's grave."

Old Thunder wasn't ready for the statement. His massive chest rose and fell before he spoke. "Well, sure, me son . . . in a month or so, ye be ready to ride. I-I buried hisself under them old cottonwoods, ye know, where y-you lads used to fight the redmen an' outlaws with y-your stick guns. I-I reckoned Shannon would like restin' there."

"No, I want to go now."

"B-But, me lad, you can't . . ."

"You can stay here. I know where it is. Shadow's

ready for a good ride, thanks to Angel keeping him in shape."

"Nay, 'tis both of us that must go. Meself will be tellin' her of our plans."

Around the corner came Angel Balta with pistols in both hands. Her face was tense until she saw the two men talking. Dropping the guns to her side, Angel smiled and said, "Well, *amigos,* you might have let ol' Balta know eet was a day for ze target practice. I thought we was havin' visitors."

Kileen's expression was the answer she got first. It was a day she knew was coming but hoped wouldn't somehow. She took a deep breath, sucking in sweet air between clenched teeth.

"W-Weel you c-come back?" she managed to say and braced herself for the response.

" 'Tis just to the . . . restin' place we go," Kileen answered, glancing at Carlow for approval. Carlow's face didn't respond.

Angel's twisted mouth indicated she didn't believe him. "Come here, *mi hijo*—and give ol' Balta a hug." She held out her arms for Carlow, and he hugged her hard.

"I don't know how to thank you, Angel. I just—"

"*Sí,* eet ees nothing. You make thees old lady *mucho* happy, jes' by being here." She wiped a tear away from the corner of her eye before it had a chance to give her away. "*Adios.* I know you must find something, but don't lose your heart finding eet, *mi hijo*. Remember, you are always welcome at Balta's house."

Carlow kissed her on the cheek and stepped away. "I'll saddle the horses, Thunder." His eyes tightened, then he turned and walked toward the barn. He didn't look back at Kileen and Angel.

Kileen repeated his claim, only more blustery, " 'Tis just to Shannon's grave we go."

"No. Today, Time Carlow weel ride into yesterday—to find heemself."

"He be too weak to fight, me lass."

"He ees the only one who doesn't know that, Beeg Thunder."

Angel folded her arms and blurted, "I ride with Silver Mallow. Two years ago, *sí,* eet was. With General Terrell an' Jesus. All theem." She cocked her head to the side and tears fingered her face as she reached out to touch him.

Kileen frowned and grabbed her hand, holding her at arm's length. "Why didn't ye tell me this before?"

Her face was drenched in hurt; her eyes flashed angrily. "I am afraid. I-I want you here with me, Beeg Thunder. I-I fear you no stay . . . if you know thees about me. Now you go—an' I know what happens next, even if you say you do not. Time Carlow, he ees going to take you into hell. You may not ride thees way again."

"Well, you don't seem to rank us very high against your Silver Mallow."

Angel frowned. "You are a good *hombre,* Beeg Thunder. A very good *hombre.* Silver is ze mad *lobo,* ze crazy wolf. Here, let me show you what Silver looks like. Eet may help."

Without waiting, she went into the small adobe house and quickly returned with a stack of drawings, thumbed through them, and held up one of the man playing a guitar. "Thees ees Silver Mallow. He looks like *mi hijo* some, I theenk—weethout ze mustache—but he ees bad. You must treat heem like wolf that keel sheep."

Kileen stared at the drawing and a deep redness boiled from his neck to his hatline, bringing with it a blurted accusation, "So this be the reason ye been so nice to me laddie, is it now?"

"What are you saying?" The words bolted from her throat, tripping on the emotions gathering there. "H-He ees *mi hijo.* I love heem because he ees part of you. I love heem like *mi* Miguel, *mi* son."

Kileen cursed loudly. He knew she had been in bed with Mallow by the twisted look on her face. With her chin jutted forward, she told him where the hideout ranch was located. His chest rose and fell; he knew Rangers had stopped there a year ago. His lower lip trembled, but no words could find their way through his hurt. In halting phrases, carried forward by choked-off sobs, she told him where Mallow and his gang were hiding. She said he loved to kill, was half-crazy but very cunning, and was strongly drawn to music. She tried to explain the disguises he enjoyed wearing. Not letting her finish, Kileen grabbed the drawing and marched away, shoving it into his coat pocket, as he headed to the barn where Carlow was preparing their mounts.

He didn't hear her groan, "Come back, Beeg Thunder. I love you." She couldn't breathe.

Four hours later the two men rode up to the familiar treeline, bursting with exuberant green leaves. The trip was far shorter when the route was direct, and Carlow had no intention of doing anything else, in spite of Kileen's suggestion that they ride carefully. Birds were gathered in the trees to discuss the wonderful fragrance of spring. A dry wind was thinning out the clouds, separating and pushing white splotches into the far corners of a blue sky. Around them was open land, as far as a man could see, with springtime's sweetness everywhere. Beside the cottonwoods, a bending creek was fat and spring happy. Neither spoke.

Kileen wanted to talk but kept silent because he felt Carlow needed it that way. Angel's drawing was folded into his coat pocket, but he hadn't told Carlow about it. To do so would mean telling him about Silver's hideout, too. It would mean talking about Angel being involved with the outlaw. The old Ranger was hopeful of returning to Angel's quickly and encouraging his nephew to rest and grow stronger. He also knew he needed to apologize to Angel and to tell her that he loved her. He didn't care who she had been with before. Silver Mallow or the Devil himself, it didn't matter.

As the two riders cleared the uneven ridge, Carlow saw the simple cross half-leaning in a mudded mound, and his breath was sucked from him. Kileen's head jerked sideways in response to the grieving sound and saw tears struggle for release in Carlow's eyes, then break through into long lines down pale cheeks. Kileen looked away to avoid embarrassing his nephew and caught a glimpse of an owl resting among the thick cottonwood branches.

Seeing an owl in sunlight was bad luck. Many Indians thought the owl was a spirit come to haunt the living. He shivered away both thoughts and hoped Carlow didn't see the sleeping bird. The huge Ranger's imagination jumped to hearing that the souls of the dead could take the shape of animals, and he was somewhat comforted. *An owl is it now, Shannon?* He mumbled to himself and looked away.

Kileen's attention was drawn to white and yellow flowers blossoming upon the grave of Carlow's mother. "Aye, look, lad. 'Tis Monday—an' we be seein' the first flowers o' spring on your sweet mither's grave. Monday means good fortune, lad. Good fortune, indeed."

Carlow was paying no attention to the land around him, or his uncle's attempt to be enthusiastic. Only the fattened piece of ground where his friend now lay could he see. He reined his horse twenty yards from the grave and studied it. His silent gaze examined the huge tree behind the resting place, letting his vision pause to remember every story that took place on every branch and around the trunk. Not far away was the granite headstone that belonged to his mother. Carlow's shoulders rose and fell as he stared at the mound, his lips barely moving. Kileen bit his lower lip and tried to think of something to say, but words weren't obliging. A flask in his coat pocket was drawing him to the freeing liquid within, but he didn't retrieve it.

Finally Carlow slid down from his horse, handed the reins to Kileen, and walked toward the grave. A robber jay screamed and swooped down at him, then swooped away to the safety of a high tree branch and continued to protest their arrival. Carlow didn't notice and half-fell, half-dived onto Dornan's grave and sobbed. Deep long sounds ripped loose from the young Ranger's soul.

Kileen waited and finally couldn't resist the waiting whiskey. A long swig, then another, extinguished some of the ache within him. He swung down from the tall horse, moving easily for a man his size and age. Leading both horses, his spurs jingled their satisfying music as he walked to the grave and the outstretched Carlow. The young Ranger lay unmoving over the muddied mound. To Kileen, it seemed the very marrow of Carlow's bones would seep into the ground. He didn't think Carlow would be able to stand—or want to.

Leaning over, Kileen touched Carlow's shoulder and said, "Me son, 'tis time to ride on from it. There be no livin' with death. It be suckin' a man's soul into the same bleemin' hole. Let's go back to Angel's."

Carlow didn't respond at first, then raised himself on outstretched arms, staring at the grave under him. His face was tears and mud streaks. Crumbles of dirt stuck to his cheek and chin. Kileen stepped back to let Carlow rise of his own accord. Unsteady, Carlow stood slowly, his gaze fixed on Dornan's resting place. Without waiting, Kileen jammed a boot into his stirrup, grabbed a handful of mane, and pulled his massive frame into the saddle. The horse spun in a tight circle in response to the returning weight, bringing Carlow's mount along with it, but quickly stopped and dropped its head. Carlow's horse stutter-stepped a defiance at being controlled, then sought the sweet grass nearby.

From a gully to the west, a gray jackrabbit appeared and bounded across the grave, skidded to an abrupt stop at the creek's bank and tore away to the north, following the water's wandering course. Both men watched the small animal retreat as if its appearance held some spiritual significance for the moment. Kileen's hand eased away from his holstered pistol, a response to the sudden movement. He didn't think Carlow had responded at all. The young Ranger seemed oblivious to everything, except straightening the wooden cross.

"Angel will be worried about us, Time. Let us be returnin' now. Can't ye jes' smell the beefsteak fryin'," Kileen said and tried to smile. He wanted another drink from his flask and wondered if it would be all right.

Carlow didn't answer. He looked at his long coat and pants littered with mud but made no attempt to brush it away. Instead, he found a downed tree branch and snapped off small sprigs and supporting branches, leaving a fairly straight four-foot stick. Returning to the grave, he scratched a rough circle around the entire earthen mound.

Panting from the rush of activity, Carlow paused to examine his work and said, "Shannon, no evil spirit will ever get to you. Not ever. You ride on now. My mother said Heaven was like the isles of Ireland. All green and sunny. And happy. Ride on, Shannon. Some day we'll meet again."

From his coat pocket he withdrew the small stone that had been their boyhood *Lia Fail*. Holding it tightly in his right fist, he stepped inside the carved circle on the ground to place the flat pebble into the grave's softened surface.

Kileen realized Carlow's intent. "Don't be doin' that, me lad. Shannon would be wantin' ye to keep the blood stone." He reached into his own pocket, past the flask and earthen pouch, and retrieved the matching rock that had belonged to Shannon Dornan. "Here, 'tis Shannon's own. I be keepin' it for ye." With his other hand he pulled a shiny badge from his left pocket, and he remembered the folded drawing there. "Here be his Ranger badge, too. Shannon would be wantin' you to keep them both."

Carlow's intense stare made Kileen blink. "Quit saying crap like that. Shannon wanted to live. That's what he wanted. He wanted to find the right woman and settle down . . . and build a place of their own together. He wanted to watch his children become strong." The young Ranger paused, shut his eyes for a moment before continuing. "He didn't want to be buried in some stinking mud under some damn tree." He turned toward the grave and motioned toward it. "Look what being a Ranger got him! A damn lonely grave."

It was Kileen's turn to stare hotly. His hooded eyes flashed with Irish temper. He squeezed both fists to eclipse the stone and badge in them as a prelude to his growling proclamation. "Ranger Dornan died doin' his duty for Texas. He be dyin' a proud death, don't ye be sayin' otherwise."

"Shannon Dornan was murdered when a dirty little town wouldn't help us because we were Irish trash."

"Aye, 'tis a sad excuse for a town, I'll grant ye that," Kileen said. "But the blood of Ranger Dornan and Ranger Wilkins be makin' Texas grow strong and tall."

"I don't give a damn about Texas."

Without waiting for Kileen to respond, he stepped forward, kneeled, and shoved the stone into the moist soil. Standing again, he went to his mother's grave. He yanked furiously at wild strands of buffalo grass, weeds and wildflowers that covered her resting place, until a small prairie rose appeared beneath the overgrowth. He had planted it years before. Tiny pink blooms responded to the clearing and stretched toward a welcoming sun.

"Bless you, dear Mother," he said quietly. "I miss you and hope Heaven is what you said it was. Look for my friend, Shannon, he'll be riding your way, Mother. Probably worrying about what to say to God. Take his hand and remember he is not as strong as he will act. Remember how superstitious he is—he was? I love you. Tell him I will miss him, too."

Returning to the horses, he asked Kileen for the stone and badge. Reluctantly the big man handed the mementos to his nephew and watched silently as Carlow walked back to Shannon Dornan's grave and pushed the second stone into the earth beside the first. The young Ranger stepped beyond the scratched circle and threw the badge into the creek. Waves of concentric circles saluted its disappearance. Then he pulled his own badge from his shirt pocket and hurled it toward the same watery destination. This time he didn't watch the circles created by the disturbance. He hurried back to his horse and swung into the saddle with only the slightest hitch in the movement.

As he settled himself into the stirrups, Carlow said, "You go on back, Thunder. Angel will be happy to see you. I think she was worried you wouldn't be coming. Give Shannon's horse to her. Tell her it is my present, will you please. She is a good woman, Uncle. That's where you should be."

Kileen looked as if he had been hit in the face with a rock. "W-What be ye sayin', me son? Angel will be welcomin' ye, too—or hadn't ya noticed her likin' for ya? She be tendin' to your wounds like ye were her own blood, she did. Don't ye know what *mi hijo* means?"

"No, I guess I don't."

"It means 'my son,' Time."

"Oh. That's very nice," Carlow said. "An' I will always be grateful to her—an' you, too. I would have died without your carin'. Now I have to go—my own way. I have to."

"B-But ye be a Texas Ranger, me lad—and the fine captain, he will be a-lookin' for us."

"No, he won't, Thunder. He'll be looking for you. His telegram said I'm not a Ranger, remember? What I have to do—is personal."

Kileen's sad eyes were the initial response, then his face brightened. "Well, then, ye an' meself, let's be goin' back to Angel's wee *hacienda*—and get ourselves ready. I'll go with ye. The captain can just be kept a-waitin'."

"No, Thunder. Your place is with the Rangers. You tell Angel good-bye for me."

"B-But, but, Time, ye be havin' no supplies, no extra hoss, no—"

"I'll get what I need in town. I've got money. Enough."

"Why be goin' back to that awful place, me son? Ye knowed they not be wantin' us Irish there. Ye knowed that, ye said so yourself." Kileen's face was as urgent as his words were choked with emotion.

"Yeah, I know. I don't intend to stay long. I've got something to do there and I'll be on my way," Carlow said and turned in the saddle toward his stunned uncle. "Thunder, this is for the best. I have to go. I just do. Please don't make it any harder for me to do this. I've been thinking about it for a long time. I can't go back to the Rangers, not without Shannon. I just can't."

"B-But where will ye go, me lad? W-Where?"

"I'm not sure. I just need to . . . I just need to. You've been my father, Thunder—and no son could ask for a better one. I will miss you somethin' fierce, but . . ." He held out his hand for Kileen to shake it. The big man's own hand trembled as it came forward.

"W-Will we be seein' ourselves together . . . again, me son?"

"I don't . . . I hope so."

In an instant it was over and Kileen watched his nephew gallop away into the flat horizon. He watched him for at least twenty minutes before the tiny black silhouette finally disappeared over the straight line that was the world. The big man took the flask from his pocket and drank from it deeply. His hand shook as the container reached his mouth. He drank again and wiped his lips with the back of his free hand. When it was finished, he stared at the emptied container as if it had betrayed him and flung it fiercely toward the trees. A branch caught the flask, bowed, and sprung it on again toward the bank.

Like a ghost, a light mist began to drift across the prairie. It reminded him of the Irish mist that comes often to the island of Inishmore where he was a boy. He let himself go there to ease his aching mind. To where the glorious lilt of a Gaelic greeting catches the morning breeze and dances with it. To where great fishing nets lay piled along the harbors, waiting for silent men to return them once again to the sea. To where laces of fog wove themselves among the happy stone-and-thatch cottages. At the bend in the creek its bubbling laughter became a woman singing an Irish lullaby, and the old Ranger cried. His massive shoulders shook and his head lay against his chest.

Gathering himself once more, Kileen swung down from the tall horse and whipped the reins around a favorable branch. The rain was growing heavier now, pelting his hat and coat. Without hesitation he jumped into the stream and waded to its swirling middle. Cold water lapped above his waist. He walked slowly, trying not to disturb its bottom. Blackness swam about him as he bent over and shoved his arm into the stream. Nothing. He swore and tried again.

This time his fingers caught the edge of a Ranger badge and quickly brought it to the surface. He examined the tin shape as if it were something holy, placed it in his coat pocket, and plunged his soaking arm back into the water for the second badge. After several attempts he finally secured it and climbed back out of the stream, fully soaked. His coat was streaked from the muddy bank and water spewed from every corner of his clothes.

He knelt beside the stream to catch his breath, not feeling the rain had turned cold and harsh. Alarmed, he remembered the folded drawing and yanked the soggy paper from his pocket. His large hand withdrew five separate pieces. Holding them in his opened palm, he laid each section on the ground and attempted to guide them into a single unit again. Only the right cheek of Silver Mallow's face remained, part of a shoulder and leg, and the bottom of his guitar; everything else was a blur or a wad of wet pulp.

Cursing in Irish, he stood, threw the wadded paper into the stream, and watched it wash away. He mumbled to himself that it symbolized his forgiveness of Angel's involvement with the man—and was actually a good sign. He reached again into his pocket and withdrew a soggy pouch. He started to throw it, too, but decided the Irish dirt would dry and returned it to his wet pocket.

A few minutes later he stood over Shannon's grave and pulled the two stones from their earthen sheath. Holding them in his mud-covered hand, a thoroughly soaked Kileen said, "Shannon, me boy, I be keepin' these for your good friend. He'll be wantin' both one day. Aye, I know he be grievin' for ye somethin' bad. I be wishin' he put on the badge meself—but I fear Satan has been talkin' to him somethin' fierce—and Time Carlow be listenin'. He be wantin' to ride into Hell—and be doin' it, I fear. Ride with me, lad. 'Tis to save your good friend from hisself, we go."

11

Time Carlow angled across a bald hill that looked like a giant grizzly's humped back. A gathering of scraggly juniper had consented to some windblown oak trees joining them along the side of the obscure trail. On both sides of his path were long ridges of rock that had escaped from the higher ridge to his right. Ahead lay granite outcroppings split into two huge shoulders to become a gateway to the open rolling hills ahead and just beyond, the town of Bennett. It wasn't far, but this was a trail few would use. He had glanced back only once, and the sight of the big silhouette that was Kileen's bothered him too much to look again.

The rumble of thunder pushed a hole through the dark clouds above him and lightning followed. Raindrops splattered on the rim of his hat; the darkening sky indicated more would follow. Loping easily along the curving trail, the proud horse was alert, ears cocked, straining to determine the extent of the advancing storm, Carlow reasoned. His voice calmed the black horse and its head lowered a little. The young Ranger rolled his neck to relieve the tension.

Rain was serious now and his first thought was an instinctive one, to keep his weapons dry. He pulled his long coat over his hand weapons and tucked the edges of the coat under his legs. His anger remained close as he rode through the thickening storm. But his mind was drawn to the images of an Irish mist that his mother and his uncle had told him about so often.

Whenever they spoke of the great island, he always envisioned a happy land and never quite understood why they had left, if Ireland was so beautiful. His thoughts swept along to Old Thunder and the look on his face when Carlow told him that he must leave. He had broken the tough man's heart—but he had to do this. He had to avenge Shannon Dornan's death. Shannon would do the same for him. Mayor Pickenson must die. So must Silver Mallow.

The image of his best friend crying out to him was a picture he tried to keep away from his thinking. It made him shiver even to recall. But that was overmatched by the cruel face of Mayor Pickenson. *There is no death cruel enough for this man,* he told himself over and over in rhythm to the horse's slushing hoofbeats.

In a strange way he could accept Silver Mallow's actions. The outlaw leader made no pretense about his intentions. He intended to turn this region into his own outlaw kingdom—with him as the ruler. Pickenson, on the other hand, presented himself as a pillar of the community, a God-fearing leader focused on making the town better. That was the worst kind of deceit, to Carlow's way of thinking.

Now he was no longer a Texas Ranger; Captain McNelly's telegram said so. Time Carlow could do anything he wanted to this poor excuse of a man, and no town lawman would dare to stop him. He wasn't bound to anyone else's code of ethics. Not even his uncle's. Of course, he didn't let his mind return to the fact that McNelly's message was standard procedure when any Ranger was wounded. It was a harsh reminder that the state wouldn't help you if you weren't in a position to help the state. Not even if you were Captain McNelly himself.

Apparently this thin trail hadn't been used for a while. Not even by the unshod ponies whose tracks he had seen earlier. A faint path wandering away from the main trail had most likely been created by longhorn seeking shelter. He rode on, watching the horizon for signs of riders. He didn't think the Mallow gang would suddenly appear, but a man didn't live in this country long without being alert. All of the time.

Gray rock formations jammed outward from the green, grassy land like giant knives cutting into a carpet. Where the land was punched upward into a series of hills, the rock structures continued, jutting out like giant umbrellas. Big chunks of loose rock and silt covered his path, laced by rows of beaten-down bushes. Carlow shook his head as he looked. At once, both ugly and beautiful. Nothing like Ireland, he was certain.

His horse was showing no signs of tiring, but the early afternoon rain was making it work harder and Carlow was nearly soaked. He pulled up alongside a rock shelf offering the closest relief from the storm. Dismounting, he leaned against the big animal for several minutes, letting the ground restore his equilibrium. His newly returned strength was limited, he realized, and nearly spent. Even the short ride to town was harder than he expected, especially after the heat of emotion left him. His wide-brimmed hat became a container for canteen water that his horse gratefully accepted.

Replacing the wet hat actually felt good on his head. Was his fever returning? *No*, he said; he wouldn't allow it. He tied the reins to a low hanging branch, allowing the horse to graze. After a swig from the canteen himself, he stretched his arms to remove the stiffness and studied the sky. The rain was definitely passing. A few minutes more and its domination would cease. He was hungry. His fingers searched his vest pockets, but only his watch and cartridges were there. Not even a piece of candy. He decided to check his saddlebags for something to eat.

Whatever was there would be old, but he usually carried jerky and corn dodgers. A can of beans might be there, too. It was better this way, he reminded himself, maybe his uncle would settle down with Angel. She certainly would keep him satisfied, he chuckled, and unbuckled the saddlebag straps, shuffled through an old shirt and a pouch of bullets to find wrapped jerky and a handful of corn dodgers. He tried not to dwell on her calling him "my son." It was a sweet expression but one that he wanted to discard.

Weariness sneaked up on him. Sleep would be a sweet escape. Just for an hour or so. His vision blurred and his mother spoke to him again from her death bed. "M-Me b-beautiful son, y-your mither must go now. 'Tis a thing I have no choice about. G-God calls to take me to a s-sweeter place. I-I love you, Time, m-more than anything. Y-Your uncle h-has promised . . . he will help you grow . . . strong. R-Remember y-you are a Carlow, y-you are your father's son. A-A warrior. H-He fought for good, me son . . . t-to help others w-who couldn't fight. Y-You must . . . always . . . f-fight for good. 'T-Tis easy to fight . . . for evil things. Be promisin' your mither. Please?"

"M-Mother, I-I don't understand. Y-You can't go. Y-You can't go!" the boy cried out, disbelieving. She was all that was right and good in his world.

She closed her eyes for a moment and he thought she was gone. Tears streamed down his young face as he stood beside her gray bed, unable to move, unable to think. She opened them again and her gaze was a gentle assurance that everything would be all right. She held out a trembling hand holding a silver chain and Celtic cross. "T-Take this, me son, and wear it proudly. 'Tis your father's. H-He would want you to have it now."

Time Carlow would never see his mother again. He cried all that long ago day. It was the last time he would do so. Until today, over Shannon Dornan's grave. Carlow staggered sideways, fighting to regain his mind and stave off the gloom that sought his courage. Long-forgotten furies had been freed by his wild ride to town. A warm wind shoved against his wet body, and he dropped the food sack.

Something behind him moved.

A muted sound, more felt than heard, yet not of the retreating rain. Staying alive meant hearing such a difference. Carlow eased his right hand inside his coat and withdrew his Colt; it was easier to cock and keep close to his body so it wouldn't appear to whoever was there that he had noticed. It would be his only edge. He took a step to his left and leaned over to pick up the sack with his left hand, cocking the pistol with his right as he moved.

A wolf!

A wet mass of black, gray, and brown fur watched him from the slit between the rocks. Unblinking eyes studied Carlow as he turned slowly toward the powerfully framed animal. Would it attack? Stories of wolves were boundless and always vicious. Kileen said most wolves were actually the spirits of evil men come back to hurt people. Dornan told of similar tales, although Carlow was certain he was just repeating what Kileen had spouted, only with added relish. Carlow didn't take to most of the claims, but was drawn to an old buffalo hunter telling him of the Comanche belief that the wolf had the soul of a man and that a warrior with a wolf for a *puhante,* a spirit helper, would be blessed with considerable courage and ability to track, especially in the dark.

Many nights he had heard the distinctive howl of this mysterious animal, along with its lesser relative, the coyote. He had to agree the wolf's cry was quite like that of a human's. He recalled the grizzled hunter saying Indians believed the wolf came and went from the spirit world and could help a warrior go there and back. Strong *puha,* strong medicine. In fact, if a war party heard four rapid wolf cries in a row, it was a warning their medicine had vanished. No warrior would go on after such an alarm.

Carlow waited, but the well-soaked wolf showed no signs of aggression. More of curiosity. The animal was just hungry, he thought, and added to himself that it wasn't interested in a former Ranger for dinner. Maybe it was lonely, too. Just like he was. *Oh, that sounds like some girl talking,* he muttered. This is a wild, fierce animal. He studied the wolf as it stood silently. The more he looked, the more he didn't think it was a wolf, or at least, not all wolf. Something about its appearance made him think it was a mixed breed; half-wolf, half-dog. While it made no attempt to growl or charge him, the animal also showed no inclination to leave. Carlow holstered his pistol and decided to give the half-wolf something to eat. Why not? It looked as lonely as he felt. This time he didn't think the observation was so silly.

He pulled the knife from his boot leggings, cut a slice of jerky, and tossed it toward the animal. Staring first at Carlow, then at the offering, the wolf took a step forward, and another, sniffed the meat, and gulped it down.

Carlow laughed and said, "Hey, did you think I would give you something bad to eat? That's Ranger food. It's good stuff, bud."

He took a bite for himself, cut off another hearty slice, and tossed it toward the wolf. After swallowing the meat, the wolf moved several feet closer to Carlow; a wiggle moved its soggy tail. He cut a third piece and knelt, holding it in his outstretched hand. Only a slight hesitation preceeded the wolf's advance. Carlow was surprised to receive a lick on his hand in appreciation. He told himself it was actually an attempt to get at the food smell, but it felt nice anyway. He rubbed the wolf-dog's neck and ears, and the animal lowered its head and stood quietly beside him. Carlow took another bite and gave the rest to the wolf-dog.

"All right, my friend, that's all I've got. If you're still hungry, you're going to have to find a jackrabbit trying to stay out of the rain. Ought to be a few around here, you know." He patted its head and stood. The wolf didn't move; its eyes held on Carlow.

"Hey, I've got to go on . . . to town. There's a bad fella waiting for me. Sort of. You run along now."

He walked to his horse, patted its neck to reassure the leery mount that the wolf-dog was no threat, and swung into the saddle. His movement was jerky, a sign of the weakness lingering within him. He sat in the saddle, drawing deep breaths to recapture his strength. Finally he looked back, expecting to see the wolf had disappeared. Instead, it sat on back legs, waiting.

"Well, we're leaving. You can come if you want to, I guess." He chuckled to himself and eased the horse back onto the trail.

Overhead, gray clouds were in full retreat from an

attacking sun. The growing afternoon warmth offered comfort to his tired shoulders. He glanced back, and the wolf was barely eight feet back, running as smoothly as his horse.

"You'd better head into the hills. They won't like you coming to town." He paused and grinned. "They won't like me coming, either." Cocking his head to the side in recognition of the comparison, Carlow shrugged and turned his attention to the meandering trail. "Don't you be following me because you think you want to be a Ranger. I'm not one anymore—an' I'm going to be a killer soon. Look for me on a wanted poster—but don't expect anything more to eat."

Fifteen minutes later he cleared a low rise and saw the town in the distance. It should have looked like home but didn't. It came to him that the only home he knew was wherever Old Thunder Kileen and Shannon Dornan were. He ached for his best friend's company. He would miss Kileen—and the Rangers—he finally acknowledged. Briefly he wondered if they would be ordered to find and arrest him, after he killed Pickenson. Probably so, and his uncle would consider it is his duty to do so. Or think he could keep Carlow from being shot.

Melancholy attacked his tired brain unexpectedly. Glimpses of playing with Dornan, fighting with the Holt brothers, following Kileen to prizefights and horse races, listening to his mother's sweet songs while she worked around their tiny sleeping quarters. But something else was there, too. He touched the silver chain under his shirt. His mother wouldn't be proud of his going after Pickenson. Not this way. He could see her frown. An idea flickered within him; dark images swallowed it. He had come too far to stop now. Pickenson had to pay. If it meant that he, too, became an outlaw, so be it.

Without thinking, he spurred his horse to reinforce his determination to kill the mayor who had been the reason for Dornan's murder. A jerky trot followed as the horse tried to respond to its rider's demand. Guilt slapped Carlow's face as he realized what he had done. He slowed the animal to a walk, then eased it to a halt. Patting its sweating shoulder, he swung down and apologized, "If Thunder had seen that, he would've whacked me good. I'm sorry, Shadow. I'm sorry."

Against his leg came weight, and he glanced down to see the wolf rubbing against his legging, hoping for attention, too. "Well, hey, I didn't hurt you." He leaned down and patted the wolf-dog on its back and scratched its ears. A lick of his hand followed, then another.

"I wonder what Thunder would say about you." As the words tumbled from his mouth, the image of Kileen telling him the souls of the dead often turned into animals swished into his mind. Would Kileen try to tell him this was actually Shannon Dornan's soul? No, that was even sillier than most of his uncle's superstitions. A chill walked up Carlow's back and out his neck.

Fatigue was real, but he had to continue. He climbed back into the saddle and recommitted himself to killing Pickenson. First Pickenson; then Silver Mallow. It would take time to track down the outlaw leader, but he would find and kill him. Those acts were burned into his soul while he recovered. Then he would ride on. Where didn't matter. Only some place where not even the Rangers could find him.

Surprising himself, he wondered if he should actually join the outlaw leader, instead of killing him. Why not? What difference did it make? The town below didn't see any, why should he? Silver Mallow might really appreciate a man who could handle himself as well as he could. But he spurred the thought away harder than he had popped his horse. Killing Pickenson might make him a wanted man, but that didn't put him on the same side as Mallow. Pickenson was a pompous, weak fool; it was Silver Mallow who was the real reason his friend was murdered. Getting Pickenson was only the beginning.

Horse, rider, and wolf-dog passed a beleaguered schoolhouse, and the town was upon them. Two-story buildings stood as unpainted testimony to Texas hardiness. A freight wagon rattled by him, headed south; its driver waved and snapped his bullwhip to make certain a team of mules understood who was in charge. To reassure himself that he really did see it, the driver glanced back at the wolf following on the heels of the rider's horse. He shook his head, cursed and snapped the whip again.

The metallic cracks of the blacksmith's hammer greeted Carlow as he trotted beside three riders who said something to each other and hurried away. Outside the livery stable, two men were hitching a buggy to matching bay horses and both were resisting the harness. The youngest man waved at Carlow but was quickly scolded by the older. A dark-haired woman from the dance hall leaned out her second-story window and gave him a comely wave. Main Street was a flurry of people, horses, wagons, and carriages. Several townspeople stopped to watch the advancing rider. Most became agitated as soon as they recognized him.

Without meeting any of their faces, he passed the long street of false-fronted stores with framed awnings and eight-foot-wide wooden sidewalks. A stagecoach rumbled into the main street, swayed to a stop in mid-block, outside the telegraph and stage office, and belched out passengers from both sides. He turned toward the hitching rack outside Pickenson's General Merchandise store. A rancher's loaded buckboard skidded onto the main street from the alley. Carlow yelled at the wolf-dog, and the animal jumped away from the wheels as they slid on the muddy street. Carlow's eyes caught the driver's face; the man recognized the young Ranger, snapped his whip over his horses, and kept going.

Outside the Lady Gay Saloon, a skinny man, wearing a dark coat that made his face appear even more yellow-toned than it was, did a double-take as he saw Carlow ride into town. Pulling the brim of his short-brimmed hat lower on his forehead, and pushing up his thick eyeglasses on his nose, he squinted into the late afternoon sun, studied the rider, and smiled.

"Well, Time Carlow, I'll be damned," Houston Holt said out loud to himself. "You're supposed to be dead. No wonder the boys didn't come back. You're as lucky as that stupid uncle of yours. Silver will be real happy to hear this."

He stepped back into the shadows so Carlow wouldn't notice him. His sudden move caused two businessmen to nearly run into him. Bowing graciously, they stepped around him, apologizing as they moved. Scowling at the slight interruption to his concentration, Holt cursed and the two men hurried down the sidewalk. Returning to the incoming rider, Holt rolled a cigarette and brought a match into flame on one of the holstered revolvers under his coat. Inhaling the fresh smoke, he waited to determine where the young Ranger was headed. As soon as he saw Carlow ride to the hitching rack outside Pickenson's general store, he took a long pull on the cigarette and went into the Lady Gay Saloon.

Dismounting, Carlow wrapped the reins around the rack with a quick flip. He turned to the sitting wolf-dog and commanded, "Now, you have to stay here. Don't cause any trouble. I'll be coming out fast." Even as he said it, the words clanked in his mind. *Am I really going to murder Pickenson? Don't I have the right to?*

"Is that a wolf, mister?"

Carlow spun around to find the person who asked the question, sarcasm close to his tongue. But the voice belonged to a small boy with a smudge on his face and a patrol of freckles across his nose. His overalls had seen better days, most likely hand-me-downs from an older brother.

Anger scurried away from Carlow's face. "Well, no, he isn't. Looks like one, doesn't he?"

"Can I pet him?"

Carlow walked over to the wolf-dog and stood beside it, rubbing its thick neck. "Well, I guess so. Let him smell your hand first. You know, a dog doesn't know whether you're a friend or an enemy right off."

Eagerly the boy stepped off the porch to the hitching rack and held out his hand for the animal to inspect.

"That's it. Now, to the side of his face. Slow-like." Carlow directed the boy's actions as if he had forgotten what he came to town to do, or was it procrastination to keep him from doing something he really didn't want to do and couldn't yet admit it to himself? He scratched the wolf-dog's ears and told him to let the boy touch him.

"What's his name?" the boy asked, running his hand gently over the wolf-dog's head and shoulders.

Carlow's lower lip pushed outward. "Hmmm, I don't know. Came up on me just by chance—and he decided to follow me to town. What do you think I should call him?"

The boy's face screwed into a tight frown. "Well, I had a dog named Blackie once. He didn't look like this, though. He was little—an' black. I liked him a lot. If'n you found him by chance, I think you should call him that. Chance."

"Chance it is, then. I like that."

"Hi, Chance, my name is Jeremiah . . . Jeremiah Beckham." The boy rubbed the wolf-dog's ears, and the strong animal watched Carlow for assurance that its actions were correct. "Aren't you a Ranger?" the boy asked, moving his own gaze from the animal to Carlow with a glint of hero worship in his blue eyes.

Something in Time Carlow wouldn't let him answer any other way except, "Yes, I am a Ranger." A sensation ran through him. He *was* a Texas Ranger—

and he was here to commit murder. How could a Ranger do that?

"Can I see your guns?"

"Huh? Oh, sure." Carlow pushed his long coat back to reveal the hand-carbine and holstered Colt at his waist.

"I want to be a Ranger when I grow up," the boy said with admiration thick on his voice. "Where's your badge?"

Carlow touched his shirt. "Ah . . . I left it . . . at my camp."

Behind them came a harsh interruption. "Jeremiah, you come here. Jeremiah. Now."

Carlow looked up and, for an instant, saw his own mother, but the image disappeared into a young woman with worry festering in her sparkling blue eyes. Warm-faced with dimples accenting both cheeks, Ellie Beckham's cinnamon hair was pulled back into a bun, covered by a plain bonnet. Her faded dress indicated a hard life, but it didn't hide the attractiveness of this young mother.

A smile crossed his face before he could stop it. "It's all right, ma'am. I'm more Ranger than I am Irish."

In spite of her concern she returned the smile and her eyes flashed. A blink later she resumed her stern posture. "Jeremiah, I said 'now.' "

"I gotta go, Mister Ranger."

"All right, Jeremiah. Thanks for stopping—and for the name."

"Bye, Chance."

After one last pat on the wolf-dog's head, the boy joined his mother on the sidewalk. She quickly took his hand and walked away. After a few steps she glanced back to see if Carlow was watching. He was. Crimson rose at her neck and she walked faster. His grin faded when he opened the door of the general store.

12

Inside the Lady Gay, Houston Holt waited for his eyes to adjust to the grayness engulfing him. Part of his hesitation was the constant worry that he would be recognized. After all, he and his brothers had lived, as children, in a tent on the edge of this settlement. He still knew some of the residents by sight even now; they hadn't changed as much as he had, Holt assured himself.

Amos Holt, his father, had been a buffalo hunter and was rarely at home. One year he never returned. His mother died three years ago, but Holt hadn't come back for the funeral. Back then, Silver was too worried about the law following him to their hideout. Now the outlaw leader kept insisting they return to hear "the Omaha Songbird," Anna Nalene, sing.

Mallow expected those with him to conduct themselves as gentlemen or they couldn't come. General Terrell told Holt the reason for the quiet approach was to keep Texas Rangers from thinking their hideout was close by—and to keep Silver Mallow from any possibility of being identified. It made sense to Holt; he wasn't interested in drawing attention to himself anyway. The town sheriff may not have the guts to do anything, but he knew from the stories Houlihan and others told, not every man in town was fearful; most had fought in the War of Northern Aggression.

Holt didn't know why Silver didn't just take this singer upstairs, like the other saloon whores, and get it over with. Instead, the outlaw leader just came to sit and stare at her, like some lovesick boy. He never even talked to her as far as Holt knew. Holt didn't think she was all that special—to listen to or look at. She never sang anything he liked anyway. And eventually someone was bound to recognize him. Mallow didn't seem to understand, or care about, the risk.

Of course, Silver's likeness wasn't on a wanted poster, like Holt's was—and Jesus's and Terrell's. There was only a description of the outlaw leader; other than wearing rings on his fingers, it wasn't specific. Terrell told him not to bring that up to Mallow, if he knew what was good for him, so he didn't. Still, it made him uneasy—and now Time Carlow was in town.

The dead Ranger was back! Holt shivered and tried to act confident. A memory of Carlow as a boy being unafraid of him, even though Holt was three years older, kept seeping into his mind. Carlow whipped him once after Holt called Carlow's mother a name. His youngest brother, Lee, kept Willie, the oldest, from going after Carlow when he heard the tale. Holt wasn't certain Willie would have gone after him anyway.

Unlike the other saloons in town, the Lady Gay was a fancy place that had immediately captivated Silver Mallow. Chandeliers glittered their golden light upon crimson curtains and all manner of tables of chance. From the upper balcony the band was musically introducing the Omaha Songbird's next song. Anna Nalene stood next to the railing, gazing down at the entranced men below. Even the faro tables stopped when she sang. Not because the dealers wanted to, but because all the men wanted to listen to—and look at—Anna Nalene. Long honey-blond hair caressed her bare shoulders, and the tight-fitted gown was a silvery coat of paint over her naked body. Every time she inhaled, while singing, at least one appreciative observer would remark loudly, "Here they come, boys!" and laugh heartily.

Below, the long bar was lined two-deep with drinkers and sprinkled with heavily made-up women in scanty dresses that showed lots of leg and bosom. When Nalene wasn't singing, the band played so the girls could earn money dancing with interested patrons. Upstairs bedrooms were reserved for more intimate performances. On the back bar was an inviting rainbow of bottles. Centered on the wall was a large French mirror flanked by paintings of erotically posed nude women.

Holt finally saw Silver Mallow sitting with the band, playing his cornet, and intently reading the music on the stand in front of him. The bespectacled outlaw waved at his leader and finally got his attention. Wearing a blond wig, Mallow was dressed impeccably in a well-tailored broadcloth coat with velvet collar, a starched white shirt, and a silk cravat; a silver watch chain crossed his matching vest. Under his coat, a pearl-handled revolver glistened from his shoulder holster. He stood quietly, laid the instrument on his chair, and walked to the balcony stairway, mouthing the words to her plaintive rendition of "Beautiful Dreamer, wake unto me, Starlight and dew drops are waiting for thee. . . ."

Walking toward Holt, Mallow was clearly annoyed to be pulled away from the music.

"Mr. Beethoven, I've got some interesting news," Holt said, using the fake name Silver liked. Mallow's frown at being interrupted slid into an evil grin as he realized the significance of Holt's news.

The only things between him and total control of this border region were two Rangers. Carlow and Kileen. He also had a score to settle with these two lawmen; they had killed eighteen of his men. Eighteen! He was certain the big Ranger had shot all the Mallow outlaws held in the jail after their failed attempt to break them out. It's what he would have done.

Spies had advised him that the main body of the Special Force of Rangers had their hands full over near El Paso. If he were rid of this nuisance of Time Carlow and his prizefighting uncle, he could solidify his stranglehold on the area. Ranchers would pay him money just to leave their herds alone. Cattleman Adrian Hooks already was. It especially pleased Mallow that he had negotiated the payment from Hooks in person, introducing himself as "Haydn from the Silver Mallow gang." At Terrell's insistence, he had taken off his rings and worn a pair of glasses to disguise himself. He chuckled at the recollection of the rancher asking him about Silver Mallow and saying that he met him several times and held no grudge against the outlaw leader whatsoever.

By the time more Rangers were sent this way, they would be met by a web of connections too entangled to overcome without great cost. Already, there wasn't a local lawman within three days' ride who would dare to mount a posse and come after him, no matter how much the area ranchers squawked. He might even buy this saloon and rename it. "The Silver Rose" had a nice sound, he thought.

Of course, several army officers had been paid to make certain their troops moved too slowly in pursuit of Mallow's rustled herds headed for the great river and Mexico. Through it all, he had managed to keep his identity, as well as his hideout, unknown to the authorities. Even the Rangers didn't know what he looked like. It was a joke he often enjoyed telling his gang. Every man laughed when he did, including Holt.

Privately, though, Holt, Jesus, and Terrell griped that they were the ones the law could identify. Out of his sight, they also discussed moving their hideout across the border into Mexico, where they thought it was safer. The ruse of the Mexican couple could only last so long, they told each other. So far, no one had brought the subject up to Mallow, though.

Of course, many townspeople suspected who he was, even though he introduced himself as "William Beethoven from over San Antonio way" and acted as a gentleman whenever he was in Bennett, usually to sit in with the band. Actually, all of the gang wanted to be selected to join him on his trips to town. It was a time when they could enjoy all the women and whiskey they wanted—and there was no worry about the local law. Sheriff Moore and his two deputies never bothered them. Only Pickenson had seemed uncomfortable with their appearance and had even talked with Mallow about it once. The result had been Mallow directing his men to fill two wagons with supplies from Pickenson's store, without paying. Pickenson never said anything again and avoided any contact with any of them when they were in Bennett.

Only Jesus dared to complain Silver Mallow was spending too much time listening to this woman sing—to Mallow's face. He thought they should take what they wanted and burn down the town instead. That had brought a hearty slap on the back and Mallow's insistence that the one-eyed Mexican be one of the gang to accompany him on this trip into town.

Mallow stood and motioned for Holt to walk with him toward the bar. "Isn't she something? I'm thinking we should ride over to Waco soon and hear that orchestra of theirs. Doesn't that sound great? You know, maybe Miss Nalene would be interested in going along. What do you think?"

Holt wasn't interested, but agreed. It was the smart thing to do around Mallow, especially where music was concerned. And now, this singer. Mallow talked of her as though she were an angel or something. It was going to cause them trouble one of these days. Pickenson didn't control this town and neither did Sheriff Moore. There were men here who could fight if they got angry enough. He remembered several of them chasing him and his brothers out of town years ago.

Mallow rubbed his chin. "I told you Houlihan hadn't killed that son of a bitch Ranger. Remember?"

Holt nodded; actually, he was the one who warned about how dangerous Time Carlow was and predicted he wasn't dead, and that was the reason the five gang members never came back. He agreed with Mallow, though, that Kileen had shot their jailed comrades.

"Would this Mick of a Ranger recognize you?" Mallow asked, returning his gaze to Anna Nalene.

Holt nodded. "Yeah, but I—"

"Go get Beathard and send him to Pickenson's. He's down there, somewhere." He pointed toward the far end of the bar. "Tell him to come and tell us when he knows what the Irishman's up to."

"What if Carlow shoots Pickenson?"

"Fine. We can buy a big general store cheap. You want to be mayor?" Mallow smiled and added, "As I recall, you probably wouldn't fit the role of minister."

Holt smiled awkwardly. "Why don't we just go in there and blast that Irish bastard to hell—and get out of here?"

Mallow's eyes narrowed and his face reddened. Holt wished he hadn't asked.

"Because I want him out in the street where we can see him—and get him in a crossfire." Mallow's voice was a snarling whisper. "Remember, he's been dead once already. Don't underrate him, Houston. I want him so dead he can't come back this time. Really dead, you hear?"

Holt nodded, relieved that he got off so lightly.

But Mallow wasn't finished. "Where's Jesus and the General?"

"Jesus . . . is upstairs. Him an' Barat, I think. With two Mex gals. General is supposed to be meetin' with, what's his name, that rancher over—"

"Drucker."

"Yeah, Drucker."

Mallow rubbed his clean-shaven chin and glanced up at Anna Nalene, pausing as the band played a bridge to the next chorus. She caught his eye and blew him a kiss. He caught the imaginary intimacy and blew one back, grinning like a schoolboy. "Did you see that, Houston? Did you see that? She likes me, said I could play better than anybody in the band."

"Of course she likes you."

Mallow's face tightened. "Anna Nalene's a real lady, Houston. Remember that."

"Of course she is. I really like her singin'."

"Do you? I do, too. Like it's coming from, you know, Heaven or something."

"Yeah, comin' from Heaven."

Mallow smiled. "That's a perfect way to describe it, Houston. I'm proud of you. You're going to like Beethoven, I promise." He shoved his hands in his pockets and scowled. "Get Barat. I don't care if the fat bastard is in the middle of it—and get him down here so we're ready."

"What about Jesus?"

Mallow grinned. "I don't think you want to interrupt him, do you, Houston?"

"I'll do whatever you want me to, Silver." Holt's chin shoved out for emphasis.

Mallow put his hand on the skinny man's shoulder. "I appreciate that, Houston, I really do. But I've got other plans for the General—an' Jesus."

At the same time Time Carlow stepped inside J. B. Pickenson's General Merchandise store and a straggling blade of sunlight tagged along. A gentle ripple of his spurs accompanied his tapping against the doorway three times with the back of his hand. A tribute to his uncle. "I won't let you down, Thunder," he muttered, then touched his shirt pocket, but his blood stone was no longer there.

Regret filled his mind and he hoped to ride back to find it after this was over. If he were able. Reality had finally overtaken smoldering anguish and anger, and he realized that he was, in effect, taking on the whole town. How would they react when he went after their mayor? But wasn't that what he really wanted? Deep down, wasn't this about punishing the community for its rejection of Shannon Dornan, his mother—and himself? He stopped, letting the store door close behind him—and allowed his thoughts to settle. Which would it be? Revenge—or justice? The easy way was revenge; the hard way, justice. Outlaw or Ranger? It was that simple and that difficult. Nothing in between offered any satisfaction.

A nagging concern tugged at the coattails of his mind. The boy outside wanted to become a Ranger. Just as he had ached to become one. The day he put on the badge became bright once more. Kileen told him that his mother was beaming with pride. "Yourself, be lookin' at the sky, me lad. See that bright shiny place—between them two fine clouds? Aye, right there. There she be. Be bettin' me month's wages on it."

Was killing Pickenson worth that much? Worth a Ranger's badge? His mother's pride?

A plainly dressed couple hesitated in front of him, uncertain whether to ask Carlow to move or not. The bespectacled husband was struggling with an over-packed box of store goods. Their presence snapped Carlow from bitter self-examination. He apologized, stepping to the side, and opened the door for them to hurry past him, avoiding eye contact. The door clicked again behind him, and familiar aromas reached out to unleash boyhood memories he preferred would remain locked away in his soul.

This store was considerably larger than the one he

remembered growing up. And much bigger than Doc Williams's cramped drugstore and doctor's clinic. Pickenson had expanded it in the back, as well as purchasing the store next door and combining the space. Carlow thought it had been a small gun shop. Samuel Jenkins, the original owner of the general store, was ambushed three years ago, returning from a trip to Austin. The killers were never found. New to town, Pickenson purchased it from Jenkins's widow for a few cents on each dollar of merchandise, enough to pay for her and her sister to travel to St. Louis. Carlow remembered Jenkins was always nice to him and his mother, letting her make purchases on credit. He wondered how payment was made, then decided he didn't want to know.

Tangy odors of vinegar and pickled fish swam with rich smells of freshly ground coffee and tobacco, the sweet perfume of new leather and old spices, the musty scent of candles and castor oil. His eyes adjusted to a gray world of contented shoppers and cluttered goods. Everywhere he looked were kegs, barrels, sacks, and displays of everything from sugar and salt, to gun powder and ammunition, to canisters of condiments and groceries. From the rafters hung hams, slabs of bacon, and cooking pots. Along one shelf were carefully placed home remedies of paregoric, Epsom salts, camphor, opium, and snake root. On another shelf was an odd collection of liquor bottles, bolts of calico, canned oysters, baby's croup medicine, bibles, and crockery. A small stack of McGuffey's Readers for school study completed the row.

Throughout the store, customers gradually became aware of Carlow's presence. Whispers of concern and contempt flitted from mouth to ear, until everyone knew who had returned.

"What are you doing here?" The accusation came from a woman with a face like a crow. A white bonnet reinforced her beady-eyed, beak-nosed appearance. "My husband is on the town council. I thought the mayor and the council told you people not to come back." She flapped her elbows twice with her fists against her chest, and Carlow couldn't help imagining her as some huge, ugly bird.

Standing at her side, the homely woman's husband tried to quiet her, but she shoved his hands away and snapped again about Bennett not wanting Irish of any kind around, not even lawmen. Carlow managed to smile, even though his temper was barely locked behind clenched teeth. He tried to tell himself that the woman's opinion of him and his friends didn't matter. He walked farther into the store, and most of the customers bent themselves away from him. *Where was Pickenson?* he thought. Surely he was in the store. Somewhere.

The crow-faced woman hurried to stand directly

in front of him. Putting her hands on her wide hips, she demanded, "Why are you here, Irishman? I asked you a question."

"Yes, you did."

He stepped past her to three people studying *Ewall's Medical Companion* to see if their symptoms, or those of their family, matched a stated illness and learn the prescriptions for curing it. He grimaced at his choice of direction. Long ago he had tried to find an answer for his mother's illness in that same book. He never found it. Even Kileen's superstitious treatments—like hanging a small bag containing three live spiders around her neck—hadn't helped. Neither did the mistletoe or the thorny bush brought into the house, or the stone with a hole in it, or twenty other things he tried. And definitely not the magical healer his uncle brought in with much fanfare. It was then Carlow was certain Kileen's beliefs were without much substance and decided not to incorporate them into his life. He did vow to wear his father's chain necklace forever, the one his mother had given him on her deathbed.

Close by the crow-faced woman sputtered, but her husband managed to refocus her attention on their shopping. A small boy was sampling crackers from the nearly filled cracker barrel but eyeing the big glass jars of striped peppermint sticks and peppermint balls on the counter. He reminded Carlow of the boy outside—and his attractive mother. Passing two women, the young Ranger heard one woman whisper to another, "I saw this in the Montgomery Ward and Company catalog. It was twenty-five cents cheaper."

Grinning at the conversation, he was thankful it wasn't about him for a change, and looked for Pickenson. The mayor wasn't in sight; his high desk and stool in the rear was empty. A high counter and shelves next to this management area was thick with dry goods and hardware. Where could Pickenson be? Perhaps in the back, where an open jug and tin cups were kept for male customers to enjoy.

Carlow eased through the store, touching the front brim of his hat whenever a lady turned toward him. Each time the gaze was easy to read: a mixture of surprise, fear, and disgust. Each time he bit the inside of his lip to keep from saying what was on his mind. Yet each time it reaffirmed the importance—to him—of acting like a Ranger.

Five men sat in a loose circle around the potbellied stove, still providing warmth to turn away early spring coolness. The cracker barrel was within reaching distance. Each man turned toward the passing Carlow. Every eye caught the belted hand-carbine and holstered Colt, barely visible under the long trail coat of the young man. Time Carlow nodded a greeting which they returned reluctantly, and that released them to the resumption of their gossiping, which now included possible reasons for the appearance of the young Irish Ranger.

A pinched-faced farmer, spending the day in town while his wife shopped, spat a long stream of tobacco juice toward the pan of ashes in front of the stove. He missed, then turned toward Carlow. "Whatcha doin' hyar, law-dawg? Didn't ya git nuff lead the last time? I thought ya was daid." He laughed at his joke, but the others didn't respond, so he went back to concentrating on his chewing tobacco. A fat townsman avoided contact with Carlow's eyes, pretending to be engaged in setting his silver watch. But a big-nosed man watched Carlow uneasily, putting a tin cup to his lips as red eyes examined the Ranger. Next to the smart-aleck farmer, a curly haired businessman in a black broadcoat suit whispered something to him. The farmer didn't like the comment, whatever it was. But Carlow wasn't interested in small talk. Or them. His objective was a singular one: find Pickenson and force him to leave town.

Yes, his mind was made up. He was a Ranger, whether Captain McNelly liked it or not, and a Ranger stood for law and order. There was no way he could arrest Pickenson for murder and make it stick. First, there was no evidence, only his strong hunch. Second, the local judge would never convict the town mayor, one of Bennett's leading citizens. If he sent for the circuit judge, the lack of evidence would make him look foolish. That left killing Pickenson—or making him leave town. Carlow had chosen the latter.

Acknowledgement of this direction was a gentle rain on his mind. It didn't matter what the town thought of him; only what Kileen—and his mother and Shannon Dornan would think. They would agree with his approach. Although all three of them would probably have insisted upon some kind of evil spirit removal ceremony to go along with it.

The brim of his Stetson was pushed up against a creased crown, and his long hair brushed against a damp, collarless shirt. His Kiowa buckskin leggings and boots were laced with mud and left a scattered trail as he moved through the store. He rubbed his eyes to clear away fatigue from a long day, combined with a weakened condition. Even with the afternoon rain drawing in townspeople looking to get out of the weather, the stale-aired store was quieter than most of the other establishments in this border settlement.

Carlow glanced again at the gathered men, drawn by a sudden curse. The young Ranger caught the glimpse of a silver-plated pistol under the black coat of the heavyset man. It made him lay his hand on his coat, over his own holstered gun, for reassurance.

"Hey, Mayor, ya got any more whiskey back thar?" yelled the farmer, glancing at Carlow, then the curly haired businessman.

Carlow barely heard the short lady with the piled-up hair complaining about the Irish to her powder-faced friend who kept trying to hush her up.

"Young man, aren't you a Ranger?"

A blonde woman, slightly beyond her best years, stepped beside him. She smiled widely. Her perfume was syrupy. She had tired eyes and a thin mouth painted red beyond the lips. Her long yellow hair was covered by a green hat with fur accents and silk ribbons tied under her chin. Her matching green dress was fitted at her waist and ballooned into a wide skirt with a large bustle.

Before he could answer, she said, "We heard you were dead."

"I was."

Carlow's light blue eyes were, at the same time, inviting and distant. His thick eyelashes were the kind any woman would desire. His responding smile was a magnet to the lonely woman.

She stepped closer and whispered, "You look alive to me. Would you like to have supper—at my place? I'd like to show my appreciation . . . for all you Rangers do. I baked an apple pie this morning. Mighty sweet." Her eyes lowered to suggest the description included other things.

Carlow was deep in thought and didn't realize the significance of her attention. "Thank you, ma'am, that's real nice of you, but I'm just riding through."

Her face cracked and her mouth shriveled like she had bitten a lemon. She spun away, her face trying to find an appropriate haughty countenance, and muttered "Low-class Irish" loud enough for others to hear.

A full-bearded man in faded Confederate pants entered the store and ambled toward the gathering at the stove. He saw Carlow and stopped. Shards of yellow light passed Carlow's face on their way to the planked floor. Realizing the hazard of his careless approach, the bearded customer's eyes searched the room and caught those of the heavyset man who shook his head. Carlow ignored the exchange and continued his search for Pickenson toward the back of the crowded building.

Sliding inside the store, a few steps behind the ex-Confederate, a short cowboy with studded cuffs and fringed chaps was tense; his eyes sorted through the room rapidly until they found Carlow. The cowboy's misshapen hat was pulled low to keep his worried face in shadow, but he pulled it even lower as he recognized the young Ranger in the back of the store. Stepping toward the closest counter, he stood and fingered cans of tomatoes without paying attention to any of them. In his waistband the handle of a revolver was evident.

Finally Carlow heard Pickenson's voice; the storekeeper was in the storeroom, addressing someone about next Sunday's church services. He wanted the couple with him to head up a drive to raise money for a new church and a regular salary for himself. From the exchange, it appeared the couple wasn't enthusiastic about either idea, but particularly the latter. All three voices became louder as they returned to the main part of the store with Pickenson trailing a well-dressed man and woman.

As they entered the shopping area, Pickenson continued pitching his cause. "Actually, Mr. Nelson, it would be a good invest—" Pickenson's comment was severed by his sudden discovery of Time Carlow standing in the crowded aisle. Pulling on the lapels of his gray suit, the store owner and part-time preacher swallowed, the furrows in his brow giving away his immediate worry.

A faint snicker eased across his face and he said loudly, "My friends, here is one of the Irish trash who almost cost us our town, bringing in those men they blatantly accused of rustling. Without proof, I might add. I'm not sure which is worse, outlaws or the Irish. I'm amazed at your gall, young man. Have you brought Satan to town this time?"

13

Laughter splattered the walls, but three people left the store in haste. The Nelsons hurried to the far side of the store, eager to be away from both the young Ranger and Pickenson's insistent sales pitch. They glanced back and pushed through the huddled gathering of curious customers to the front door and left.

"Looks to me Satan is already here—and he's wearing a nice gray suit." Time Carlow locked hard eyes onto Pickenson's face.

Pickenson bit his lower lip and looked at the men sitting around his stove. There was something about this young man he hadn't expected. Something different. This Texas Ranger was changed from the cocky young Irishman he'd seen at the jail last winter. Time Carlow appeared older, more focused, yet there was more. Pickenson couldn't pinpoint what it was, but the transformation made him shiver.

Surely some of the men in the store would step up

to help. They hated the young man's type as much as he did. His sermon last Sunday had been about keeping bad influences out of town, and he had made it clear he meant Irish, Negroes, and Mexicans. Many of his neighbors had praised his words afterward. But, so far, none had moved to confront the young Ranger.

Pickenson saw the short cowboy with studded cuffs standing behind transfixed customers and knew who he was. The storekeeper's eyes asked for his help, then his frown wondered why the Mallow outlaw didn't respond. On the edge of Pickenson's tongue was a scream to "shoot the son of a bitch!" But a fearful sense, about what this intense young man might do, kept the words from being unleashed.

A thought jerked into the storeowner's mind that Silver Mallow himself was likely in town. Although it always made him uneasy, Pickenson took satisfaction in deciding that the appearance of the Mallow outlaw was an indication Silver knew the Ranger was here, too. There was no way Silver Mallow would let this upstart Irishman hurt him. No way.

After all, it was Pickenson who alerted Mallow about the Rangers' capture of some of his gang and helped him with the attack. Their relationship went back four years, when Mallow was gaining a reputation for a hot temper and a fast gun, and Pickenson was just another haughty, transplanted Yankee businessman looking for a way to get wealthy quickly. It had been a good match. Pickenson kept Mallow informed of happenings in the area, especially when the Rangers had come to the territory, and the outlaw leader slipped him occasional contraband goods taken from raids on ranches.

Of course, lately it seemed Silver was becoming bolder in his dealings with the town—but Pickenson knew the outlaw leader counted on him for support. He shook his head to stave off the recollection of Mallow's men driving away, laughing, with two wagons of goods from his store a few months ago.

Since no help was immediately forthcoming, Pickenson remembered the shotgun under the counter in front of his stool. He would talk to Silver later about his man's slow-coming action to help him. Anyway, all he had to do was step over there, and this nightmare would be over. The foolish Ranger would never know what hit him. What an idiot he was anyway to come riding into a place where everyone hated his kind, and coming alone to boot.

Casually Pickenson stepped to his right, talking as he moved. "Bennett has no use for the likes of you or your Irish friends. I would appreciate it if you'd leave my store now—and let my friends enjoy themselves."

"If you touch that shotgun, you'll never touch anything again," Carlow said. His words were cold, matching his eyes.

Wildly Pickenson looked at the assembled customers, seeking a friendly face, any friendly face, and mouthed "Help me" to the crow-faced woman. She responded immediately; her eyebrows arched and she pointed at Carlow. "Are you threatening our mayor? I'll have my husband bring this up to the council."

"Yes, I am, ma'am, you do that. The council's going to have to pick a new mayor. Pickenson is wanted for helping Silver Mallow murder two Rangers."

Pickenson froze and hated the visible shiver that followed. "What? I-I did no such thing."

"You heard me, Pickenson."

"W-What do you want? T-Take the money from my register. T-Take it and go!"

"No, Pickenson, I'm not like you," Carlow growled. He sensed movement to his right. "Tell your fat friend with the shiny gun . . . he isn't that good—and that you'll die first, if he tries."

"P-Please, please, H-Henry—do what he says. He's crazy!"

"No, not crazy, Pickenson, just interested in justice," Carlow said loudly for the entire store to hear. "You helped Silver Mallow get his men into town. How did you do it? Through that back door?" He studied Pickenson for the flinch that told him he had guessed correctly. "You had my friend, Texas Ranger

Noah Wilkins, killed. You got him to your store to be ambushed. . . ."

"N-No, no! I had no idea they were—"

"Save it for the fools that listen to you preach. I know what you did. So do you. You just didn't think any of us would live to tell about it. Well, you guessed wrong, Pickenson; now you're going to pay."

A half-smile entered the storekeeper's face as he realized the local judge was a slipshod attorney from Ohio who owed him a sizable amount of money from his wife's extravagant purchases. Pickenson hadn't pressed for payment, figuring there might come a time when such leverage might pay off bigger.

"You're going to leave town. For good. You're going to leave now."

Pickenson's smile vanished. "B-But I can't . . . I . . ."

"Yeah, you can—and you will. You and I are going to ride to Silver Mallow's hideout—and then you're going to leave the region. And if I ever see you again, you will die."

"I don't know where his hideout is."

"This isn't the time to lie, Pickenson. I know you do."

Carlow saw the stocky man leave from the corner of his vision and glanced in the direction of the slamming door. He didn't put significance on Shorty Beathard disappearing down the street, and turned his concentration back to Pickenson. The store-keeper's face collapsed into white fear as he realized what the outlaw's leaving meant: Mallow didn't care what happened to him. Pickenson whispered, "I-I didn't have any ch-choice. P-Please, they would have killed me. P-Please, I meant no h-harm. I didn't have a choice. I tried to warn you. Remember?"

A slump-shouldered rancher in a weather-battered hat and a stained canvas short coat stepped from the back of the crowd. His deeply lined face matched his hat for hard wear. He pushed his wide-brimmed hat back on his forehead and drawled, "So, ya did what the Ranger hyar said ya did."

"Don't get involved, Wallace," his wife whispered.

"Silver Mallow dun stole our cows, Maggie."

Ignoring the rancher's remarks, Carlow's face was stone. "I remember you had Ranger Dornan and Ranger Wilkins murdered. I remember you got this store right after old man Jenkins was murdered. Quite a coincidence, don't you think?"

The rancher pulled a small penknife from his pocket, flicked it open, and matched it with a to-bacco square from his other pocket. Deftly he cut off a wide slice and placed it inside the side of the cheek. Satisfied with his action, he proclaimed, "Now, that do make sense. Bin a-chewin' on that since ol' Jenkins were kilt." His wife tugged on his arm. The rancher looked around the room; his eyes sought agreement to his statement, and a few nodded.

Pickenson sobbed; huge tears flopped from his pained eyes and ran down his cheeks. "I-I c-can't leave m-my store. I-It's all I have. Th-These people need me . . . I-I'm their minister. I-I bring them the Word of God."

"You should've thought of that before you set up my friends to be shot down. The last time I checked, the Word of God was about love, not murder. As far as your store is concerned, that's all Jenkins had."

"H-He's going to k-kill me! I-Isn't anybody going to do anything—to help?"

"I'm not going to kill you. I should, but I won't—not unless your buddies over there get stupid." Carlow crossed his arms, as if having an everyday conversation. The action emphasized the distance between his hands and his guns. But no one moved or spoke. One man coughed and it drew angry stares.

Pickenson stared at the floor. "P-Please . . . d-don't."

"It's a lot better than you deserve. If you really do pray, I'd suggest you thank the Lord I remembered I was a Ranger. I'm just going to see that you get a good head start—to somewhere else—after you show me where Mallow's hideout is." He cocked his head to the side. "You won't be back."

Carlow looked around the room, catching the eyes

of the bravest customers. "Folks, you're going to need a new mayor—and a new preacher. Looks like there'll be a store for sale, too. This man is a murderer, and Bennett doesn't like trash, I understand." He looked again, but most were staring in other directions. "Of course, I know murderers are considered a better level of trash than the Irish."

The same blonde woman who had invited him to supper spoke up. Her voice trembled slightly. "S-Sir? W-We didn't know anything about this. The Rangers are always welcome here. H-He told us that you were trying to hurt the town, because . . . well, for the way we treated your mother. He told us the men you arrested weren't really rustlers."

A Scotsman with lamb-chop sideburns chimed in, waving his arms for emphasis. "H-He told us that we should stay inside that night—an' everything would be all right . . . again. W-We didn't know."

Pickenson glared at the man and he quit talking. The blonde woman glanced at the frightened man and shuffled forward to make certain Pickenson saw who was talking. "Mr. Pickenson, you can evil eye all you want. But we know the Ranger is telling the truth. You tried to have them killed."

A chorus of supporting comment joined her statement and she beamed. Even the frightened man with lamb-chop sideburns acknowledged she was right.

Staring at her with wicked eyes, Pickenson said, "Widow Webster, you should talk. Men are coming an' going from your house day and night."

She blushed, glanced at Carlow, and snarled, "Oh, really, and how are you doing with Widow Snyder these days? Did she pay for this store—like she did the church?" Laughter snapped the tension from the room.

The rancher pulled his hat back in place, pushed the chaw into a new place with his tongue, and growled, "You townspeople are damn fools. What do you think that Mallow bunch has been doin' to our herds? I've already lost over five hundred head—an' your Sheriff Moore don't give a damn. Neither do any of them army boys around. You folks figger it ain't your worry—'bout what's happenin' to us ranchers. Wal, one o' these days Silver an' his bunch o' devils is gonna come ridin' in hyar an' take over ever'thing. It'll be too late then. I figure we got one chance—and that's with these Rangers. Or do you folks think Silver Mallow's just gonna walk away one day?"

He paused, savored the tobacco, and took a half-step toward Carlow. "I'm Wallace Porter. Me an' my wife, Maggie, got a spread north o' hyar. We know you dun growed up hyar, Ranger. We don' have nuthin' ag'in you Irish. We don' take to Mexicans and coloreds none, but we don' figger yo'al are of that ilk." The rancher smiled at his wife and stepped back. There were more affirmative reactions to his short speech, and he looked around the room, absorbing the support.

"You know, I lost my best friend because none of you in this room would help us," Carlow said, his eyes narrowed. "Shannon Dornan grew up here. He was a son of this town. He spoke well of it, in spite of the way you treated him. He became a Ranger to help you—and the rest of Texas—live peaceful, good lives."

A sob from the blonde woman interrupted him. Pickenson stood with his hands clasped in front of him, his head down, trying to think. Three steps away was a barrel of long ax handles. The storekeeper's mind registered on the handles, and he blinked away his stare before Carlow noticed them as well. Instead, the young Ranger was seeing only Shannon Dornan being riddled by bullets.

He swallowed away the nightmare and continued. "Shannon Dornan didn't want to die; he wanted to live. But he was willing to put his life on the line—for you. But you didn't give him a chance to live. You killed him just as much as the Mallow gang did. All of you were as guilty as Pickenson." He paused and said, "I'm taking him—but I should put a torch to this whole miserable excuse for a town."

The room exploded with gasps, prayers, and admonitions of innocence and muttered threats against Carlow. The young Ranger walked over to the men sitting around the stove and demanded the pistol from the heavyset townsman. He quickly handed it over, adding that he would have never used it against Carlow. The young Ranger told him the gun would be on the sidewalk and shoved it into his belt.

The curly haired businessman stood and ceremoniously handed Carlow a Civil War Navy Colt dragoon with "CSA" hand-carved in the walnut handles. Carlow saw the marking and told him to keep it. The businessman smiled and glanced at the tobacco-chewing farmer. After returning the gun to his waistband, he crisply saluted. Carlow returned the greeting with a self-conscious salute of his own. The others nervously assured him they weren't armed, and the farmer volunteered that his wife carried a derringer and offered to point her out. A brown spit aimed at the spittoon followed, and most of the spittle missed. Carlow said pointing out his wife wouldn't be necessary.

The sudden wide-eyed expression on the former Confederate was enough of an alarm. Carlow spun to meet Pickenson's desperate charge, swinging an ax handle grabbed from the barrel. Sidestepping the vicious, downward swing of the ax handle, Carlow drove his right fist into the storekeeper's face as the weapon brushed along the Ranger's left arm.

Blood flooded from Pickenson's nose and the sound of crunching bone crackled in the taut room. His hands popped open and the handle thudded on the floor. A blur behind the first blow came Carlow's left uppercut that lifted Pickenson off his feet. He crashed into the barrel, careening handles like loose matches, and lay there unmoving. One handle spun wildly on its end in a tight circle before collapsing.

"You can't do that to our mayor!" the crow-faced woman screamed, placing her hands on her hips. "Stop that this instant," she demanded of Carlow, not yet realizing the fight was already over.

"Yes, ma'am," Carlow responded quietly, shaking his right hand to ward off the pain. He walked over to the downed store owner, grabbed his coat, and yanked him upright. He stood weaving, held up by Carlow's firm grasp. Pickenson's face was plastered with blood; long red strings ran down his neck onto his white shirt and suit. Other than the woman's agitated outcry, no one had attempted to stop Carlow. He expected them to try something. His attention appeared to be on Pickenson, but his peripheral vision sought unusual movement anywhere.

Through the crowd burst Jeremiah Beckham. Carlow's wolf-dog was trotting right beside him, quite happy to be included. The freckle-faced boy skidded to a stop a few feet from Carlow and examined the scene, uncertain of what he saw. With its tail in full wag, the wolf-dog continued on to Carlow and stood affectionately against his leg.

From the doorway the boy's mother yelled, "Jeremiah, did you come in here? Jeremiah, where are you? Come here!"

Carlow looked at the boy and smiled. "Jeremiah, your mother wants you."

"I thought you might need help, Ranger. I brought Chance with me. Is he a bad man?"

"Thanks for coming." Carlow nodded. "Yes, he is. A very bad man."

"Are you going to shoot him?"

"Jeremiah, come here!" The woman's voice was closer. Ellie Beckham edged her way through the tightly gathered customers and was surprised to see Carlow standing there. "Oh, it's you. I should've known." Her gaze took in Pickenson's wobbly stance and bloody face. "Is that what Rangers do? Beat up ministers?" Her eyes flashed angrily.

Immediately the crow-faced woman told her what had happened, using her fists to simulate Carlow's action, and said her husband was on the town council and would take proper action against Carlow. She left out Pickenson's initial attack with the ax handle, but her husband picked up one from the floor and completed the story, even explaining Mr. Pickenson had evidently been involved in the ambush that killed the Rangers last winter. The crow-faced woman seemed surprised at hearing these aspects of the fight. Carlow's wolf-dog caught her attention, and suddenly she had a new cause. "My God! It's a wolf! Someone shoot it quick—before it kills us all!"

"Lady, that's not a wolf, he's a dog, and his name is Chance. He's the Ranger's dog, but he likes me, too. Maybe he'd like you—if you didn't yell at him," Jeremiah said matter-of-factly.

Ellie stepped next to Jeremiah. Her arms draped over his shoulders and she held him to her, studying Carlow as if she were seeing the Ranger for the first time. In a quiet voice she said, "So that's why Mr. Pickenson told all the men to stay inside that night, that no one would get hurt—if we just let the outlaws go. I heard that one of the Rangers was killed in a cross-fire in the mayor's store. Was he . . ."

"He was Ranger Noah Wilkins. They also killed . . . my best friend, Shannon Dornan. He grew up here, like I did."

"I'm sorry. I was rude earlier. I just worry about Jeremiah . . . too much. His father died two years ago."

"I'm sorry. A boy needs a father."

"Can you be my father? Huh, can ya?" the boy exclaimed excitedly and glanced up at his mother. She blushed, her eyes dropped to Jeremiah, and she patted his face, partially out of love and mainly out of embarrassment.

"No one can take the place of your father, Jeremiah. I have to leave town with Mr. Pickenson now, to find Silver Mallow." Carlow pulled on the neck of Pickenson's coat for emphasis. "But when I come back, I'd like to be your friend. If it's all right with your mother."

Ellie looked up and their eyes connected again and danced for an instant. No one else was in the room for that moment. "Of course it would be. I-I'd like that."

Carlow smiled. "Thank you, ma'am."

"It's Ellie. Ellie Beckham."

Touching the brim of his hat, Carlow said, "Time Carlow. I'm very happy to know you . . . Ellie."

Ellie Beckham stood alone as the crowd began to dissipate, many wondering what would happen to the store and if they could make purchases anyway. Jeremiah didn't wait for more. He dashed toward Carlow's wolf-dog and held it around the neck. "You hear that, Chance? You an' me—an' the Ranger—are goin' to be buddies."

The dog responded by licking the boy's face.

"Can me an' Chance lead the way?"

Carlow yanked on Pickenson's coat again; this time to keep him upright. "I'd like you to stay in here and help your mother. Until this is over."

Jeremiah frowned. "Can Chance stay with me?"

"Not this time. He's got work to do."

The wolf-dog looked up at Carlow as if it understood. Before the young Ranger could direct Chance further, a tall man in a wrinkled suit stepped out from behind two women and lashed out, "Ranger, you're just mad that Silver Mallow outsmarted you. I'd stake my life Mayor Pickenson wouldn't do anything like you've accused him of. Get out of here, Mick! You're bringing Hell down on us!"

Chance growled and the tall man froze in place. Holding the dazed store owner upright by the back of his coat, Carlow told Chance to be quiet and stepped toward the businessman, who now wouldn't look at him.

"That's a mighty big bet, mister," Carlow said and reached out with his free hand to lift the man's chin until he was staring at him, holding it with an iron grip. "You yelled the same thing last winter but didn't have the guts to face me then, either. Look at me when you accuse. But I'd be careful what I put on the line, friend." Carlow released his hold and pushed the storekeeper toward the door. "Let's go. We'll get you a horse at the livery." He paused in front of Ellie. "Wish I could stay . . . an' get acquainted. This is something . . . I've got it to do."

"I understand," she said and reached out to touch his arm. "You will be careful. You promised my son that you'd return, you know."

"I never break a promise." His freed left hand

reached for her fingers on his arm. He squeezed them gently while his eyes embraced hers.

"W-We . . . I'll . . . be waiting," she said.

At the doorway Carlow turned back to the frightened customers. One man was fanning his wife's pale face with a magazine he had grabbed. The crow-faced woman was arguing with her husband; she wanted him to find a gun.

"Don't worry about Pickenson, folks. I'm certain Silver Mallow will be glad to see him . . . again. One of you better go get his clerk." Carlow touched the brim of his hat and told Chance to lead the way.

Eagerly the wolf-dog bounded through the opened door. Carlow didn't know what to expect outside. His presence was no secret by now, and the town would sense something was going on. He figured the abrupt appearance of this beast would keep most at a distance. Shoving Pickenson out of the store, the young Ranger was surprised to see the sidewalks filling with people on both sides of the main street. None were close, however, and Chance stood on the sidewalk as if he was ready to attack anything that moved toward them. All were curious to see if the wild tale flying through town was true: the Irish Ranger who grew up here was taking the mayor away.

"In case you're wondering, Pickenson, this here's an Irish wolfhound," Carlow's mouth twisted upward in one corner. "Special trained to attack storekeepers who set up murders. I suggest you not provoke him."

Pickenson muttered he was sorry and retched. Both Carlow and the wolf-dog jumped to avoid the onrushing vomit. Swinging into the saddle, his taut command put the store owner into a wobbly walk down the main street northward toward the open prairie. Carlow remembered the silver-plated revolver in his waistband, pulled it free, and removed the cartridges. An easy toss placed it on the planked sidewalk. Pickenson was too dazed to resist or even wipe the blood continuing to ooze from his nose or the vomit attached to his chin.

At Carlow's side trotted the wolf-dog. He looked down at the eager animal and said, "Glad you're with us, Chance. You like that name—Chance?"

Movement at the general store doorway became an eager Jeremiah who waved energetically. Behind him with a worried face came Ellie. She had given up trying to keep her son inside. She, too, waved and mouthed, "Come back." Carlow touched the brim of his hat and forced himself to study the assembled crowd.

People watched them pass with whispered observations and widened expressions. A cowboy paused beside his horse at a hitching rack in front of the Red Horse Saloon; he watched the young Ranger pass and nodded his appreciation. A buckboard came around the corner faster than it should have, and its horses swerved to avoid Pickenson, who did an awkward jig and fell down. Carlow should have been annoyed, but he couldn't help smiling. He was enjoying this parade through town; it was compensation for the way he and his mother had been treated. He reminded himself to stay alert; some townsman might want to do more than yell.

"Get up, Pickenson. We're going to the livery, not the dance hall."

Chance growled at the storeowner in support, then looked at Carlow for approval.

Somewhere came a loud curse: "Get outta here, Irishman! We don't want your kind around here." Then another, "Your mother was a whore!"

14

Only the flicker of Carlow's eyes showed he heard the curses, reinforced by "Go away, Irishman." The anonymous demand was followed by the familiar voice of Mrs. Jacobs shouting, "Thank you, Ranger. Thank you for protecting us. God bless you."

Carlow tried not to smile; she was some kind of woman. Her support brought an equally supportive bellow from Wallace Porter, the rancher from the store. Carlow recognized the distinctive gravelly voice but didn't see him. "Thanks for coming, Ranger. We need ya real bad."

A well-dressed man in a fashionably cut suit appeared in the doorway of the Lady Gay Saloon. Inside, the band was playing an uptempo "Jeanie with the Light Brown Hair" as a break in Anna Nalene's performance. The pounding rhythm hurled itself onto the sidewalk. Silver Mallow watched Carlow and Pickenson pass, keeping himself in the shadows so the storekeeper wouldn't fall to the temptation of pointing him out.

Mallow muttered to himself. "Today, it ends."

Hurrying to see what was happening, a bowlegged cowboy in a crumpled coat pushed past him. Beer splashed from his mug onto Mallow's suit sleeve. Mallow glared at the stain, but the cowboy didn't notice either the splashing or Mallow's anger.

"Ain't that somethin'? *Hiccup.* One man again' a whole town. *Hiccup,*" the cowboy observed, nudging Mallow with his elbow. " 'Course that one man are a Ranger. *Hiccup. Hiccup.* Makes me almost feel sorry for . . . *hiccup* . . . Silver Mallow." He laughed at his joke and took a deep swallow from his beer glass.

Mallow politely chuckled, wiping the beer foam from his suit, and forced himself to remain quiet. He stepped away from the drunken man to the middle of the sidewalk and gazed upward as if to check to see where a reluctant sun had hidden. His eyes took in the second-floor window of the Red Horse Saloon next door and saw that Shorty Beathard was in position. Barely visible, the ugly end of his Winchester slithered between the white lace curtains. Mallow smiled and glanced toward the far alley, where the obese Lyle Barat leaned against the far wall. The man nodded in response to Mallow's attention. Directly across the street, Houston Holt nervously fiddled with his hands as he waited in the shadows of a real estate and law office.

Satisfied, Silver Mallow returned to the shadows of the saloon doorway. The cowboy had already reentered the Lady Gay, singing loudly and off-key with the band. The outlaw leader retrieved a cigar from his inside pocket, bit off the end, and snapped a match to life on the door frame. White smoke encircled his handsome face as he waited. *Would Sheriff Moore—or someone from the town council—try to stop the Ranger?* he wondered to himself. That would allow a perfect distraction for Barat and Holt to kill Carlow.

But if the sheriff didn't show, and the man rarely showed any backbone, they would kill him anyway. Beathard would be the backup if everything else went wrong. Neither Barat nor Holt were aware of Beathard's orders. General Terrell and Jesus were waiting for their instructions inside. Mallow didn't think the lawman knew he was in town but didn't care if he did. As long as Sheriff Moore didn't bother him or his men. By showing such smart judgment, Mallow would leave him alone. Why take a chance on a more aggressive sheriff?

Mallow smiled and drew on his cigar. "I'm too good for you, Time Carlow. Too bad you'll be dead before you know the truth of it."

On the far right-hand side of the street, a badge

sparkled within the burgeoning crowd. A slump-shouldered man in a three-piece suit and a wide-brimmed white hat pushed through the curious line of people and stepped off the sidewalk into the muddy street. In his crossed arms was a Winchester.

"Halt in the name of the law, mister," came the order from Sheriff Titus Moore. "Where do you think you're going with our mayor?"

Carlow didn't stop or even look at the town constable. "Keep moving, Pickenson, or I'll shoot you down right here. Sheriff, this man set up the murder of a Texas Ranger. He's leaving town."

"On whose orders?"

"Mine."

Sheriff Moore cleared his throat, not liking the young man's confident manner. He had thrust himself into a position where everyone could see him, and now he wished he had stayed busy in his office, like he always did when he heard some of Mallow's men were in town. Sheriff Moore tried to recall a simpler time before he succumbed to the implied threat of Mallow's gang. Bennett wasn't paying him to face even one of them. He was hired to jail drunks and keep the town bank safe. Not to take on a mad-dog killer like Silver Mallow or someone like Jesus that he'd seen in the wanted bulletins. He certainly didn't want to know what Silver Mallow looked like, either. It was safer that way. For the town, too, he told himself. If Mallow got angry with Bennett, he'd simply wipe it out. Surely the town council understood that. If not, he would tell them. If Mallow's gang minded their own business, that was good enough for him.

He knew who this rider was with the mayor walking in front of him. One of those cocky Texas Rangers who scared him into finding an excuse to leave town when they brought in some of the Mallow gang last winter. What bothered him most was that he thought they had all died, except that massive bull of a Ranger who used to win prizefights around the county. But this was Time Carlow, the Irish lad who had grown up here.

Aware of the crimson that was crawling from his neck toward his hat, Sheriff Moore cleared his throat again and tried to keep up with Carlow's continued advance. "I'm the law in this town, Ranger. Not you." Moore was impressed with the resonance in his voice and inhaled to expand his chest. "Nobody takes our mayor."

"Really. I'm taking him. You going to stop me?" Carlow brushed his coat away from the holstered hand-carbine with his freed right hand.

"I-I have two deputies."

"They the same ones that cut 'n' ran when we brought in the Mallow gang?" Carlow said. "Like you did?"

A murmur, laced with laughter, meandered through the crowd. Moore didn't like it. Most of his authority came from the respect people had for his reputation with a gun. A bloated reputation built on a decade-old story of killing a drunken cowhand who wouldn't surrender his handgun. Still, it was a reputation he had used effectively, letting others embellish the story until it had become three men coming at him blazing.

Where were his deputies? he asked himself nervously. There! He caught a glimpse of one deputy as he disappeared into the Corao Saloon, hopefully headed for an upper window and not a whiskey or a whore. The other deputy was at the other end of town, where Moore had sent him. Wearing a long coat and holding a shotgun, he stood on his tiptoes in the middle of the street, trying to see what was going on. Moore waved angrily at him to come forward and the lanky Deputy Terwelliger began to run toward him. Smiling at his new assessment of the situation, the sheriff turned his attention back to the young Ranger.

Carlow appeared uncaring about the lawman and unknowing about his deputies; the young Ranger's back was nearly turned to Moore as he rode toward the end of town. Pickenson wandered in front of him, shuffling his feet and staring at the uneven street. No one was close enough to tell the young Ranger was pale and trembling from weakness. He was chilled from the earlier rain and weak from pushing his body beyond its readiness. His mind, however, was set on this. It was the least he could do for Shannon Dornan and Noah Wilkins. He would make Pickenson pay for his part in the ambush by losing his reputation and all he owned. He would find Silver Mallow, too.

Moore smiled and cocked his Winchester, but the clicking was like a shout above the chatter on the crowded street. The sound brought a growl from Carlow's wolf-dog, long and deep in his throat, and he spun away from Carlow's horse and ran snarling at the sheriff. Moore saw the dog coming, hesitated, and fired at Chance too quickly. The bullet tore into the street.

From behind the sheriff came a familiar voice. "Me thinks ye better not be doin' that again. 'Twould be a better idea if ye be droppin' that fine gun. Me thinks 'twould be good if ye did it right 'bout now."

It was Old Thunder Kileen. His pants and part of his coat were damp and wrinkled. The big Ranger was standing ten feet behind Sheriff Moore, brandishing a cocked Henry rifle. Time Carlow shouted at Chance to stop. The wolf-dog arched his back and stutter-stepped to a stop a few feet from the terrified sheriff. A mouthful of white teeth greeted the lawman, and Carlow couldn't help smiling as Moore quickly let his gun fall from his opened hands.

Half a block away the lanky Deputy Terwelliger skidded to a stop, uncertain of what he should do. Carlow saw him and waved him forward.

Kileen cheerily added, "Come ahead, lad, an' be joinin' the party. The scattergun ye be leavin' ri't there, in the street." The deputy looked down at the gun in his hands as Kileen continued, " 'Tis better the fine gun be layin' in the street, lad, than yourself."

"Drop the gun, Elias, you fool!" shouted Moore.

The deputy threw the gun like it was hot and walked briskly toward Moore and Kileen. Moore cursed the deputy's wide smile, and Kileen told the sheriff to shut up, that he liked seeing a man who liked his job. Out of the corner of his eye Carlow realized Jeremiah was trying to get his attention without everyone else seeing. Turning his head slightly toward the red-faced boy, Carlow nodded his awareness of Jeremiah's intent. Biting his lower lip, Jeremiah crossed his arms, passed in front of Silver Mallow, and pointed with his finger toward the fat man in the alley on the other side of the Lady Gay Saloon. Mallow whispered in Anna Nalene's ear, and they disappeared into the saloon, unnoticed by either Ranger.

Carlow resisted looking directly where the boy indicated, letting his gaze slide there without moving his head. He saw Barat leaning against the alley wall and knew the fat outlaw was trouble. Under Barat's crossed arms, Carlow glimpsed the short barrel of a revolver. On the opposite side of the street he sensed movement and the flicker of sunlight off steel. Cross fire!

As planned, Barat jerked out the gun and fired. But Carlow was no longer on his horse. As the outlaw's shot tore into the space where Carlow had been, a second shot from the far side of the street attacked the same emptiness. But a trigger pull earlier, Carlow swung his right leg up and over the saddle, kicked free of the left stirrup, and landed with his feet spread apart. All in one smooth motion. His horse masked his back to the other side of the street, stopping as he ordered. In his right hand was the hand-carbine, its lever spinning the gun into readiness.

Bracing the gun against his hip, Carlow levered three fast shots into the stunned fat outlaw. Barat's revolver fired again, this time into the alley dirt, and the man spun sideways and slid along the building wall, leaving a long smear of blood. Without waiting to see the result of his shooting, Carlow pitched himself sideways, almost a continuation of his rapid dismount, ending up under his horse's belly, facing the other side of the street. His eyes searched immediately for the second assailant there, somewhere. Along the street was an explosion of screams, shouts, and people scurrying for any kind of cover.

Houston Holt's eyes were wide as he hurriedly

cocked his pistol to fire a second shot at Carlow. Inside his brain was whirring the awful realization that he had done a stupid thing. Shots from Kileen's rifle and Carlow's hand-carbine hit Holt at the same time, slamming him against the glass window of the real estate office and shattering the pane. His cocked pistol thudded into the sidewalk, triggering a shot that ripped away a shard of wood and spat splinters in all directions. Two more shots made Holt shudder. His shirt caught on a sharp piece of glass and held up his quivering body for an instant before it crashed to the sidewalk.

"At the window, me son!"

Orange flame spat from the window as Kileen fired into the curtain-lined space. As if connected to Old Thunder's shot, Carlow's bullet slammed into the silhouette frozen there. The two gunshots were one roar. Ahead of Carlow, Pickenson grabbed his chest and stumbled to the street. At the window, a hand grabbed the curtain and disappeared, leaving a bloody mark in the middle of the white drapery.

Levering his gun, Carlow yelled, "Get a doctor—for Pickenson!"

The young Ranger caught movement behind him on the sidewalk. Spread-eagled on the street, he spun his hand-carbine toward a businessman pushing his hand inside his coat. Surprised at Carlow's sudden attention, the man jerked his hand free and turned his quivering palm outward to show he was merely after a cigar. Carlow knelt beside his horse, hearing Shadow paw the ground nervously.

His hard gaze studied the remaining windows, alleys, and shadows for more trouble. Here and there a person stood, usually slowly and with hands clearly displayed to show he was not a part of the ambush. His mind registered on Houston Holt and knew this was another Mallow ambush. How many more were in town? Was the sheriff involved?

As if on command, another townsman left his hiding place behind a water trough, explaining his actions loudly for Carlow to hear. He rolled Pickenson over and examined his still body. "Too late, Ranger. He's dead." On the sidewalk a woman moaned and fainted, drawing an immediate gathering of concerned onlookers.

Carlow's mouth twisted into frustration. Pickenson was his only chance to find Silver Mallow's hideout. His shoulders rose and fell, and weakness seeped through his body as the adrenaline of battle sped away. Strength was waning fast, and he needed to move on before the town realized it, or he fainted. From his kneeling position, he leaned over to retrieve the dropped reins. Slowly he stood and patted his black horse. "Good job, Shadow. Good job, boy."

"Where be that other fine deputy?" Kileen demanded of Moore as the first deputy jogged up beside them. The big Ranger levered his rifle, spitting a smoking cartridge and readying the hammer again. A wisp of smoke trailed from the ugly end pointing at Moore's stomach. Like Carlow, Kileen's eyes scurried up and down the street, looking for a man who might look like Angel's drawing.

"Oh, Langdon? He were interested in that red-haired gal . . . in the Corao," Deputy Terwelliger answered before Moore could respond. Laughter followed from the crowd, and the deputy looked around, surprised at the reaction to his statement.

Kileen's eyes glittered. "Aye, and 'tis a fine thing he be doin'. The lass be needin' a lot o' protection, for sure." More laughter followed.

"Oh, she wasn't needin' no protection, he was needin' a screw," the deputy advised. Moore frowned and told him to shut up. Main Street activity was reenergized as people resumed their lives; most finding a reason to be elsewhere. The town undertaker-and-barber was the next to examine Pickenson, then the two dead outlaws in the street. The one upstairs in the hotel would be removed later.

"Sheriff, after ye be removin' your handgun, ye walk over to the dead storekeep an' be sayin' your last farewells to the son of Satan. For all I know, you are part of this evil day."

Moore shook his head vigorously to assure his innocence.

"Next ye be tellin' Ol' Thunder that yah didn't know Mallows were in town." Kileen's eyes continued their search for more waiting guns. "I may be Irish, but I ain't no potato. Be any more Mallows around? How about Silver hisself?"

"I-I didn't know they were here, Ranger. H-Honest."

" 'Honest?' Ye don't know the meanin' o' that word. If we find Silver—or any more of his devils— I'm goin' to come for ye afterward, Sheriff. It won't be to chat about the wonder of the day."

Moore winced visibly, told his deputy to unbuckle his pistol belt, and did the same to his. Kileen watched them walk toward Pickenson as he strolled over to Carlow. The young Ranger was again kneeling, letting the dizziness pass while he hugged an excited Jeremiah. The huge wolf-dog had already joined them, splashing the boy's arms and Carlow's hands with sloppy licks. Kileen smiled at the encounter and saw Ellie standing on the sidewalk. Her arms folded, she watched both Carlow and the boy. Kileen pursed his lips and shook his head. His eyes again sought a certain face among the passersby. None caught his attention. *Were there more Mallow outlaws waiting? Where? Was Silver himself in town? Why?* Questions shot through his mind faster than bullets.

"I hope ye not be mad at Ol' Thunder for followin'," Kileen said. "I couldn't be lettin' ye go that way."

Carlow's smile was wide. "Your voice was about the prettiest sound I ever heard." He stood with his arm around Jeremiah. "This here's my new friend, Jeremiah. He saved my life."

"Aye, 'tis a brave thing you did, laddie. Jeremiah, is it? Could that be your mither there? Bless her fine-lookin' self."

Jeremiah turned and waved at Ellie. "Yessir, that's my mom. Come here, Mom! Are you a Ranger, too?" he asked Kileen.

"Aye, 'tis a Ranger I be."

"Boy, this is my lucky day!" Jeremiah exclaimed. "Two Rangers!"

Kileen started to say something but realized his nephew wasn't paying any attention. Ellie was rushing toward him. "I-I w-was so worried . . ."

"Jeremiah saved my life," Carlow said and took her in his arms, pulling his horse to one side as he moved. She held him tightly; their cheeks pushed against each other's. Neither wanting the moment to end. Standing on the sidewalk, the blond woman from the general store watched, made a snorting assessment, "Hussy," and marched on. Ellie's lips pressed against Carlow's cheek, and his mouth edged toward hers. Behind him, Carlow's horse whinnied and pushed its nose against his elbow as if to encourage the process, but neither Carlow nor Ellie noticed, lost in each other's closeness.

"Aye, 'tis a busy boy ye've been this fine day," Kileen observed with a knowing grin and clapped Carlow on the shoulder enthusiastically.

The young Ranger staggered from the blow, and Kileen realized his beloved nephew was very weak from the day's battles. The thumping broke their embrace, and Ellie stepped back quickly, brushing her hair with her hand and trying to think of something to say. She glanced around to see if anyone was watching.

"Be mighty proud o' ye, me son," Kileen continued without any indication that he had interrupted something special. "Thought ye might be intendin' to shoot down that murderous bastird Pickenson. Mighty glad to see ye be doin' the right thing." He made no mention of Carlow's acrobatic move to turn a cross-fire ambush to his advantage, even though the savvy ex-prizefighter was swelled up with a mixture of pride and concern.

"I was going to kill him, Thunder," Carlow said. His eyes sought Ellie's, but she was concentrating on holding Jeremiah to her side and deliberately keeping her eyes on her son. "But I couldn't. Too much Ranger in me, I guess. You taught me well, Uncle."

Kileen's tongue pushed against his cheek, extending it, before responding. His eyes glinted with guilt, and he looked away as he spoke. "Aye, an' too much Carlow. Your father be a man like that. Fight like the devil hisself but not if'n the man ag'in him couldn't be standin'." He acted as if he wanted to say something more but didn't.

Carlow glanced at the dead Pickenson. "Well, I was hoping to get Pickenson to tell me where Silver Mallow is. Figured he'd know." He pointed in the direction of the slumping body below the window. "That's Houston Holt over there. The others had to be Mallow men, too. You think there's more in town? How'd they know I was here? Did they follow me? Did you see Silver?" Carlow knew his last question was silly and shook his head. "Sorry, I'm a little wound up, I guess."

"Nay, 'tis a sorry thing to admit, me son, that Silver Mallow could just as well be a trooper fairy or a wee leprechaun." Crossing himself, Kileen studied the people moving again on the sidewalks and crossing the street as if Silver Mallow would magically appear. Silently he cursed his misfortune with Angel's drawing in the stream. Carlow's questions were rushing through his mind; he remembered the old Mexican saying Mallow and his men actually came into Bennett every now and then. That thought brought him to Angel's sorrowful face when he stormed away.

"How come you're so wet? Did you get caught in the storm?"

"Aye, the storm."

"Do you think Silver's in town?"

Behind them came a stranger, and both Rangers

turned toward the movement, levering their guns to
ready them.

"Oh, oh, my! Sorry. Sorry. I just came over to say
how impressed I was by all that." The middle-aged
stranger in a rumpled suit tipped his hat and introduced himself as Howard Norfield, a pottery and
china salesman from Iowa. He said that he'd never
seen a gunfight before and how thrilling it had been.
"Can't wait to tell Mary . . . that's my wife, Mary . . .
that I saw an honest-to-goodness gunfight. I mean it
was something to behold! My God! Did you know
they were there? I mean, one second you were on
your horse—and the next, you know, you were down
on the ground, shooting . . . and what is that gun?
I've never seen a gun like that!"

Howard Norfield continued talking, and Carlow
wasn't certain the salesman was ever going to stop
long enough to let someone else talk—or, better yet,
get away from him. The salesman asked who would
be taking over ownership of the general store; if the
town would appoint a new mayor or hold a special
election; and if there was someone in town who
could take Pickenson's place as a minister and conduct the church services, adding that he went to
church, even when he was traveling. It was Kileen
who finally ended the one-sided discussion by interrupting Norfield with the statement that the fight
might not be over and he was in danger standing so

close to them. Norfield turned around mid-word and hurried to the safety of the Lady Gay Saloon. Carlow watched him go, catching the strains of a brassy song as the salesman entered.

Kileen shook his head. "I knew it were gonna be a good day, laddie. I be seein' a white horse right over there." He pointed at a dirty white horse tied to the rack. "Then I spit an' didn't say a word until I saw a dog, like you're supposed to. It was your dog I be seein', Time. I knew the day was going to be a lucky one."

"I'm glad to hear it." Carlow tried to keep from smiling. "I think we should search the town. Silver himself might be here. Or more of his men."

Kileen glanced and nodded at a passing wagon, noting to himself that the driver actually smiled at them. " 'Tis unlikely, me lad. Let's go where ye can be sittin' down for a wee bite o' supper. When did ye last eat, me son? 'Tis weak in your face, you be." Kileen motioned toward Ellie and Jeremiah. "Should ye be invitin' . . . your new friends . . . to join us?"

Carlow turned back to Ellie, wishing he could hold her again, but her face was not readable. Was it just the moment that brought her into his arms? Just fear that he might be shot down? He couldn't remember feeling this way about a woman before. There was Jessica Crawford behind her father's barn when they were both sixteen, but that lustful exploration didn't feel like this. All he could think of was having Ellie close to him.

"Why don't you be askin' the lass? While I be goin' to see about the fella who shot Pickenson . . . from that window." Kileen put his hand on Carlow's shoulder. "Ah, 'tis no husband we should be worryin' about, is there?" He winked.

"She's . . . a widow, Thunder—and a nice lady. W-We just met. Her son liked . . . my dog."

" 'Tis a dog now ye be havin'. Would've bet a month's Ranger pay that it be a wolf. Where'd he join up with ye?"

Carlow explained what had happened, but his gaze barely caught Kileen's face; his eyes wanted Ellie to look at him again. Jeremiah was petting Chance and telling her about the wolf-dog. She petted the beast, glancing up occasionally at Carlow.

"Was it just after ye . . . left Shannon's grave, bless his soul?"

"Awhile after." Carlow glanced at Kileen. "It's just a dog, Thunder. Just a dog that might be part wolf."

"Aye, just a dog . . . that 'tis a wolf." The big Ranger answered, but his eyes didn't agree. He looked away at something only he could see, then blinked back to Carlow. "Got some things for ye." Kileen reached into his pocket and retrieved a Ranger badge and the two blood stones.

Carlow stared at the them in the big man's massive hand. "I-I was plannin' on goin' back to . . . get the stones. I-I shouldn't have left them." He stared at Kileen's pants. "So that's why you're so wet."

Kileen nodded.

"But I'm not a Ranger. Remember the captain's telegram?"

It was Kileen's turn to smile. "Well, that not be so, me lad. In me pocket is a second telegram from McNelly hisself. You be a Ranger again."

"B-But . . . how?"

"I send the captain a wire when I got to town—an' he be answerin' right off." He reached into his pocket and withdrew the folded copy of the telegraph message.

"You mean you've been here?" Carlow's face was a question mark. "How long? Why didn't—"

"Wanted to be sure meself were in the right place," Kileen said. "Ye know, watchin' me nephew take on a whole town be a sight to see." He patted Carlow three times on the shoulder and pinned the badge on the young Ranger's shirt. Carlow unfolded and read the telegram. It was brief:

BOTH ARE RANGERS STOP . . . MAIN FORCE IN EL PASO STOP . . . YOU AND CARLOW GET MALLOW STOP . . . JOIN US AFTER STOP.

"Well, McNelly doesn't want much, does he?" Carlow refolded the paper and returned it to Kileen, then took the stones, eased each one into his shirt pocket, and patted the memory. Kileen motioned that he should tap the stones two more times and Carlow did, smiling. The big Ranger patted his own pocket and said he also had Dornan's badge, and Carlow nodded his appreciation. Beside him, Carlow's horse jerked its head, wanting to leave. Carlow yanked the reins and told it to be still.

"I be the one who told Captain McNelly that we would capture Silver Mallow and his gang, lad."

Carlow stared at his uncle and shook his head. "Weren't you the one just giving me trouble about taking on a whole town? How many guns you think Mallow's got?"

"Hold on a minute, me boy. Just how many Rangers did ye figure were goin' after hisself, Silver Mallow, and his bunch o' hoodlums . . . a few minutes ago," Kileen countered, shoving new cartridges into his Henry rifle. He skipped over the thirteenth bullet in his belt loops and took the next one. "Least me eyes are playin' tricks on this old man, one Ranger I be countin'—before I said 'howdy.' "

"Yeah, well, lots of luck with Pickenson dead."

Kileen stared at his nephew. "Well, now, ye be thinkin' Pickenson be the onliest man in town that knows where the bastird be?"

Carlow stared at him and burst into laughter. "It's Angel, isn't it? I should've known. Why didn't you—"

"No chance ye be givin' me to tell ye much of anything." Kileen didn't mention the drawing or his angry departure. "Be loadin' that big gun o' yournself now, a'fore ye be forgettin'." He smiled a jack-o'-lantern grin. "The thirteenth bullet, ye be skippin' over."

Carlow shook his head, started to reload the hand-carbine, and was aware the wolf-dog was again at his side. He looked up to see Ellie walking away, holding her reluctant son's hand. His mind ran after her. Would she wait? Why should she? His heart told him to hurry, and he heard himself yell, "Ellie . . . Jeremiah . . . wait, please!"

Shoving the not-yet-reloaded hand-carbine into its holster, he ran after her. He pulled on the reins of his horse to get the well-trained mount moving faster. An ache was seeping into his head, but he tried to ignore it. If there was any concern about more Mallow outlaws in town, it was forgotten for the moment. Ellie was the only thing he could see.

Ellie bit her lower lip to keep from turning around and making a fool of herself again. Behind her, she heard rapid footsteps and walked faster. Jeremiah pulled hard on her hand and broke free, but she regrabbed his arm and walked faster.

15

The big Ranger shook his head, watching his nephew run after the woman and her son. He was more worried about Time Carlow than Silver Mallow. His nephew was as courageous as his father ever was, but he was also weakened from the savage attack and needed to ease into duty, not charge it headlong. Kileen smiled when he replayed Carlow's gunplay from minutes earlier in his mind; there weren't many men who could have duplicated that. Where had Carlow met this woman and her child? Maybe she could convince him to rest before going on. The thought of this woman and his nephew in bed together seeped into his mind. He chuckled and decided there wouldn't be much resting.

That brought Angel Balta to his mind. Among her last words to him were that Silver Mallow was headquartered at a small ranch everyone thought was owned by a Mexican couple. He knew where it was, had been there himself, looking for the outlaw gang, and had been greeted by the older man and wife. He still couldn't believe the connection, but it did make sense. A perfect hiding place—right in an open valley, no less.

Angel having been with the gang shouldn't bother him, he told himself; he didn't love her; nor she, him. They just found comfort within each other's arms. Just comfort. He shook his head vigorously to remove the images of Angel with other men and tried to recapture the drawing of Silver Mallow in his mind. He should have been more careful with the drawing. Maybe the spirits didn't want him to have it; water nymphs could be particularly mean when they wanted to, he reminded himself.

Finally Ellie stopped. At Jeremiah's insistence. She turned toward Carlow, trying to keep her face from showing how pleased she was that he came after her.

"Ellie, my uncle and I . . . we'd like you and Jeremiah to join us for supper later, if you would. Please." Carlow took off his hat to reinforce his invitation, bowing slightly.

"That would be swell, wouldn't it, Mom?" Jeremiah hopped on one foot, then the other.

"I would understand, of course, if you thought it wasn't a good idea. Us being Irish and all," Carlow added.

Ellie's perky smile became a thin line. "Mr. Carlow, don't you think I can take care of myself and my son?" Her eyes sought his for the right answer.

"Oh, no, I didn't . . . I just . . . well, I would really like you to . . . but . . ." He stopped and laughed at himself. "Shoot, you make a fella have trouble with his tongue."

She giggled and touched his arm. "I'm sorry. You've been through a lot—and I'm acting like some spoiled brat."

"Oh, no . . . Ellie . . . you're just . . . real fine." Carlow felt redness dawning from his shirt collar.

"I'm sorry about Mr. Pickenson. I didn't like the man. I didn't trust him. Still, it's awful to see someone die like that," Ellie said. "Who were those men who tried to . . . kill you? My God, that was so frightening!"

"Looks like they were part of Silver Mallow's gang. The one over there is, for sure." He pointed in the direction of the dead Holt.

"Ohmygoodness! I-Is Silver Mallow here? In Bennett?"

Carlow's chest rose and fell with a long breath. "I wish I knew. I don't know what he looks like. Neither does Thunder . . . ah, Ranger Kileen. I guess he could be watching us right now." His eyes reconnected with hers, and he forgot what he was talking about. "Ah, what was I saying?"

She giggled. "You were telling me about Silver Mallow. Goodness, well, there are always strangers coming through. The stage brings a loadful three times a week." She bit her lower lip and continued, "But I work in Mrs. Jacobs's shop, and I don't think anyone like him would be coming in there."

"You do? I think she's one terrific lady."

"Yes, she is. She told me about you, said you grew up here. She thinks a lot of you. I expected Ranger Time Carlow to be eight feet tall."

He laughed, Ellie smiled, and he didn't want to move. Reminding himself that he was a Ranger with work to do, Carlow said, "Well, I'll walk you over that way and tie up my horse outside, then I'm going to catch up with Ranger Kileen. He doesn't know it yet, but we're going to search the town. Is it all right if Chance stays there, too—with my horse? Will you wait . . . please?"

"Jeremiah would like that, I'm sure. Of course we'll wait. Jeremiah and I will be in the millinery store."

Chance followed after them, nipping playfully at Carlow's Kiowa leggings. Running her hand along her hair, Ellie walked beside him, caught herself, and glanced about the busy sidewalk. No one was paying any attention to them, except for the yellow-haired woman standing outside the general store with her arms crossed. Ellie glimpsed the massive Kileen tap on the door frame of the Red Horse three times with his rifle and enter.

After securing his horse at the rack, Carlow reluctantly excused himself, told Chance to remain with Shadow, and walked back across the street. Sheriff Moore and Deputy Terwelliger were examining the body of the outlaw in the alley; they had retrieved their guns as Kileen had told them. Deputy Langdon had finally showed up, sporting a half-smile and an embarrassed look on his face. He cheerfully tried to engage Carlow in conversation as the young Ranger paused beside the other lawmen. Carlow's mind wouldn't let go of the possibility Moore and his men might have been in on the ambush.

"The two dead ones are Barat and the last of them Holt brothers," Deputy Langdon pronounced proudly. "Silver Mallow's men. We've got papers on them. Wanted for rustling an' murder. Lord-a-mercy, Silver will be madder'n hell when he hears about this. You Rangers better ride hard outta here."

Carlow's fierce stare changed the deputy's expression from concern to fear as the young Ranger stepped beside the sheriff. "Moore, how do I know you weren't part of this?" Carlow laid his hand on the lawman's back and Moore jumped.

Moore stood slowly, trying to compose himself. When he turned toward Carlow, his face was white.

"C-Come on, Ranger, I-I had nothin' to do with this. Ya have to believe me."

"Is Silver Mallow in town?"

"I-I wouldn't know. Never laid eyes on the man far as I know."

"I'm sure you work real hard at it, too."

Moore's face flushed. "Look, Ranger, I get paid to haul in drunks and keep the bank from being robbed. That's it. I don't give a damn what happens out on the range. That's your job. Silver's never hurt this town. But I-I have to live here, you don't."

Carlow glanced at Moore's deputies, then back at the sheriff. Carlow's eyes locked onto Moore. "I want all three of you to stay in your office until we leave town. I don't want to see any of your faces again. If I do, I'm going to assume you're with Mallow—and shoot you down like the yellow dogs you are. Do you understand?"

Moore didn't look at either deputy. He glanced away and muttered, "Y-Yah. W-We won't get in your way, Ranger, I promise."

"No, you won't."

On the second floor of the Red Horse Saloon, Old Thunder Kileen kicked open the door of a drab room. His quick examination took in a single bed covered by a stained quilt, a dresser with a missing drawer, and a lamp empty of both oil and wick. He levered his Henry and stepped inside the gray space usually rented by the hour. A dead Shorty Beathard lay slumped below the opened window. The outlaw's last attempt to live had resulted in one curtain ending up across his back like a white half-shroud. The other remained, streaked with his blood.

Kileen's first instinct was to make certain the door was open to let the spirit leave; the window was obviously ready for such a release. Even a bad man deserved such treatment, he thought. Actually he was concerned more about leaving a ghost for others to deal with. He smiled when he considered the idea of a saloon whore and her patron being interrupted by a nasty specter. Still, giving the soul an opportunity to leave was the right thing to do. He hoped someone would do that for him when the time came.

He shoved Beathard's rifle away from the body and studied the unseeing face. The dead man was familiar to him. Beathard was a known rustler, last seen running with the Silver Mallow gang. The bigger question in Kileen's mind was why the man was here. Today. The would-be assassin in the alley had to be Barat—and it was definitely Houston Holt across the street. Why were they in Bennett? Had they seen Time Carlow headed this way and followed him? If so, why hadn't he seen them—or their tracks? He reminded himself that he wasn't a great tracker. Maybe he just missed the signs.

Did this mean Silver Mallow was here? Would he still be in town somewhere? Is that why Beathard killed Pickenson—so he couldn't identify the outlaw leader? Should they scour the town for someone who could identify him? Or did everyone in Bennett know him but was afraid to talk?

Kileen looked around the room as if it could give him answers to the questions burning in his mind. He put out his hand to lean against the faded flower-patterned wall. One answer settled like new snow. Likely Mallow was worried about the storekeeper leading Carlow to his hideout—or pointing him out, if he was in town somewhere. That had to be it. Certainly he wasn't concerned about Pickenson volunteering his connection to the outlaw leader; Mallow wouldn't have cared, at that point.

Kileen laid his own rifle against the wall and rubbed his unshaved chin. It all came back to timing: *Why were the Mallow men here? How did Mallow, or his men, know what was happening? They had to have seen Carlow coming to town and guessed what it meant.* Kileen shook his head in agreement with himself. He picked up the rifle enthusiastically as if a considerable problem was resolved and tapped the wall three times. But it only brought more questions.

If Silver Mallow himself had been with his men, was he still here? Where? Or would he have left after giving his men orders? Of course, it also meant Mallow now knew, for certain, that Ranger Time Carlow hadn't died—and was after him. Kileen dismissed the fact that the outlaws knew he was there, too. He cursed aloud that he didn't know what Silver Mallow looked like and shut his eyes to try to recall Angel's destroyed drawing. It was too much to endure because it always ended up with his seeing her in bed with some man without a face. Opening his eyes, he slammed a fist into the wall, creating a bowl-like dent. The impact sent pain shivering through his arm, and he stared at his bleeding knuckles and cursed again. "May ye never find a friend in this life or the next, Silver Mallow!"

Angry at himself, he leaned out the window to yell down for Sheriff Moore and his deputies to come up and get the body. He immediately noticed Ellie and Jeremiah were not in sight, and that made him sad; maybe she wouldn't wait for his nephew. Foolish lass, he muttered and tried not to think of Angel. He didn't see the sheriff or his deputies, either. Only Carlow walking toward the saloon.

Brisk rhythms from the Lady Gay Saloon next door reached Kileen's ears and then his mind. Music! Silver Mallow was in town to hear music! It had to be. Music! Silver Mallow loved music—that's what Angel said! That's why Mallow men were in town. Of course. Why didn't he think of that before?

Carlow saw Kileen, and the big Ranger waved that

he was coming down and to wait for him. " 'Tis a grand day to get me son back, 'tis," Kileen muttered, stepped away from the window, and took a swig from the whiskey flask from his pocket. He patted the tiny pouch of Irish earth in his other pocket. "I be thankin' ye, spirits. 'Tis good work ye do." He took another swallow. "Now ye be keepin' a close eye on hisself." He paused, took another drink. "An' I be thankin' ye, Shannon Dornan, for comin' to his aid—as a wolf-dog."

Outside, Kileen told his nephew what he suspected. He skipped over the drawing but told about Angel describing Mallow and his love of music. Quickly they decided on the best way to enter the Lady Gay. Kileen would enter the saloon from the front. Carlow would go around to the back, in case Silver Mallow tried to escape.

"Reloaded your gun, did ye?" Kileen asked.

Grinning sheepishly, Carlow shook his head and quickly added new cartridges to the sawed-off Winchester. Kileen watched, counting bullets out loud.

"Now I'm ready."

"Got your acorn, lad?" Kileen asked.

"Sure," Carlow said over his shoulder, shoving his hand into his pocket.

Kileen slipped inside the saloon; he couldn't remember being in a fancier bar. Pretending to listen to Anna Nalene's forceful finale to "The Yellow Rose of Texas," he studied the audience carefully. Anna Nalene's song finally reached Kileen's mind. His first thought was to ask if she knew an Irish ballad. Would she be knowing "Heather on the Moor"? He hadn't heard anything wonderful like that in a long time. He needed something to remind him of the green isle. That and, perhaps, just a touch of Irish whiskey.

Would he know Silver Mallow if the man was here? Would something burn within to tell him that here was Angel's former lover? Would her drawing suddenly come alive in his mind? All he saw were entranced men watching the woman sing from the balcony, and none fired up his insides.

Holding his rifle at his side, Kileen strode to the bar, shoving between two customers, spilling their drinks on themselves and the floor. The taller of the two started to raise his fists to challenge the massive Ranger but quickly lowered them, acting as if he always intended to wipe the whiskey from his coat and shirt with his hands. Blubbering about people not having any manners anymore, the second man rubbed furiously at the whiskey on his face. When he opened his eyes and saw who had caused the trouble, he shivered and timidly asked if he could buy Kileen a drink.

The big Ranger ignored them both and grabbed the arm of the closest bartender and yanked the frightened man off balance toward him. "Would there be a man here earlier? Dark hair and light blue eyes, maybe wearing rings on his fingers. Handsome, he be, and listening to the lady sing."

Eyeing the huge hand grasping his arm, then glimpsing the Ranger badge, the bald-headed bartender swallowed, but found his courage. "I don't spend much time looking at any man's eyes. Every man in here was watching her. Who wouldn't? Look around, Ranger. Sounds like half the men in the place, except the 'handsome' part."

Chuckles and supporting remarks trickled along the bar. The fourth man down said, "One o' these times, she dun gonna pop outta that dress—an' I'm gonna be ri't hyar to see them." A knowing chuckle and a nudge with his elbow came from the man standing next to Kileen. "Ya oughta spend your time lookin' at her, instead of some blue-eyed guy."

Kileen glowered at him, but the man was too drunk to realize the significance of his remarks or who they were aimed at. The bartender tried to pull away, but Kileen's fist held his arm in a lock that wouldn't let him move. "Ranger, really, I don't know. Is that all you got? Who's this man you're lookin' for, anyway?"

" 'Tis Silver Mallow I be seekin'."

Color left the bartender's face and he ran his tongue across his lower lip, leaned forward, and whispered. "Please, Ranger, please. I don't know if it was Silver Mallow, but there was a stranger in here—earlier. He was yellow-haired, though. Sat in with the band and played a horn." He made an offhand motion toward the balcony. Kileen looked and saw an empty chair among the band. "Charlie, he's the band leader, ya know, Charlie says the guy plays real good. He's not from Bennett. Been here a few times before. Always polite. Always asks if he can join in with the band." The bartender hesitated and glanced around the bar. "Dresses—like a gentleman, but wears a lot of rings. Said he was in freighting—or something like that. From San Antonio, maybe, I'm not sure of that. The girls liked his looks and tried to get him upstairs a few times, but he doesn't seem interested in them, only Anna. Don't know his name. Wait, yes I do . . . Beethoven, that's it. Beethoven. Heard a man today call him 'Mr. Beethoven.' Does that help?" He glanced down the bar to see if anyone was paying attention. Every man's eyes had returned to the balcony where Anna Nalene was beginning a new song, "Dixie." Everyone at the bar knew it by heart and sang along.

"Aye, that it does," Kileen said over the roar, ignoring that the bartender obviously knew it was Mallow. "When did he leave? Where did he go?"

"Left in a hurry, come to think of it. Right after the shooting outside." The bartender motioned toward the back door but tried to do it casually so no one would see his indication. Kileen released his shirt, brushed it three times to remove the wrinkles, then reached into his pocket and laid a gold piece on the bar. "Be givin' these two gentlemen a bottle of your finest Irish whiskey—and I be askin' fer your forgiveness for spillin' your drink."

Kileen touched his hand to his wide-brimmed hat and stepped away from the bar. Both men gurgled their understanding and appreciation as he walked over to the back door. He took a deep breath, levered his rifle, and pulled open the door, holding the weapon like a pistol with his right hand. Timid late-afternoon sunlight greeted him. The open alley behind the saloon was completely empty except for some stacked boxes and crates, and fresh manure where several horses had stood. He walked into the empty alley and saw horses' tracks heading away. Silver Mallow was long gone now. Kileen's chest rose and fell.

16

A jingle of spurs announced Time Carlow's appearance. He held the hand-carbine cocked but at his side. "Nobody on this end. Looks like horses left from back here. Fast."

Swinging his rifle like a walking cane, Kileen told him what the bartender had said.

"Well, if it is Silver, he's got a good lead on us—but we know where he's headed, thanks to Angel."

"Aye, and he be headed toward the rest o' his men—and nightfall be lookin' over our shoulder in two hours." Kileen hoped to talk Carlow into staying in town for a few days before they went looking for Mallow's hideout. Rest would let the young Ranger gain back strength and give them both a chance to think through their next action. It was one thing to talk about finding Mallow's hideout; it was quite another to know where it was and go there anyway.

"I'd say we be holin' up in Bennett for a few days,"

Kileen said as casually as he could manage. "Find out more about his habits. Angel said he likes music—and the bartender says he comes to listen to that glittery lass in there. A man's habits can trap him, ye know. We could wait for him to come back. Maybe put out a flyer about a big music party goin' on here."

"Let's check around town some more to make sure. If we don't find anything, we ride out in the morning, Thunder."

"He be waiting for us at his ranch, like a fine Irish sunrise."

"We'll think of something."

"Let's get some supper—and then we'll be havin' us a search. How about the pretty lass and her laddie?"

"Sure, I asked . . . Ellie . . . Mrs. Beckham and her son to join us. She's over at Mrs. Jacobs's. She works there. But we'll look around first. I'll go get her when we're through—and you can get us a table—at that place across the street. How's that sound?"

Kileen knew the discussion was over, but he insisted Carlow had to return the way he came; otherwise, the young Ranger would be forced to return through the back door and have bad luck. One must always leave by the same door he entered, Kileen reminded his nephew. Carlow smiled and walked around; Kileen reentered the saloon.

Smiling and thanking the big Ranger again for the

bottle, the two drinkers he had pushed aside quickly backed away from the bar as the big Ranger approached. "Tell me, laddie, did this Mr. Beethoven have a friend dressed like a Confederate officer with him? Or have ye seen a fella in such garb today?"

The bartender nodded toward the end of the bar. "Well, sure. Leonard Barnes. He's right down there, drinking. Was a major with Hood. Wears his stars and bars every single day—since the surrender."

Kileen glanced in the direction indicated and saw a haggard-looking man in a butternut uniform that appeared unwashed for years. He shook his head. "Terrell, I know. That ain't him."

Bending over as if he was picking up something, the bartender whispered, "What shall I do if . . . this man comes back? Whenever?" His hushed voice barely cleared Anna Nalene's throaty ballad about "The Ship That Never Returned."

"If there be a Ranger in town, go find him, or send someone to find him."

"B-But what if there isn't?"

"I'd be prayin' she sings what the bastird likes." Kileen motioned toward the balcony and left.

Kileen stomped outside, not hearing the continued thanks delivered by the two drinkers with damp clothes nor the greeting from the Iowa salesman at a nearby table. Outside, the two Rangers talked briefly, then split up to search the town separately.

An hour later they decided the town was safe. Carlow headed for Mrs. Jacobs's millinery, and Kileen went on to the small eatery down the street. Late-afternoon sun stroked the big man's hard face as he paused in front of the restaurant window and read the handwritten sign perched inside the glass: NO NEGROES. NO MEXICANS. NO IRISH.

Turning back to see Carlow walking with Ellie and Jeremiah, the big Ranger waved his arm and said, "Lookie here, lads and lasses, 'tis a fine dining establishment that be wantin' to change its wicked ways."

With that announcement, he bounded inside, not waiting for them. Carlow had asked Mrs. Jacobs if she would join them for supper, but she graciously declined, referring to a dress that needed completion. Jeremiah wanted the wolf-dog to come with them, but Carlow assured him that wasn't something they should do. By the time Carlow, Ellie, and Jeremiah reached the door, a pale restaurant owner greeted them with a nervous bow. "Ranger Carlow, Missus Beckham, and Master Jeremiah, how good to see you today. Ah, your associate is already at your table. Would you care for coffee? Milk, Master Jeremiah?"

Nervous beads of sweat bubbled along the man's forehead as he motioned toward a table in the back of the room. Dimly lit with gas lamps, but recently scrubbed clean, the restaurant was nearly empty.

Two townsmen doing business while eating were at the closest table; an army officer and another businessman occupied the far corner table, and their expressions indicated they were discussing something serious. A young woman was giggling with an enraptured young man at the table next to them.

Kileen had taken a table in the other corner. His rifle lay beside his chair. From there, one could watch both the main doorway and the back kitchen door. Carlow guessed the location had been Kileen's idea. The big Ranger waved at them, smiling widely. In front of him was a large glass of whiskey. Carlow smiled and whispered to Ellie, "Sometimes having a prizefighter for an uncle is a good thing."

She laughed, touched his hand, and said, "Oh, he seems like such a gentleman. He makes me feel safe—like you do."

The scent of her surrounded his mind, a musky blend of soap, lavender, and woman. Carlow couldn't think of a response except to say, "I'm glad you waited."

Ellie smiled, then looked down at herself involuntarily. "Bennett shouldn't be this way. I'm sorry they haven't been . . . nice to you." Ellie wanted to hold him in her arms but settled with touching his hand, by his side, with her fingers.

Carlow cocked his head to the side. "Well, we're Irish—so they don't like us. Simple as that. I don't know how Mrs. Jacobs has made it all these years. They don't like Jews, either—but she's a saint."

"Yes, she is a good lady. I think it's because . . . well, the town likes the way she sews, I guess. She's been very good to me since my William passed. I don't know how we would have made it." Her fingers were dancing with his, and it was difficult to concentrate on what she was saying. Feeling a need to explain more, she added, "We stay at the Hawkens boardinghouse. I do the laundry—as a trade."

Carlow couldn't help the sense of guilt, or was it anger, as the comparison to Ellie's situation and his late mother's passed through his mind. He shook his head slightly to remove the thought. At the table Kileen stood while Carlow seated Ellie and Jeremiah climbed into a chair beside the big Ranger. Carlow removed his long coat, hung it over the chair next to hers, and sat there. His spurs clinked against the chair spokes creating a metallic introduction to an initial awkward silence. Jeremiah broke it by asking if the Rangers were going to fight any more today. Both men assured him the trouble was over for a while with Carlow adding that they would ride to Silver Mallow's hideout in the morning, and Kileen suggesting again that they should wait. Then everyone started talking at once.

Kileen's was the only comment everyone heard, that he had already ordered for everyone. Outside on the street, two women were leering through the window to see if it were true that the Widow Beckham was with the young Ranger. Carlow waved and they scurried away. Their curiosity slapped his mind with the realization of their vulnerability. Instinctively he drew his hand-carbine, cocked and eased the hammer to rest, and laid the gun on the floor beside him.

"Company ye be expectin'?" Kileen said, then added, "Forgive us, lassie, 'tis old habits we have. There be no danger now."

Carlow looked at her, smiled, and almost forgot what he wanted to say. "I'm sorry, I didn't mean to . . . I shouldn't have . . ."

"I understand." She surprised herself that she actually did, and even more surprised that she wasn't afraid, not with Time Carlow so near.

Her closeness was heating his whole body, and all he could think of was her. He had barely slumped into the chair before their meals were served. The dumpy waitress had little interest in handing out their food, except when it came to Carlow. She batted her eyes while placing his plate in front of him; he seemed unaware of her attention. But Ellie noticed and was pleased at his lack of response.

Kileen immediately asked for his steak to be cooked "a wee more" and only then asked Ellie and Jeremiah if what he had ordered—steak, potatoes, beans, apple pie, and milk for the boy—would be all right. She assured him it was a good selection. Carlow whispered to her that it was probably the only choice and she nodded. Kileen looked disappointed at the comment and asked if either he or Ellie wanted whiskey. The big Ranger said they had bottles in the back; both declined. Within minutes the waitress brought back Kileen's revised edition, obviously annoyed by the extra effort required.

"No feast 'til there be a toast," Kileen roared and immediately broke into one, holding up his glass. "Health and life to ye; the mate o' your choice to ye; land without rent to ye; and death in Ireland." Carlow held up his coffee mug to touch Kileen's glass, and Ellie did as well, biting her lower lip to keep from laughing. Puzzled but excited, Jeremiah grabbed his glass of milk and clinked it against the others enthusiastically. Kileen nodded at each of them, emptied his glass with one long swallow, and set it down with emphasis.

"Aye, 'tis a fine meal we have before us—an' even finer company."

"Thank you, sir," Ellie said shyly. "Jeremiah and I are most thankful to be invited."

Nudging Jeremiah with his elbow, Kileen told the boy that before slicing a new loaf of bread, to make the sign of the cross on it. And that a loaf should never be turned upside-down after a slice had been cut from it. Carlow glanced at Ellie and rolled his eyes, but she shook her head and smiled. She found the big man's superstitions rather delightful and, at the least, thought-provoking. The men ate heartily on large steaks and potatoes, steaming platefuls of beans, plus most of the loaf of freshly baked bread— and the better part of an apple pie. Ellie ate slowly, savoring the closeness of this strangely handsome man beside her. No one talked while they ate, except for Kileen. His was a nonstop dissertation about superstitions, Ireland, leprechauns, and fairies, mostly directed at Jeremiah.

Bursting into the restaurant came a bronze-faced rancher in trail-worn chaps and long coat and a short-brimmed hat curled at the edges. A cigarette lay in the corner of his stern mouth, and his dark eyes darted around the room. Carlow's hand moved toward his Colt, but Kileen cautioned him. "Easy, me lad. 'Tis only his own trouble he brings."

The agitated rancher almost knocked over the closest table before seeing what he came for. Carlow and Kileen watched his bowlegged approach. He strode to their table, crossed his arms, and proclaimed, "Rangers, I need to talk with ya. Jes' saw Porter. Wallace Porter. An' he said I should come an' see ya."

He waited for their response, blinking his eyes rapidly.

"How can we help you, sir?" Carlow asked.

Kileen smiled at the use of "sir." It made him proud to hear his nephew speak politely.

"Name's Drucker. I own the Bar Six spread. Out south o' hyar," Drucker said. "Just finished our spring roundup an' half my herd's bin a-run off this winter." He took a long drag on his cigarette and let the smoke curl across his face and fade away at his hat line. It seemed to prepare him for his direct concern. "Are you goin' after Silver Mallow an' his bunch?" Drucker waved his arms to accent his question. "Or should I start payin' him to leave me alone, like Hooks is doin'?"

Carlow answered first. "Mr. Drucker, our job is to get Silver Mallow. That's what we're going to do. You can do anything you're man enough to do—and we will, too."

Kileen reached out and touched Carlow's arm. "Ranger Carlow, maybe Cattleman Drucker would be willing to bring his men along to help us? 'Twould make the numbers a bit more appealing—for the two of us."

Drucker's eyes widened and he looked as if he had been hit with a fist in his face. He took the cigarette from his mouth and started to speak, but nothing came out. He swallowed and walked out. Ellie watched Carlow for his reaction to the rancher's fear, but none came.

It was Kileen who observed dryly, "Probably saw

somethin' on our table that spooked him." Immediately Kileen returned his attention to Jeremiah, as if the rancher's appearance had never occured. " 'Tis much to learn, me lad. Why, in this wee diner alone, there be spirits watchin' an' waitin'. If ye be droppin' your fork, a man be comin' to visit."

"If I drop it now, will it mean you—and Ranger Carlow—will come to my house?"

Ellie bit her lower lip as Carlow said, "We'd like to do that . . . some day real soon . . . and you don't have to throw your fork. Remember, Jeremiah, this is just . . . make-believe. Isn't it, Thunder?" His question carried an edge that Kileen ignored.

"Now, lad, if'n ye be spillin' salt, it means bad luck be comin'. Ah, but ye kin change it, jes' by throwin' a wee pinch over your left shoulder, your left, mind ye, and into the face of the devil hisself standing there."

Jeremiah looked around but saw nothing and Carlow chuckled. Ellie leaned into the boy and whispered something and he grinned.

"What if I spill the pepper instead?" Jeremiah asked.

"Aye, 'tis not as bad. But a serious argument— with your best friend, no less—will ye be havin'."

Kileen looked at Ellie and told her that if she ate the last piece of bread on her plate without speaking, she would have a rich husband. And if she tossed the last piece of bread, before eating it, she would have good luck. But that whoever ate the very last piece of bread on the table would either have a handsome partner or die unmarried, but none knew which it would be.

"My goodness, that's a lot to remember," Ellie said. "Should I talk—and toss—at the same time?"

Carlow laughed. "Sometimes I wonder how my uncle gets through a day with so many things to remember."

"Aye, 'tis why I do, me lad, why I do."

The restaurant door opened and closed and two work-weary cowboys wearing worn coats, filthy chaps, and misshapen hats entered. Their faces and clothes were dirt-streaked, and the brims of their hats barely cleared their lowered eyes. The taller man with a dark beard walked with a limp and had on spectacles with a crack across one glass; the stockier cowhand wore faded Confederate pants. Neither man appeared to be armed and they were escorted graciously by the owner to a table close to the door.

Both Rangers eyed them briefly, then went back to their conversation. Kileen wondered aloud if the two men had the money for their meal from the looks of their clothes, or how the one fellow could even see through eyeglasses like that. Carlow chastised him for judging people by their appearance, adding that the two of them weren't exactly dressed for a ball. He suggested telling the owner that they would pay for the poor men's meals.

Kileen frowned. "I don't recall nobody ever buyin' Old Thunder supper 'cause I looked like I might need it."

"Well, the way you act, it's no wonder," Carlow teased.

"Would you like more pie?" the dumpy waitress interrupted, without much interest in the question or the answer.

"No thank ye, me lady, three's my limit these days," Kileen said with a wink, "but I be havin' a mite more o' that fine coffee."

Carlow and Ellie agreed that more coffee would be good. Jeremiah asked if he could have more pie, and Kileen assured him that he could. Carlow told his uncle the boy's mother should make such a decision; she said it was a special day, so it would be all right. Slowly the taciturn waitress filled the cups without further comment. She left to wait on the businessman and army officer at the corner table.

Halfway through his third cup of coffee, Time Carlow heard Chance bark from outside. More of a threatening growl. Carlow put the cup down and listened. Chance growled again, long and deep in his throat. Maybe someone was messing with his horse. Before he could move, the wolf-dog yelped. Somebody was trying to hurt him! The young Ranger sprang from his chair. "I'll be right back."

"Be gentle, me son, 'tis likely a townsman thinking

he's a wolf," Kileen advised as Carlow hurried to the door and past the two cowboys drinking coffee; neither glanced in his direction.

As Time Carlow burst outside, Kileen turned toward Ellie and added, "Should never be askin' a question of a dog; he might answer, ye know—and if he does, the questioner would surely die."

She wondered if this big Irishman was serious about some of the strange things he said, but she was soon capitvated by his sharing the young Ranger's near-death battle last winter, the loss of his best friend in the fight, about the blood stones they both kept for luck, and that he had raised Carlow after his mother and father died.

Kileen didn't tell her that he was worried about Carlow pushing himself too fast after his recovery, or that he hoped to convince his nephew they should wait a few days before riding to Mallow's hideout ranch, or that there was no way they wouldn't be heavily outnumbered when they eventually did. None of this was conversation suitable for a woman's ears, especially when they were eating.

Ellie was drawn to the big man's gregarious manner and felt comfortable in his company. She couldn't remember feeling quite this happy for a long time. Was it simply the fascination of this powerfully built man's intriguing brogue? Or was she captivated by the cavalier manner of Time Carlow and the way he faced danger? Or was her heart trying to tell her this was something more? She glanced at her son, almost out of a need to reassure herself that she wasn't acting foolishly. When the thought entered her mind about what the church women might think of her being with two Irishmen, she blinked it away and concentrated, instead, on Kileen's rhythmic Irish phrasing as he continued to praise his nephew. After a long pause the big Ranger began to tell her about Angel Balta.

17

Outside, Carlow hurried toward his tied horse and Chance; his hand dropped to his empty hand-carbine holster, and it registered that he had left the gun, cocked and ready, beside his chair. His hand moved on to the reassurance of his Colt. He stopped a few feet from both animals, relieved to see they were there. But even from a distance he could see the wolf-dog had two long bloody marks across its back. Carlow's anger soared. Someone had whipped him! He couldn't believe how terrible some people could be. Wasn't it enough that they didn't want him and his uncle in town; did they have to take their hatred out on a dog? He ran to Chance and knelt beside him. The animal whimpered its affection while Carlow gently touched the wound to determine its severity.

Suddenly the wolf-dog tensed and growled.

Time Carlow belly-flopped against the ground as

Jesus fired his pistol. His shot tore into the street inches from Carlow's waist. The one-eyed Mexican bandit emerged silently from the shadowed crease between buildings, where he waited for the young Ranger to respond to his whipping Chance with a quirt. He remained hidden until the last moment to keep the wolf-dog from giving away his presence by coming after him—and to give himself a good shot at an unsuspecting Carlow.

As he rolled, Carlow drew his Colt, and his own shot was a continuation of the outlaw's firing. Jesus's second bullet struck Carlow at his chest, and he flattened to the ground. A metallic whine trailed the roar of the gun, like a ricocheting bullet. Carlow's return shot clipped Jesus in the shoulder and made him drop his gun. Chance snarled and exploded at the kneeling outlaw. Jesus tried to hit at the brown fury with the quirt in his left fist. White teeth grabbed the swinging arm and smashed through to the bone. Jesus struggled wildly to get the enraged animal away from him. Frantically the Mexican outlaw grabbed his dropped gun, cocked, and brought it toward the powerful wolf-dog.

Propping himself up on his left forearm, Carlow's Colt fired again and again. The outlaw's hand shivered and became limp; his pistol slammed against the sidewalk, roared, and clipped the edge of the tie rack. A second later Jesus slumped and his head thudded against his unmoving chest, between crossed bandoliers. Chance continued his assault until Carlow said weakly, "I-It's all right, Ch-Chance. L-Let him go."

The young Ranger's arm gave way and his gun oozed from his quivering hand. He was dizzy and couldn't keep his head from falling against the street. His body jerked and was still. Whimpering again, Chance came to his side and shoved his nose under Carlow's unmoving hand to receive attention that didn't come.

Inside the restaurant Kileen reached down for the rifle at his feet. The two cowboys at the front table stood; pistols appeared in their hands.

"Don't touch the rifle, Ranger—or we'll kill the lady and her son," Silver Mallow, disguised as one of the dirty cowboys, warned. He waved his pistol at Ellie and Jeremiah. "Pull that six-gun with your fingers. Do it slow."

Smiling, Mallow tossed the eyeglasses to the floor and cocked his head confidently to the side. "We'll wait here for Jesus to join us. He's going to drag the dead body of your young friend in here. I want to know he's really dead—this time." He paused for effect, glancing at General Terrell, dressed as the second cowboy. "Then I'm going to blow your head off. You two have caused me no end of trouble. I didn't even get to hear the end of Anna's performance." He looked again at Terrell and added, "And I lost three good men today."

Kileen cursed in Irish but stood without moving further.

Mallow's mouth jerked involuntarily at the corner. "I want to watch your eyes when you see your nephew is dead. He is your nephew, isn't he? Houston told me all about his whore mother and you raising him. Oh, that would have been your sister, wouldn't it? It was all very touching. Like Beethoven's Fifth. Do you like Beethoven, Ranger?" Mallow's eyes narrowed and his mouth jerked again. "Too bad you won't hear any music again. Your nephew's death will be the last thing you'll ever hear. I hear he looks a little like me. I find that a fascinating coincidence, don't you?"

Kileen's silent stare didn't move from Mallow's face. Slowly he drew his handgun, gripping it with two fingers, and let it fall to the floor. "The lady and her boy are not part of this. Let 'em go, Silver. Let 'em leave. They can't hurt you."

"I'll make the decisions here." Mallow's eyebrows flared. "So you finally guessed who I am. Brilliant, Ranger. Just brilliant. How'd you like our coming right in here. Right in here—under your noses. It was all my idea. The General here was against it at first, weren't you?"

General Terrell's eyebrows twitched nervously,

and he hunched his shoulders to shake off the emotion. He said something to Mallow that Kileen didn't hear, but the outlaw leader smiled and ordered Terrell to disarm the army officer and to see if anyone else was armed. Mallow continued to explain how they had taken the coats and hats from two drunks they coaxed into the alley. He added it was the first time he'd used the beard and asked how Kileen liked it, but didn't wait for an answer. Laughing shrilly, he then asked Kileen if he liked music and immediately began describing his favorite songs.

Terrell grinned triumphantly, pointing his pistol at Kileen's stomach as he passed. "Come on, big boy, I'd love to put a slug in your gut. A great way to die, getting gut shot. Come on."

Kileen's glare bothered Terrell enough that he transferred his attention toward the army officer and the businessman. Behind Kileen, Jeremiah whispered, "Mother" and his eyes went to the hand-carbine beside Carlow's empty chair. Ellie took a deep breath and slowly stood.

"Sit down, young lady. I'll tell you when to move." Mallow's voice was almost apologetic, then it changed as his eyes narrowed and his chin rose. "You can go with us—to our place. The boys need a little entertainment. You can sing, can't you? Let's hear . . . ah, 'Yellow Rose of Texas.' You know, 'There's a yellow rose of Texas, that I am going to see, no other soldier knows her—no soldier, only me. She cried so when I . . .' " Mallow stopped, pursed his lips.

Crossing her arms, Ellie sat down, only in Carlow's chair this time, hoping her dress covered the gun, and Mallow didn't notice or care about the switch. Her face was taut, but she patted Jeremiah's leg and told him to be quiet.

"Don't know that one, eh?" Mallow continued without waiting for her to respond. "Do you know 'Utah Carrol?' That's a fun one. No? How about, ah, 'Beautiful Dreamer?' Maybe 'Goober Peas?' " He was becoming exasperated. "No matter, the boys'll like what's underneath that dress. Maybe I will, too. General, let's bring along that other young woman, too."

The young man stood defiantly. "No, you won't."

Mallow's gun answered, then swung back to Kileen. The young man gurgled and fell forward across the table. Screaming, his girlfriend leaped across it to her lover, sending plates and cups crashing. His eyes fluttered and he reached for her, but his hand lost its direction and flopped on the table's growing crimson pool.

Terrell finished disarming the customers, forcing the army officer to get on his knees beside the table and stay that way. Neither of the townsmen at the closest table were armed, and the haughty-faced man asked Terrell if they might leave since this was no concern of theirs. He laughed, picked up the man's plate of food, and dumped it on his lap. In the far corner the waitress was sobbing on the short owner's shoulder, and he was trying to comfort her while trying not to retch. Her mumbled words indicated she was more upset about Mallow not wanting to take her along with the other two women than about the violence erupting within the restaurant.

Terrell returned to Mallow's side with a wide grin on his face. "I want Carlow's woman. Unless you do, Silver."

Mallow glared at him. "Go see what's with Jesus. I don't want him scalping Carlow on the street. He can bring the body along and do whatever he wants with it later."

Hesitantly Terrell asked if he should watch for the sheriff or townspeople curious about the gunshots. Mallow snorted his disgust at the suggestion. "There's no way Moore or his deputies are going to come this way, General. Or anybody else in this town. I own it now." Mallow snorted again. "Get Jesus in here so I can watch the big Ranger. It's going to be more fun than killing him."

Terrell had seen this look in Mallow's eyes before and didn't want to risk the outlaw's madness descending upon him. He saluted briskly, strode to the door, and slipped outside. Mallow liked the military tribute, chuckled, and saluted back, laying his gun barrel against his forehead, then quickly brought it back to aim at Kileen's stomach.

Standing outside and peering down the street, Terrell yelled, "Carlow's dead! He's layin' in the street."

"Where's Jesus?"

"Can't see him. Oh, oh, he's down, too, Silver."

"Well, go check on him."

Terrell headed past the restaurant window and down the street. Mallow looked at Kileen and said softly, "You look like a man who will take a lot of killing. I didn't expect it of the other one. But, surely, the state of Texas didn't expect to stop me with just two Rangers. I'm insulted." He laughed shrilly. "Did you like the limp? A nice touch, I thought—and the mud on our faces? You know, I can disguise myself so well—even as a woman—and the Rangers who come after you're dead won't have the faintest idea of who I am. Isn't that great? Wouldn't I look great as an orchestra leader?"

Before Kileen could respond, the swinging doors to the kitchen slammed open, thudding against the wall. Mallow spun his pistol toward the noise and fired into empty space. Somewhere in the kitchen, the bullet clanged off a pot and whined away. His attention came too slowly back to Kileen. The big Ranger lunged at him, grabbing the wrist of Mallow's gun hand forcing it against the wall. The recocked gun went off, driving a bullet into the adobe wall. A blink behind came Kileen's powerful right fist exploding into Mallow's face, smashing his nose and showering both of them with blood.

Dazed, Mallow struggled to free himself from Kileen's control of his right wrist. Kileen stepped closer and slammed a right jab into the outlaw leader's rib cage. Mallow's air left his body and his gun bounced against the floor and skidded under a table. Releasing Mallow's empty gun hand, Kileen's left fist hooked into his exposed chin, shoving his fake beard to his nose and breaking off two teeth that clattered on the floor. The outlaw leader swung a wild haymaker that grazed Kileen's face and enraged him further.

The big Ranger lifted Mallow and threw him bodily over a table, clattering two chairs across the floor. Kileen yanked the defenseless Mallow to his feet and held him upright with his left hand as he continued to pound him with his right. "That is for bein' with me Angel . . . and this be for Shannon . . . an' this for Noah . . . an' this, this is for . . . takin' the life of me son."

In the kitchen doorway was Carlow with a gun in one hand and the broom he used to open the swinging doors in the other. His face was pale and his voice soft. Too soft.

"I'm right here, Thunder."

Fury commanded Kileen's attention and he didn't hear or see his beloved nephew. Carlow walked unevenly toward Kileen, who continued to beat the senseless Mallow. The young Ranger repeated, "I'm right here, Thunder. I'm all right."

It was Ellie who yelled, "Look! Time's alive! Look!"

Kileen's fist stopped in mid-strike and he released the bloody Mallow, who collapsed like a dropped garment beside an overturned chair.

"Saints be praised," was all Kileen could utter and hurried to Carlow, wrapping him in an emotional bear hug. Carlow hugged him back and Kileen cried unashamedly.

"Shannon saved my life—or you did, Thunder. The Mexican's bullet hit a blood stone. I think it was Shannon's. Right here in my pocket. And it glanced away. Would've hit me in the heart." He dropped the broom, holstered his gun, and reached into his shirt pocket to withdraw the stones. A large chip was gone on one, showing white where once there had been a dark stain.

"Lord be praised. 'Twas the curse of the thirteenth bullet that saved ye, laddie. 'Tis a bad piece o' lead, like I be tellin' ye."

Carlow nodded agreement, rather than pointing out Jesus shot at an angle and the bullet raked the hard surface, instead of penetrating. Still, it made him silently thank his childhood friend for protecting him.

Kileen took the chipped remembrance from Carlow's shaking hand and rubbed it, unable to speak. His face changed from joy to worry. Jabbering in Irish, the big Ranger unbuttoned Carlow's shirt and stared at the red-and-purple imprint on his chest, to the left of his Celtic cross.

"I-I thought I was dead, Thunder. It hurt like hell—and everything in me quit."

"Your heart, it be stopped, Time."

"You mean I was dead?"

"Aye, sort of."

Carlow noticed Kileen's bloody hands. "You'd better soak those hands, Ranger Kileen, we've got a lot more work to do—they'll be as big as potatoes by morning. Irish potatoes, no less." He smiled thinly.

Kileen saw his bruised-and-cut knuckles for the first time, but his mind was elsewhere. He reached into his pocket and pulled out the small pouch of Irish soil. Opening it, he dipped his fingers into the soft, fine earth and drew a circle in Irish dirt around Carlow's bruised heart area, avoiding the cross.

" 'Tis a special circle from the Green Isle itself," he said, not looking at Carlow. He wiped a stray tear from his cheek, leaving a red smear.

The young Ranger frowned. "I figured to come in

shooting, after I used that broomstick to push open the doors, but you didn't seem to need—"

"There were two devils after you," Kileen interrupted. "General Terrell be the one wearing old clothes an' sech. Mallow and him, they fooled us. Came right in here, they did. Jesus, you know him, the one-eyed bastird." He gradually moved his gaze up to Carlow's face. "Are you all right, me son?" Kileen's fat fingers tenderly touched the cross.

"Jesus is dead. That second fella sorta lost his nerve and dropped his gun when I politely asked him to. Right now he's lashed to the hitching post—with Chance watching him."

Behind them came movement. A blood-soaked Mallow raised his pearl-handled pistol toward Carlow. The roar of Carlow's hand-carbine followed. Carlow and Kileen looked first at Mallow grabbing his shoulder and dropping his gun, then at Ellie, holding the smoking weapon. Her face was white; tears weren't far away.

"I-I sh-shot him. I-I sh-shot a man," she mumbled and threw the gun on the table. Jeremiah jumped from his chair and held her.

Carlow's pistol was again in his fist and aimed at the wounded Mallow. "I'll take that fancy gun, Silver. You won't be needing it again." Carlow walked over and picked up the pistol.

"Good work, Rangers. You, too, ma'am." The army

officer stood, retrieved his own revolver on the floor, and brushed himself off. "Is that . . . Silver Mallow?"

"Aye, 'tis the devil hisself—and the others be Jesus and General Terrell, two o' the worst heathens this side of the Rio Grande."

"I thought Silver Mallow liked to wear a bunch of rings. You know, silver rings. I didn't know he wore a beard."

"It's a fake. I imagine you'll be findin' 'em rings in his pocket, soldjur," Kileen said. "An' I imagine you'll be findin' two poor cowlads in some alley—missing their coats an' hats, bless their poor souls." The big Ranger yanked the loosened beard from Mallow's face, then thrust his hand into Mallow's coat pocket and withdrew a fistful of silver rings.

The army officer walked toward Kileen and held out his hand. "I'm Colonel Fletcher of the Fourth. We've been trying to catch up with that bastard, too. We're always a bit slow, it seems."

"Get up, Silver. You an' that General of yours be headin' for jail—and some fine new ropes." Kileen reached down and yanked Mallow to his feet.

The outlaw leader grimaced and Kileen whispered, "Please be givin' me one more reason to knock your head off your scrawny neck. I knew who ye be the minute ye walked in. Disguise, me ass. Ye forgot Angel Balta drew a picture of yourself." Kileen laughed and it came deep within his chest.

"Angel? A-Angel Balta? Why did—"

"She be my woman." Kileen interrupted proudly.

Returning to the table, Carlow knelt beside the sobbing Ellie. "I-I thought . . . I don't know what I-I thought . . . then Jeremiah reminded me of y-your gun . . . and I-I sh-shot a man . . ."

"Thank you, Ellie, for saving my life."

"I-I d-didn't know what else to do." She stopped and rubbed her upper arm. "Oh, my, that . . . gun has an awful kick."

Carlow laughed and ruffled Jeremiah's hair. "Thank you, again, Jeremiah. That's twice you've saved my life."

"Is Chance all right?" the boy asked.

"Well, yes, he's going to be. Maybe you can help me put some medicine on his back. A bad man hit him—to make me come out."

"Oh, I'd better go."

"I think you'd best stay with your mother—for a little longer," Carlow said, brushing a long tear from Ellie's cheek.

She touched the encircled mark on his chest, then the cross, telling herself that she was only concerned about the Ranger's well-being. Slowly she raised her eyes to meet his. "Time Carlow, I don't know if there is a charm—or something I can say—but I hope you will ride back here when this is all over." She paused, swallowed, and said, "I will be waiting."

"It's almost over. Thunder and I will ride out to Mallow's hideout tomorrow morning. With him an' General in jail—and Jesus dead, they shouldn't put up too much of a fight." He grinned and added, "I hope."

Kileen looked at Ellie, wishing she might say something, anything that would keep his nephew from going. Then he turned back to Colonel Fletcher. "Colonel, we know where Mallow's hideout is—and the rest of his bloody bandits. Can you ready a company to go with us?"

"Wish I could, Ranger. Wish I could. But I get my orders from Washington. I can wire them tonight. Maybe in a week."

"Aye, a week."

Quietly the emphasis shifted to stabilizing the wounded boyfriend while the restaurant owner went for a doctor. Carlow stopped the chest wound from bleeding with napkins, and Ellie calmed his girl-friend. Kileen marched Mallow and Terrell to jail and instructed Moore to handle the dead Jesus. The sheriff thought he was joking, at first, but quickly re-alized the foolishness of his ways. Twice, he brought up the subject of rewards, but Kileen didn't respond. The big Irishman was only interested in Mallow and Terrell being secured; Carlow decided both Rangers would stand guard in the jail during the night.

Stunned by the events of the day, the town was

awash in rumor. More than a few gossiped that the Rangers had been fooled into arresting a cowboy and that Silver Mallow had escaped. Three boys told the Rangers of finding six horses and two dead cowboys, wearing only long johns, in an alley behind the Corao. They also brought a Confederate general's uniform, fine dress clothes, and an encased cornet. Carlow sent Moore to put the Mallow horses in the stable. Reluctantly Doc Williams dressed Silver Mallow's wounds, straightened his broken nose, and bound his broken ribs, but could do nothing for his broken teeth. Mallow asked to see the judge, pleading that he was just an innocent cowboy; Kileen told him it didn't matter who he was, he was wanted for attempted murder of a Ranger, and the outlaw leader spoke no more. Anna Nalene brought over a dinner basket for Mallow and left quickly when Carlow searched it and found a revolver. Kileen kept the food and ate it himself, proclaiming loudly that it was excellent. Carlow made him share some of it with Chance.

Neither Kileen nor Carlow slept much. Kileen knew they still faced a considerable fight. At least a dozen armed men would remain at Mallow's ranch. He tried not to look at Mallow because it brought up images of Angel with the outlaw leader. Time Carlow's mood, triggered by returning to the jail, was a mirror of memories, sad and happy, drawn first to hazy pictures of his best friend. In his hand were both blood stones. He couldn't put them down. His chest throbbed and his head ached. The thought of leaving Ellie Beckham behind was even stronger. Over and over, he replayed their kiss in a quick moment when they were alone after the fight. Whenever he closed his eyes, she was there. His whole body tingled with the feel of her against him.

Only the dawn's pink underbelly reached them as the two Rangers walked alone through the sleeping town to the livery. Trotting beside Carlow, Chance appeared a little stiff but eager to go. Moore had kept his promise, to both Rangers' surprise, and showed up to stand watch at the jail, along with both deputies. Kileen was uncharacteristically silent; Carlow was glad for the lack of conversation; he didn't need to be reminded of what waited for them at Mallow's ranch, even without the gang's leaders.

Earlier, over coffee, the big Irishman had talked endlessly about charms Carlow could use to make Ellie Beckham love him. There was butter on a new-made dish, but it had to be given in the presence of a mill, or a stream, or a tree, and accompanied by special words that Kileen kept forgetting. Carlow suggested that a couple in that setting would likely not need any butter, or any charms for that matter.

Powdered evergreen needles mixed in food or drink would also produce great love, Kileen suggested. Or Carlow could hold a sprig of mint in his hand until the herb was moist and warm, then take Ellie's hand. As long as their hands touched the herb, she would follow him. No special words were necessary. In fact, the two must be silent for ten minutes to give the charm time to work. When Carlow commented that neither Kileen nor Angel could have possibly been silent so long, the big Ranger harrumphed and said the young man should not scoff at things that were beyond his imagination.

Finally, as they saddled their horses in the stable, Kileen shared his parting with Angel, her drawing of Silver Mallow and its destruction in the stream. Carlow told his uncle that he had reacted poorly to Angel; that she had put their love on the line to help them. Kileen's face agreed even though no words supported it. Chance growled and Carlow said, "Someone's outside."

"Or 'tis an evil spirit he be seein'." Kileen nodded his head authoritatively and continued tightening his cinch. "Dogs can see evil spirits, ye know. We can't see 'em but a dog can. That's why they bark sometimes at nothing."

There was a scuffling sound outside then a horse's whinny. Carlow frowned at Kileen and drew his handcarbine. "Doesn't sound like a spirit to me, Thunder. Maybe the town's coming to run us out."

Kileen nodded, pulled the Henry from its saddle

sheath, levered it into readiness, and went to the heavy entrance doors.

"Could just be the livery boy, getting an early start at his mucking," Carlow said.

"Sure, an' 'tis red shamrocks we be findin'." Kileen motioned for his nephew to position himself behind a bale of hay, where he had a good line of fire.

"Ranger Carlow! Ranger Kileen! It's Mrs. Jacobs. Please open the doors. I've got some good news."

"Time, it's Ellie. Please!"

Carlow stood and told his uncle to let them in. Tapping the door frame three times with his rifle, Kileen swung open the door wide enough for the two women to enter. Behind them in the street were twenty waiting riders. Kileen jumped back, closed the door, and raised his rifle.

"Mrs. Jacobs, what brings ye here this fine morn?" Kileen frowned and touched the brim of his hat. "Did ye come to warn us? 'Tis nice o' you—but appears the townsmen are already waitin'. A lot o' them will die this day."

"Some of the townsmen are here . . . to ride with you to the Mallow hideout," Mrs. Jacobs said, lifting her chin defiantly. "They want to help. Bennett owes you plenty. Consider this a down payment."

Kileen looked around for Carlow, but he was already standing next to Ellie. They were talking quietly, as if the rest of the world had gone away.

"Time, me lad, did you hear this?"

"Ah, Mrs. Beckham . . . just told me."

"Aye, and that be the first thing she be tellin' ye, I'm sure."

Carlow smiled. "Let's go outside, Uncle."

Even in the gray morning light, both Rangers recognized many of the waiting riders. Rancher Wallace Porter and several townsmen they'd known; and many faces they'd seen only in passing. The restaurant owner was there, proudly carrying a double-barreled shotgun. And Sampson, the grocer, and Orville Frederick, the blacksmith. And Doc Williams. Even the bald-headed bartender from the Lady Gay. Each man was mounted and carrying a rifle; some had pistols shoved into their waistbands. In the back were two of the cowboys who'd helped Kileen attack the Mallow gang last winter.

"And to what do we owe the pleasure of this fine company?" Kileen asked, lowering his rifle.

Carlow saw the curly-haired businessman from the general store, decked out in his full Confederate uniform. Beside him was a friend Carlow didn't know in similar attire. Both men saluted Carlow when his gaze met theirs; he returned it with a smile. The young Ranger waved at three townsmen he knew as a boy, then recognized the crow-faced woman's husband sitting on a long-legged bay. He had a bandolier of bullets across his buttoned coat and a rifle butt rested on his thigh, pointing skyward. He spoke for the group.

"We thought you might need a hand, Rangers. If you'll have us, we'd like to go with you to Mallow's hideout." The councilman motioned with his hand to include the group and continued. "Mrs. Jacobs and Mrs. Beckham came to me last night. They can be . . . rather persuasive. Some of us are . . . well, embarrassed about the way we've acted toward you men. You risked your lives—for us . . . an' we owe you better treatment than you got. I hope you can find it in your hearts to forgive us."

Carlow holstered his hand-carbine. "Let's ride."

From the shadows of the livery, Jeremiah stepped to join his mother. The boy saw Carlow and Chance, said something to Ellie, and ran for them. The wolf-dog barked happily to see the approaching boy.

Wide-eyed, a townsman saw the animal, blinked, and asked, "My gosh, is that a wolf?"

Jeremiah stopped, turned toward the man, and advised solemnly, "No, sir, that's an Irish wolfhound." He hurried to pet Chance as Kileen and Carlow laughed at the description the young Ranger had used with Pickenson yesterday.

Throwing his shoulders back, Wallace Porter spat a brown stream of tobacco juice toward the ground and hollered, "Anybody who's thinkin' about backin' out this hyar shindig, you'll have to answer to Mrs.

Jacobs." He grinned at his pronouncement, then glanced to his right, and Carlow saw the rancher, who introduced himself as Drucker in the restaurant, obviously wishing he were somewhere else.

"Mighty good work getting Silver Mallow, Rangers!" the curly-haired businessman shouted. "Most of us thought he was going to take over Bennett."

More accolades followed, and in the middle of the riders, someone shouted, "Long live the Irish!" That was followed by "Long live Dixie!" Another grumbled, "I still don't want them Irish livin' next to me." "Me, neither" came a whispered response.

Kileen looked at Carlow and winked. " 'Tis a fine day for Irishmen, me son. 'Tis a fine day. I knew it the moment we entered the stable an' saw a black horse standin' there, big as you please."

"That was my horse, Thunder. That was Shadow."

Carlow looked over at Ellie. She was holding something in her hand. He squinted to make it out. A piece of bread! She smiled at him, threw the bread slice into the air, caught it with both hands, and began eating.

Kileen nudged his nephew playfully with his elbow. "Looks like we'll be ridin' back this way, me son."

"Looks that way, Thunder."

Kileen smiled broadly, letting his missing teeth

show. "I should'a gone back an' told me Angel that I was sorry fer actin' so. Bless her lovin' soul."

"She'll be waiting for you."

"Got your acorn?"

"Sure do. Let's ride."

Kileen looked down at the wolf-dog now waiting next to Carlow. "Well, what are you waiting for, Shannon? Let's take 'em."

ROUND 'EM UP!

CAMERON JUDD

THE CARRIGAN BROTHERS SERIES

Shootout in Dodge City
0-7434-5708-0

Revenge on Shadow Trail
0-7434-5709-9

COTTON SMITH

THE TEXAS RANGER SERIES

The Thirteenth Bullet
0-7434-7568-2

GARY SVEE

SPUR AWARD-WINNING AUTHOR

The Peacemaker's Vengeance
0-7434-6346-3

Spirit Wolf
0-7434-6352-8

Showdown at Buffalo Jump
0-7434-6351-X

Sanctuary
0-7434-6350-1